F
COS

The sun was spinning faster, that fact was undisputed by the world's leading astronomers. And they had discovered the cause: a force-beam of terrible potency, coming across the void from Neptune and pushing against the sun! As the spinning increased, it would cause the sun to infallibly divide into a double star, destroying most of the solar system and bringing an end to all life. Time was running out for humanity.

The World Government had to find out what was behind this impending disaster and, ultimately, how to stop it in time. So they assigned a team of four brave men to undertake a dangerous journey across the wilds of deep space to the planet Neptune. There they hoped to find the answers so desperately needed to save the Earth and the rest of the solar system. The mighty ray of doom must be stopped—and failure was not an option!

ABOUT EDMOND HAMILTON

Edmond Hamilton...

...started writing science fiction when he was 20 years old—all the way back in 1924. Many of his first sci-fi stories were published in *Weird Tales,* but he wrote for all the major pulp and digest magazines for the next several decades. In his career he wrote hundreds of stories and dozens of novels.

Hamilton was born in Ohio in 1904 but lived for many years in Pennsylvania. One of his oldest friends was another master science fiction storyteller, Jack Williamson.

In 1946, Hamilton married fellow sci-fi writer and enthusiast, Leigh Brackett. They lived for many years in a 130-year old farmhouse in the old Western Reserve of Ohio.

Edmond Hamilton is known as one of the great sci-fi authors of the 20th Century. There was probably no author better equipped at writing space opera and tightly written science fiction adventure. Some of his best known works were *The Star Kings, City at World's End,* and *The Haunted Stars.*

Edmond Hamilton passed away in 1977.

THE UNIVERSE WRECKERS

By
EDMOND HAMILTON

ARMCHAIR FICTION
PO Box 4369, Medford, Oregon 97504

*The original text of this novel was first
published by Experimenter Publications, Inc.*

Armchair Edition, Copyright 2015 by Greg J. Luce
All Rights Reserved

*For more information about Armchair Books and products, visit our
website at...*

www.armchairfiction.com

Or email us at...

armchairfiction@yahoo.com

CHAPTER ONE
A Warning of Doom

IT WAS ON the third day of May, 1994, that the world received its first news of the strange behavior of the sun. That first news was contained in a brief message sent out from the North American Observatory, in upper New York, and signed by Dr. Herbert Marlin, the observatory's head. It stated that within the last twenty-four hours a slight increase had been detected in the sun's rotatory speed, or rate of spin, and that while that increase might only be an apparent one, it was being further studied. That brief first message was broadcast, a few hours later, from the Intelligence Bureau of the World Government, in New York. It was I, Walter Hunt, who supervised the broadcasting of that message at the Intelligence Bureau, and I remember that it seemed to me of so little general interest that I ordered it sent out on the scientific news wave rather than on the general news wave.

Late on the next day, however—the 4th—there came another report from the North American Observatory in which Dr. Marlin stated that he and his first assistant, an astronomical student named Randall, had checked their observations in the intervening hours and had found that there was in reality a measurable increase in the sun's rotatory speed, an increase somewhat greater than had been estimated at first. Dr. Marlin added that all the facilities of the observatory were being utilized in an effort to determine the exact amount of that increase, and although it seemed at first glance rather incomprehensible, all available data concerning it would be gathered. And at the same hour, almost, there came corroborative reports from the Paris and Honolulu Observatories, stating that Dr. Marlin's first observations had already been confirmed independently by their own observers. There could be no doubt, therefore, that the sun was spinning faster!

To astronomers this news of the sun's increased rotatory speed became at once a sensation of the first importance, and in the hours following the broadcasting of Dr. Marlin's first statement, we at the Intelligence Bureau had been bombarded with inquiries from the world's observatories regarding it. We could only answer those inquiries by repeating the statement already sent out on the scientific news wave and by promising to broadcast any further developments instantly from our Bureau, the clearing house of the world's news. This satisfied the scientifically minded, while the great mass of the public was so little interested in this slight increase in the sun's rate of spin as not to bother us with any questions concerning it. I know that I would have taken small interest in the thing myself, had it not been for a personal factor connected with it.

"Marlin!" I had exclaimed, when the Intelligence Chief had handed to me that first report for broadcasting, "Dr. Herbert Marlin—why, he was my astronomy prof up at North American University, two years ago."

"Oh, you know him," the Chief had remarked. "I suppose then that this statement of his on the sun's increased rate of spin is authentic?"

"Absolutely, if Dr. Marlin gave it," I told him. "He's one of the three greatest living astronomers, you know. I became good friends with him at the University, but haven't seen him for some time."

So that it was with an interest rather unusual for me, that I followed the reports on this technical astronomical sensation in the next few days. Those reports were coming fast now from all the observatories of Earth, from Geneva and Everest and Tokyo and Mexico City, for almost all astronomers had turned their interest at once toward this unprecedented phenomenon of the sun's increased rate of spin, which Dr. Marlin had been first to discover. The exact amount of that increase, I gathered, was still somewhat in doubt. For not only did the sun turn comparatively slowly, but the problem was complicated by the fact that it did not, like the Earth or like any solid body, rotate everywhere at the same speed, but turned faster at the equator than at its poles, due to its huge size and the lack of solidity of its mass. Dr. Marlin, however, stated that according to his observations the sun's great fiery ball, which had rotated previously at its equator at the rate of one rotation each 25 days, had already increased its rate of spin, so as to be turning now at the rate of one rotation each 24 days, 12 hours.

This meant that the sun's rotatory period, or day, had decreased 12 hours in three Earth-days, and such an unprecedented happening was bound to create an uproar of excitement among astronomers. For to them, as to all, who had any conception of the unvarying accuracy and superhuman perfection of the movements of the sun and its worlds, such a sudden increase of speed was all but incredible. And when on the fourth day Dr. Marlin and a score of other observers reported that the sun's rotatory period had decreased by another 4 hours, the excitement of the astronomers was unprecedented. A few of them, indeed, sought even in the face of the recorded observations to cast doubt on the thing. The sun's rotatory speed, they contended, could be measured only by means of the sunspots upon its turning surface, and it was well known that those sunspots themselves often changed position, so that this sudden increase in speed might only be an illusion.

This contention, however, found small support in the face of the indisputable evidence which Dr. Marlin and his fellow astronomers had advanced in the shape of numerous heliophotographs and time-recordings. The sun was spinning faster, that was undoubted by the greater part of the world's astronomers—but what was making it do so? Was it due to some great dark body passing the solar system in space? Or was it due to strange changes within the sun's great fiery sphere? It was the latter theory, on the whole, that was favored by most astronomers, and which struck me at the time as the most plausible. It was generally held that a great shifting of the sun's inner layers, a movement of its mighty interior mass, had caused this sudden change in speed of rotation. Dr. Marlin himself, though, when questioned, would only state that the increased rate of spin was in itself beyond doubt but that no sound theory could as yet be formed as to the phenomenon's cause.

AND while the astronomers thus pondered and disputed over the thing, it had begun to arouse repercussions of interest in the non-scientific public also. More and more inquiries concerning it were coming to us at the Intelligence Bureau in those first few days, those inquiries becoming so numerous as to cause us to switch the news on the thing from the scientific news wave to the general news wave, which reached every communication-plate in the world. It was, no doubt, out of sheer lack of other topics of interest that the world turned thus toward this astronomical sensation. For sensations of any kind were rare now in this peaceful world of ours. The last mighty air war of 1972, which had ended in the total abolition of all national boundaries and the establishment of the World Government with its headquarters in the new world capital of New York, had brought peace to the world, but it had also brought some measure of monotony. So that even such a slight break in the order of things as this increase in the sun's rate of spin, was rather welcomed by the peoples of the world.

And now, the thing had passed from the realm of the merely surprising to that of the astounding. For upon the fifth and sixth days had come reports from Dr. Marlin and from the heads of the other observatories of the world that the strange phenomenon was still continuing, that the sun's rotatory speed was still increasing. In each of those two days, it was stated, it had decreased its period of rotation by another 4 hours, the same daily decrease noted previously. And the exactness of this decrease daily, the smoothness of this strange acceleration of the sun's spin, proved that the acceleration could not have been caused by interior disturbances, as had at first been surmised. A great interior disturbance of the sun might indeed cause it to spin suddenly faster, but no such disturbance could be imagined as causing an exact and equal increase in its speed of spin with each succeeding day. What, then, could be the cause? Could it be that in some strange way the universe was suddenly running down?

But while Dr. Marlin and his fellow astronomers discussed this matter of the phenomenon's cause, it was its effects that had begun to claim the attention of the world at large. For that increase of the sun's speed was already making itself felt upon Earth. Even the great storms in the sun's mass, those storms that we call sunspots, indeed, make themselves felt upon Earth by the intense electrical and magnetic currents of force which they throw forth, causing on Earth electrical storms and auroras and strange weather changes. And now all the usual phenomena were occurring, but enhanced in intensity. On the third day of the thing, the 6th of May, there occurred over the mid-Atlantic an electrical storm of such terrific power as to all but sweep from the air the great airliners caught in it, the Constantinople-New York liner and a grain-ship bound from Odessa to Baltimore having been forced down almost to the sea's surface by the terrific air currents. Great auroras were reported farther south than ever before, and over all our Earth changes in temperature were quick and sudden. And among the other new phenomena called into being, apparently by the sun's increased spin, were the new vibrations discovered at that time by Dr. Robert Whitely, a prominent physicist and a colleague of Dr. Marlin's at North American University.

Dr. Whitely's report, though rather obscured in interest by the central fact of the sun's increased speed of spin, was yet interesting enough to physical students, for in it he claimed to have discovered the existence of a new and unknown vibratory force, emanating apparently from the disturbed sun. This was, he claimed, a vibration whose frequency lay in the octaves between light and Hertzian or radio vibrations, an unexplored territory in the domain of etheric vibrations. Dr. Whitely himself had for some time been endeavoring to push his researches into that particular territory, but though he had striven with many methods, he had been able to produce or find no etheric vibrations of that frequency until the strange increase of the sun's rotatory speed had begun. Then, he stated, his instruments had recorded new vibrations somewhere out in space toward the sun, whose frequency lay between the light and Hertzian frequencies, and which seemed a force-vibration of some sort, weak reflections from it only being recorded by his instruments. It seemed possible, he stated, that this strange new force-vibration was being generated somewhere inside the disturbed sun itself, and he was studying it further to determine the truth of this theory.

This discovery of Dr. Whitely's, however interesting though it was, seemed to be but a side issue of the real problem, the acceleration of the sun's rotation. After the sixth day, there were no further reports from Dr. Marlin and his fellow astronomers. During all the seventh and eighth and ninth days there came no word to the Intelligence Bureau regarding it, from any of the astronomers who had formerly reported to us on it. And though we got into touch with Dr. Marlin and the others by communication-plate, none of them in those three days would make any statement whatever on the thing, saying only that it was being carefully studied by them and that a statement would be issued soon. It was evident from this universal sudden silence on their part that the astronomers of the world's observatories were acting in conjunction, but why they should want to withhold from an interested world the news on this strange acceleration of the sun's spin, we could not understand. The great electrical storms and temperature changes that had prevailed over Earth continued, and we were anxious to know how much longer we might expect them to continue.

"One would think that Dr. Marlin and the other astronomers had some great secret they were keeping from us," I remarked to Markham, the Intelligence Chief, and he shook his head.

"Secret or not, Hunt, they're doing us out of the first unusual news subject we've had for a year," he said. "Why don't they give us whatever they've learned about this change in the sun's rate of spin?"

It was a question repeated by more than one in those days, for the great public having become interested in the matter was irritated by this silence on the part of Dr. Marlin and his fellow scientists. Whatever they had learned or guessed as to the thing's cause, why did they not give their information to the Intelligence Bureau for distribution to the world? It was hinted freely that the whole matter was a hoax devised by Dr. Marlin, which had duped the astronomical world for the time being, and which they were reluctant to acknowledge. It was suggested also that the World President or the World Congress should take action to make the astronomers give out their usual reports. The public was quickly working itself into a state of indignation over the matter, when there suddenly burst upon it that doom-laden and terrible statement by Dr. Marlin, which was to loose an unprecedented terror upon the peoples of Earth.

IT was on May 13th, the tenth day after Dr. Marlin's first announcement of the thing, that he gave to the world through the Intelligence Bureau that epochal statement, and in it he referred first to his silence and to the silence of his fellow astronomers in the preceding few days. "In those days," he said, "every observatory in the world has been engaged in an intensive investigation of this acceleration of the sun's rotation, which I discovered. And in each of those days the sun's rotatory speed has continued to increase at exactly the same rate! In each day that speed has increased so much as to cut down the sun's rotatory period 4 hours more, so that now, ten days after the beginning of the thing, its rotatory period has been cut down by 40 hours. In other words, ten days ago the sun turned as it had always turned to our knowledge, at the rate of one turn in every 25 days, at its equator. Now the sun's rotatory speed has increased to the rate of one turn in every 23 days, 8 hours.

"And that increase of rotary speed continues. With each passing day the sun's rate of rotation is growing greater by the same amount, with each passing day it is lessening its rotatory period by 4 hours. And that steady increase of rotation of the sun, if it continues, spells destruction for the sun as we know it! All know that the sun in rotating generates in its own mass a certain amount of centrifugal force, force which tends to break up its mass. That force is not large enough, however, in our own sun to affect its great mass, since our sun's speed of rotation is not great. We know that over vast periods of time a sun's rotatory speed will increase, due to the slow shrinkage of its mass, and that when the speed has increased to a point where its centrifugal force is greater than its own power of cohesion, the sun breaks up like a bursting flywheel, breaks up or divides into a double or multiple star. Thousands upon tens of thousands of the stars of our universe are double or multiple stars, having been formed thus from dividing single suns, whose speed or rotation became too great.

"But as I have said, our own sun seemed in no danger of this fate, since the natural increase of a sun's rotatory speed, due to the shrinkage of its mass, is so unthinkably slow, requires such unthinkable ages, that it is out of all concern of ours. For our sun has rotated once in 25 days at its equator, and it has been calculated that it would need to reach a rotatory speed of once in one hour before its centrifugal force would be great enough to divide it, to break it up. And because of that eon-long slowness of a star's natural increase of rotatory speed, there seemed, indeed, no slightest peril of our own sun dividing or breaking up thus, because before it could reach that speed of rotation required, unthinkable ages must elapse.

"But now, due to some cause, which none of us have been able to guess, some great cause utterly enigmatic and unknown to us, our sun's rotatory speed has begun suddenly to grow greater, to increase! Faster and faster every day the sun is spinning, its speed of rotation increasing by the same amount each day, its rotatory period decreasing by exactly 4 hours each day! You see what that means? It means that if the sun's speed of spin continues to increase at that steady rate, if its rotatory period continues to decrease by that amount each day, as it shows every sign of doing, within 140 days more the sun's rate of rotation will have increased so much that it will be turning at the rate of one turn in one hour, will have reached that speed at which our calculations show that its great mass can no longer hold together! So that 140 days from now, if this increase of rotatory speed continues, our sun will infallibly divide into a double star!

"And that division means death for Earth and almost all its sister planets! For when the sun divides into two great new suns, the first force of their division will send those two mighty balls of fire apart from each other, and pushing thus apart from each other, they will inevitably engulf in their fiery masses all the inner planets and most of the outer ones! Mercury, Venus, Earth and Mars will undoubtedly be engulfed in the fires of the two dividing suns upon their first separation, their first division. Jupiter and Saturn and very probably Uranus will be drawn inevitably into fiery death also in one or another of those great suns, if they too, are not overwhelmed in the first separation. Neptune alone, the outermost of all the sun's planets, will be far enough out to escape annihilation in the dividing suns when the terrific cataclysm occurs. For if the sun continues to spin faster, as it is now doing, that cataclysm must inevitably occur, and must as inevitably plunge our Earth to fiery doom and wreck our solar system, our universe!"

CHAPTER TWO
To Neptune!

"DOOM faces us, a fiery doom in which the dividing sun will annihilate Earth and most of its sister planets! Panic even now grips all the peoples of Earth, such panic as has never been known before, as that doom marches inevitably toward them. Yet inevitable, inescapable as that doom seems, we of the World Congress, we who represent here all the gathered peoples of Earth, must endeavor to find even now some last chance of lifting this awful menace from us."

The World President paused, his dark, steady eyes searching out through the great room at whose end, upon a raised platform, he stood. Behind him on that platform sat a row of some two-score men and women, garbed like himself and all others in the modern short and sleeveless garments of differing colors, while before him in the great room stretched the rows of seated members of the great World Congress, the twelve hundred men and women who represented in it all the peoples of Earth. Just beneath the great platform's edge sat Markham, the Intelligence Chief, and myself; before us were the switches that controlled the communication-plates throughout the room that broadcast all proceedings in it to the world. And sitting there, I could glance up and see among those two-score behind the World President two figures well known to me; the strong figure of Dr. Marlin, with his intense gray eyes and gray-touched hair; and the lounging, dark-haired form of Dr. Robert Whitely, his somewhat sardonic countenance and cool eyes turned now with keen interest toward the World President before him. And as the latter began again to speak my own gaze shifted toward him.

"It has been just three days," the World President was saying, "since Dr. Herbert Marlin and his fellow astronomers gave to the world a warning of this doom that hangs above it, gave to us a warning that in less than five months more, if the sun's rotatory speed continues to increase, it must inevitably divide into a double star and in so doing wreck our universe and plunge most of its planets into fiery death. I need not speak now of the terror that has reigned over Earth since that announcement. It is sufficient to say that the first wild riots, inspired by that terror in Europe and Northern Asia, have been suppressed by the dispatch of police cruisers, and that throughout the world order is being maintained and most of our world's activities are being carried on as usual. Yet it is clear to all that the panic which that statement inspired has not subsided, rather it is growing in force over the Earth's surface with the passing of each day. For each day is bringing our Earth nearer to death.

"For each day, each of these three intervening days, the sun's speed of rotation has continued to increase by the same exact amount. Each day its rotatory period has decreased by 4 hours more. It cannot be doubted then that whatever is causing this strange acceleration, it will keep on, until in a mere 137 days from the present, the sun's rotatory period will have reached the figure of one hour. When that occurs our sun will, as Dr. Marlin has warned us, divide into a double star. Nothing in the universe can save our Earth or its neighboring planets then. Our one hope, therefore, to save ourselves, is to prevent that thing from happening, to halt this acceleration of the sun's spin before it reaches its critical point 137 days from now! For it is only by halting that steady increase of its rotatory speed that we can avoid this terrific cataclysm that means death for us!

"But can we halt this acceleration of the sun's spin when none of our astronomers has been able to ascertain its cause? That is what you will ask, and in answer to that I say, some hours ago two of our scientists *did* ascertain that cause. They learned at last what great, what almost incredible cause is responsible for this acceleration of our sun's rotatory speed. Those two scientists are well known to all of you, for they are Dr. Herbert Marlin himself, who first discovered the fact of the sun's faster spin, and Dr. Robert Whitely, his physicist colleague, who has been studying the new vibrations recorded by his instruments since the beginning of that acceleration of the sun's rotatory speed. These two men have found, at last, the terrible cause of our sun's strange behavior, and it is that you might hear it that I have called you of the World

Congress together at this time. It is Dr. Marlin himself, then, who will tell you what he and his fellow scientist have discovered."

The World President stepped aside, and as he did so Dr. Marlin rose, stepped forward to the great platform's edge, and looked quietly out over the great room's occupants. I was aware as he did so of a quality of utter tension in all the hundreds in that room, of a hushed silence, in which the slightest sound seemed unnaturally loud. Through the great windows there came a deep hum of sound from the sunlit surrounding city, but in the big room itself was silence almost complete until Dr. Marlin's strong, deep voice broke it.

"It was thirteen days ago," he said, "that the acceleration of our sun's rotatory speed was first noted, thirteen days ago that it first began to spin faster. In those days we of the world's observatories have sought unceasingly for the cause, whatever it was, that was behind this strange acceleration of the sun's spin, and have sought for that cause even more intently in the last few days, since it was recognized by us, that this increasing rotatory speed foreshadowed the division of the sun and the doom of almost all its planets. That acceleration of speed was too exact, too uniform each day, to be the result of interior disturbances. It could not be the result of the influence of some dark body passing the solar system in space, for such a body would affect the planets also. What, then, could be the thing's cause? That is what I and all astronomers have been seeking to solve in the last days. That great enigma has finally been solved, not by an astronomer, but by a physicist—by Dr. Robert Whitely, my fellow professor at North American University.

"It will be remembered that when the first great effects of the sun's increased spin became apparent on Earth, the great electrical storms and temperature changes that still are troubling Earth, Dr. Whitely announced the discovery of new vibrations which were apparently emanating from the troubled sun also. That new vibration lay in frequency between the Hertzian and the light vibrations, an unexplored territory in the field of etheric vibrations. It seemed, Dr. Whitely then stated, a force-vibration of some sort, the weak reflected impulses from it, that reached his instruments, affecting them as tangible force. It seemed reasonable to suppose, therefore, that this new force-vibration or ray was being generated inside the sun's disturbed mass, just as light-vibrations and heat-vibrations and cosmic ray-vibrations and many others are generated by and radiated from the sun.

"IN the next days, however, Dr. Whitely continued to study this new vibration, and endeavored to trace it accurately to the sun by using recording instruments which recorded it as strongest or weakest in various quarters of space. By means of these instruments, he was able to plot the course of this force-vibration or ray in space, to chart the path of its strongest portion in space. And by doing this he found that this new force vibration, contrary to his expectations, was not being radiated out equally in all directions as one might expect. It was being shot forth in a great force-beam or ray, one which cut a straight path across half our solar system! And that mighty force-ray, whose weaker reflected pulsings only struck his instruments here on Earth, was not being generated and shot forth by the sun, but was *striking* the sun! And tracing its path out across the solar system by his charts he found that the great force-ray was being shot out from the planet Neptune, was stabbing across the great gulf from Neptune, the outermost planet, and striking the sun!

"And it was that giant force-ray, as Dr. Whitely and I soon saw, that was and is making our sun's rotatory speed steadily increase! For that great ray, as we found, is one that can stab across space and strike any object with terrific force, as though it were solid and material! You know that even light rays, light vibrations, exert a definite pressure or force upon the matter which they strike. Well, these force-vibrations, of greater wave-length than the light vibrations, also exert pressure and force upon any matter which they strike, but they exert an infinitely greater pressure, can stab across the vast void and strike any object with colossal and unceasing pressure. In this way, then, this great force-vibration or ray hurtles across space and strikes all matter in its path with terrific force, as though a solid arm were pushing across the gulf.

"And this terrific ray of force, stabbing in through the solar system from Neptune, was striking our sun just at its edge, just at its limb, at its equator. It struck that edge turning always away from Neptune, and striking that turning edge of the sun with terrific force as it did, the great pushing ray made it turn even faster away from Neptune at that edge, made the sun turn faster and faster! Pressing always upon the turning sun's edge with the same great power, this mighty force-ray has made the sun rotate faster each day, has made its rotatory speed increase by the same amount each day. And since that great ray is still stabbing across the gulf from Neptune to the sun, is still accelerating the sun's spin, it is to that ray that we will owe the division of our sun into two parts, 137 days from now, and the consequent wrecking of our solar system!

"For Neptune alone will escape the cataclysm that will take place when the sun divides, and it is from Neptune, from intelligent beings on Neptune, there can be not the slightest doubt, that this great force-ray comes. For it cannot be doubted for an instant that this mighty force-ray is the work of intelligent creatures upon Neptune. Never in all the many discussions concerning the possibility of life on the other planets have astronomers conceded any possibility of life on Neptune, the outermost of the sun's worlds, for though we have always known it to have air and water, its great distance from the sun must needs make it so cold a world as to be unable to sustain life. That was our belief before, but now with this great ray from Neptune swiftly wrecking our solar system before our very eyes, we can no longer doubt that life, intelligent life, exists there!

"It is the beings of Neptune, therefore, the creatures of the sun's outermost world, who are making the sun spin faster and faster, who are deliberately planning to make our sun divide into a double star, to wreck its universe! What their reason is for doing this, we cannot now guess. We know that Neptune, almost alone among the sun's planets, will survive the great cataclysm of its division, and we can but hazard the thought that it is for some great advantage to themselves that the Neptunians are engaged upon this colossal task. Neither can we guess just how, exactly, they are doing it, how they are able to push against the sun with such colossal force without Neptune itself being pushed out into the void by the tremendous reaction from that push. But these things are not of the greatest interest to us now.

"The thing of greatest interest to us now is this: Can we halt this acceleration of the sun's rotation, can we thwart the doom which the Neptunians would loose upon us? To do that there is but one remedy! That is to bring an end this great force-ray which the beings of Neptune are playing upon our sun's edge, with which they are making that sun turn faster. And to bring that ray to an end, to destroy it, it is necessary that we go out to Neptune, to the source of that great ray. For it is only at its source, whatever that source may be, that this force-ray can be destroyed! And it is only by destroying that force-ray that Earth and its sister planets can be saved!

"This proposition, this plan to go out to Neptune itself, may seem to you impossible. For greatly as our scientific knowledge has risen in the last decades, we have been unable to bridge the gulf to even the nearest of the planets. True, we have managed to send rockets to our moon and explode flares there by means of them, but never yet have any of us reached even the nearest of our neighboring planets. And thus to propose to go out to Neptune, the farthest and outermost of all the planets, the last outpost of our solar system, may appear to you quite senseless. But it is not so, for now, at last, there is given to us the power to venture out into the gulf of space to other planets! And that power is given to us by the very doom that now threatens us, since it is the force-ray or vibration with which the beings of Neptune are turning our sun faster, which we can use to cross the gulf of space!

"For since his instruments first received and recorded that vibration, the weak reflected pulsings of the great ray, Dr. Whitely has studied it intensively, and has been able, by reversing the hook-up of his receiving and recording instruments, to produce similar vibrations, a similar ray, himself! He has been able to devise small generators which produce the same force-ray, and on that principle larger generators also can be devised and constructed, to shoot forth a force-ray of immense power. With such a force-ray, generated from inside a strong, hermetically-closed flier, one could shoot out at will into the great void! For if such a flier, resting on Earth, turned its powerful ray down upon Earth, that ray would strike Earth with terrific force. Being so vast in mass, and the flier from which the ray is shot down being so small, it would not be Earth that would be perceptibly moved by the ray, but the flier itself would be shot instantly up and outward into space by the ray's great pushing reaction!

"It would be necessary only to head the space-flier out toward the desired planet upon starting, and the pushing force of the great ray, constantly turned on, would so accelerate the flier's speed that it would be pushed out toward that planet at a terrific velocity, a speed which could be controlled by the power of the pushing ray. To escape the attraction of other planets among which it might pass, the space-flier would need only to shoot a similar great force-ray out toward whatever planet was attracting it, and the pushing force of that ray would hold the flier out from it. And when the space-flier neared the planet that was its goal, it could gradually slow its progress by means of a ray shot ahead toward that planet, braking its forward rush thus, and being able to land smoothly and without harm upon that planet!

"Such a space-flier as that might be built and operated in that way, with the great force-ray or vibration of the beings of Neptune to propel it, and in such a flier it would be possible to go out across the gulf to Neptune itself. Such a flier, pushing itself out into space with a great ray, could be brought to such colossal speeds that the journey out through the gulf to the distant planet could be accomplished in but a score or more of days. We have the power to build that flier, we have at last, at this tense moment, the power to send such a space-flier out into the void. And I propose that such a space-flier be built with the greatest speed possible and be sent out to Neptune to locate and if possible to destroy the source of the mighty force-ray whose colossal power is spinning our sun ever faster, threatening Earth and most of its sister planets with a final doom!

"A SINGLE space-flier capable of holding three or four men and their equipment and supplies, could be built in a month or more, if all energies were concentrated upon it, and if the great generators of the force-ray which it would need could be constructed in that time. That single flier, when built, should be sent out to Neptune at once! For little enough time remains to us before the break-up of our sun; little more than four months indeed. And that single flier, going out with its occupants at once, could locate the source of the mighty force-ray on Neptune, and if it could not destroy that ray's source, could at least return to Earth with exact knowledge of its position. And in the interval, there could be constructed here on Earth a fleet of such space-fliers, so that with a knowledge of the great ray's source these might be able to destroy it. All depends, however, upon constructing and sending out that first space-flier, while there is yet time!

"It would not be possible to construct a large space-flier in the short time of a month that I have mentioned, but a small one capable of holding four men, say, could be built in that time if all efforts were concentrated upon it. And I myself will be one of those four! For upon disclosing this plan to the World President, I was asked by him to be the commander of such a space-flier on its venture out to Neptune; and I accepted! Another of that four must be Dr. Whitely, whose discovery of the great force-ray from Neptune has shown us whence our doom is coming, and which discovery has alone made such a space-flier possible. It is my intention to take as a third my own assistant, Allen Randall, and as the fourth person to make this momentous voyage it would be best, no doubt, to have some younger member of the Intelligence Bureau, so that a complete report on the great ray's source and on all else encountered could be brought back, in case we were unable to destroy the ray ourselves.

"This, then, is the one chance for our Earth, that in such a space-flier or fliers we of Earth can go out to Neptune and put an end to that mighty force-ray from Neptune that is spinning our sun ever faster. For if we can do that, if we can construct such a space-flier or fliers and reach Neptune and bring an end to that ray before the 137 days left to us have elapsed, we will have halted this acceleration of our sun's spin, will have prevented its division. But if we cannot do that, if we are unable in the short time remaining to us to accomplish the task of destroying that mighty force-ray, then the beings of Neptune will have accomplished their colossal purpose, will have caused our sun to divide into a double star and will have sent all its planets except Neptune to a fiery doom!"

Dr. Marlin's strong voice ceased, and as it did so an utter silence reigned over the great room for some moments, broken at last by the voices of the twelve hundred members of the great World

Congress—breaking into a vast, indistinguishable roar! My heart was pounding at what I had heard, and I turned, spoke swiftly to Markham beside me, and then as he nodded was leaping up myself upon the great platform! Was leaping up to where Marlin was standing now with Dr. Whitely and the World President, the whole great room trembling now with the cheering shouts with which those in it greeted Dr. Marlin's announcement. And there I was speaking rapidly to the World President, and to Dr. Marlin.

"The fourth man, sir!" I cried. "The fourth man that's to go in the space-flier—let me be that fourth!"

The World President, recognizing me, turned inquiringly toward Dr. Marlin, who nodded, placing a hand on my shoulder. "Hunt is from the Intelligence Bureau," he said, "and he's young and has had scientific training—was one of my own students. We could have no better fourth."

My heart leaped at his words, and then the World President nodded to me. "You will be the fourth then, Mr. Hunt," he said, shaking my hand. And as I stood there on the platform with Marlin and Dr. Whitely, the World President was turning back to the hundreds of shouting members, a sea of faces extending back to the great room's walls. Cheering as they were at this last chance to save Earth and its peoples that had been proposed to them, this last hope given to them to halt the terrible doom overshadowing them, their great uproar yet stilled for a moment as the World President turned toward them, as his voice went out to them over the great room.

"You, the members of the World Congress," he said, "have heard that which Dr. Marlin has told you. With this last hope in view, it is unnecessary for me to tell you to bend now all the world's energies toward that one chance, toward the construction of the first space-flier. For since upon that space-flier rests the only chance to save Earth, to prevent the sun's cataclysmic division, which this great ray from Neptune is accomplishing. I have no fear but that in a month from now that space-flier will be completed. Have no fear but that in it, a month from now, Dr. Marlin and his three friends will start on their unprecedented and momentous voyage out from Earth into space; will start on their great flight out through the void—to Neptune!"

CHAPTER THREE
The Space Flier Starts

"THREE more days and the last work will be done—the space-flier will be finished!"

It was Dr. Marlin who spoke and Whitely beside him, nodded. "Three more days," he said, "and we'll be starting."

We four, Marlin and Whitely and Randall and myself, were standing on the flat roof of the great World Government building, that gigantic cylindrical white structure that looms two thousand feet into the air at the center of the new world capital, New York. All around us there stretched the colossal panorama of New York's mighty cylindrical buildings, each rearing skyward from its little green park, extending as far away as the eye could reach, many of them rising on great supporting piers out of the waters of the rivers and bay around the island. In the late afternoon sunlight above them there swirled and seethed great masses of arriving and departing aircraft, unfolding their helicopter-vanes from their long hulls as they paused to rise or descend, seeming to fill the air, while away to the south the great Singapore-New York liner was slanting smoothly down toward the great flat surface of the air-docks. Yet it was to none of these things, nor to the masses of humans that swarmed and crowded in the city's streets far beneath us, that we four were giving our attention at that moment, for we were gazing intently at the great object that stood on the roof before us.

That object was a great gleaming metal polyhedron that loomed in a supporting framework beside us like a huge ball-like faceted crystal of metal. This great faceted ball of metal, though, was fully thirty feet in diameter, and here and there in the great, smooth, faceted, plane-surfaces of it were set hexagonal windows of clear glass, protected by thick raised rims of metal around them. There were also set in six of the facets six round openings a foot in diameter, one of these being in the faceted ball's top, one in its bottom, and four at equidistant points around its equator. In one of the flat facet-sides, also, was a screw-door of a few feet diameter that now was open, giving a glimpse across a small vestibule-chamber inside through a second open screw-door into the great polyhedron's interior. That interior seemed crowded with gleaming mechanisms and equipment, attached to the inner side of the great metal shell.

Marlin was contemplating the great thing intently as we stood there on the roof beside its supporting framework. "Finished—in three more days," he repeated. "Everything's ready for the last generator."

"That will be done in two days more," said Randall, beside me. "Everything else at the World Government's laboratories has been suspended in order to get these generators ready for us."

"They've worked fast to get three of the generators in the flier already," Marlin acknowledged. "Especially since Whitely here, in directing them, had only his own first crude models to work on."

"Lucky we are to get the generators completed and the space-flier finished in the month we estimated!" I exclaimed. "If the whole world hadn't centered its energies on the space-flier's completion we'd never have done it—and even so it's been a tremendous task."

It had, indeed, been a period of tense and toiling activity for Marlin and Whitely and Randall and me, that time of four weeks that had elapsed since Marlin had proposed his great plan to the World Congress. In those weeks all our efforts, and all the efforts of the world too, it seemed, had been concentrated upon the building of that space-flier in which we four, first of all men, were to venture out into the great void, to flash out to Neptune in our attempt to halt the great ray that was spinning our sun ever faster to its destruction and to ours. For each day of those four weeks the rotatory speed of the sun had grown ever greater, its rotatory period decreasing by an exact four hours each day. The instruments of Dr. Whitely, too, showed that the mighty force-ray was still playing unceasingly from Neptune upon the turning sun's edge, spinning that sun ever faster. Already the terrific pressure of that great ray had lowered the sun's rotatory period to 18 days, 4 hours, and in hardly more than a hundred days more, we knew, would have brought the sun's rotatory period down to that critical figure of one hour at which it could no longer hold together, at which it would divide into a double star and plunge Earth to doom and wreck the solar system.

And with that knowledge, all the world had sought to aid in the construction of our space-flier. Dr. Marlin had directed that construction, aided by his assistant, young Randall, whom I had met for the first time and had found a sunny-haired fun-loving fellow of my own age. And it had been Dr. Marlin who, after consultation with the world's greatest engineering authorities, had chosen for the flier the form of a great polyhedron. Such a form, it had been found, could resist pressure from within and without much better than the spherical form that had been at first suggested, and it was realized that this power of resistance would be necessary. For upon venturing out from Earth's gravitation field into gravitationless space, the very interior stresses of such a space-flier would tend to explode it unless it was braced against those stresses. Also the space-flier was to be shot out through the void and maneuvered in that void by the pushing reaction of its own great force-rays against the Earth or other planets, and though that force would thus hurtle the flier out at terrific speed, it would also crumple the flier itself unless it were strong enough to withstand the force-ray's terrific pressure.

WITH the space-flier's form decided and the plans for it drafted, work upon it had begun at once. At the World President's suggestion, it was being set up on the great flat roof of the World Government building. From over all Earth had come the world's most brilliant engineers and scientists to aid in its construction, for the world lay still beneath the great shadowing wing of fear that had been cast over it, when the peoples of Earth had learned first of the doom that Neptune and its beings were loosing upon the solar system. So that though the world's first wild panic had subsided, it had been replaced by a waxing realization and dread that had made the peoples of Earth and their representatives offer to us their help in this plan of ours, which alone held out any chance, however slender, of escape from the annihilation that was nearing Earth. Laboring ceaselessly day and night therefore, in picked crews of workers that every few hours replaced each other,

Dr. Marlin and Randall and myself and our eager workers had swiftly brought the great space-flier's metal shell into being.

That great crystal-like shell, at Dr. Marlin's suggestion, had been made double-walled, the space between the two walls being pumped to as complete a vacuum as possible so that vacuum might insulate the flier's interior from the tremendous differences in temperature that it would meet in space. For where the sun's heat-radiations struck the flier in space it would be warm, hot even, but those parts in shadow would be subjected to the absolute zero of empty space. Each of these thick double walls, in turn, was itself built up of alternate layers of finest steel and of non-metallic, asbestos-like insulating material, pressed and welded together by titanic forces into a single thickness. And the great faceted wall-sections of the flier, when in place, had been so welded and fused one to the other by the new molecular-diffusion fusing process, that the great ball-like faceted flier might have been and was, in fact, a single and seamless polyhedron, its strength enormous.

In one of the flier's facets was the round screw-door, admitting one through a small vestibule-chamber, and then through a second hermetically-sealing door into the flier's interior. In that interior, all the flier's mechanisms and equipment had been attached directly to the inner side of its great crystal-like ball, with hexagonal windows, made double and of thick unbreakable glass, here and there in the walls, between the mechanisms. Just inside one of those large windows, at what might be called the ball-like flier's front, were ranged on a black panel of several feet in length the space-flier's controls. The most central of these controls were six gleaming-handled levers which controlled the flier's great force-rays, shooting them forth from anyone of the six ray openings in its sides, to send the flier hurtling through space by reaction, or to use against asteroids or other objects as a great weapon. Supported from the wall in front of those levers was a metal chair that swung on pivots and on sliding pneumatic shock-absorbing tubes, a metal strap across it to hold its occupant in it. And the occupant of that chair, with the six force-ray controls before him, thus controlled the flier's flight through space, and could, if necessary, use its great rays as weapons.

To the left of those controls were the recording dials and switches of the four great generators. Those four gleaming cubical generators themselves were attached to the other side of the flier's hollow interior, along with the marvelously compact and powerful Newson-Canetti batteries. Operating from those batteries whose power-stores were almost exhaustless, the generators, when turned on, would generate the great force-vibrations which, of a wavelength higher than that of light vibrations, exerted a terrific pressure or force beside which the pressure of light was as nothing. These vibrations were carried by thick black cables running between the flier's double walls to the projecting mechanisms inside the six ray-openings, and from those openings the great force-vibrations were released as great force-rays by the operator of the flier's six controls. These great force-rays, we had found, almost equaled the speed of light itself in the velocity with which they shot out from the flier's ray-openings.

In front of the generators' recording dials and switches was suspended a metal chair like that of the control-operator, while between those two was a third chair before which, on the control-panel, were ranged the instruments recording the space-flier's conditions of flight. There was a space-speed indicator, working by means of ether-drift, a set of dials that accurately recorded the gravitational pull of celestial bodies in all directions, inside and outside temperature recorders, inside and outside air-testers, and beside others the controls of a number of the necessary mechanisms attached at different points inside the hollow faceted ball of the flier. Among these were the controls of the flier's air-renovator, which automatically removed the carbon-dioxide from the flier's breathed air by atomic dissociation and replaced it with oxygen from the compact tanks of compressed liquid-oxygen; the controls of the heating-mechanism, which beside its own heating coils was to utilize the heat of the sun on the flier's side in space; and the control of the hooded lights set above the flier's control panel and mechanisms.

To the right of the control-operator's chair, too, there was a fourth similar chair before which were ranged on the control panel a compact but extremely efficient battery of astronomical instruments. There was a ten-inch refracting telescope, its lens set directly in the big hexagonal window over the control panel, the tube of the telescope, thanks to the new "re-reflecting" principle, being but a score or so of inches in length. There was also a small but efficient spectroscope similarly mounted, a micrometric apparatus for accurate measurements of celestial objects, and a shielded bolometer for ascertaining the radiated heat of any celestial body.

These four metal chairs, suspended there in front of the long control-panel and with the big hexagonal window before and above them, were mounted all upon special shock-absorbing tubes of pneumatic design which would enable us to withstand the pressure of our flier's acceleration upon starting, and the pressure also of its deceleration upon slowing and stopping. Seated in them, we would be able to look forth over the space-flier's controls into the void before us, and since gravitation would be lacking in the flier, once out in space, metal straps across them would hold us in them. Here and there among the mechanisms that lined the ball-like flier's interior, too, were hand-grips by which we could float without harm among the mechanisms and equipment, while the metal bunks attached at one point to the flier's interior were provided with metal straps to hold us in them during sleep.

RANGED among the mechanisms, that lined the flier's interior, were the cabinets that held our stores and special equipment. Among these were ample stores of food in thermos-cans, kept hot thus and obviating all necessity of cooking, the tanks of compressed water, and the extra liquid-oxygen tanks. Also attached to hooks on the walls were the four space-walkers that had been constructed for us to enable us to venture outside of the flier into airless space, if necessary. These space-walkers were cylindrical metal structures seven feet or more in height and three in diameter, tapering at the top to a smooth dome in which were small vision-windows. Each held a small generator of force-vibrations, and an equally small air-renovator. There were two hollow metal jointed arms that extended from the upper part, and on entering the cylinder and closing its base-door one thrust his own arms inside those hollow metal ones. They ended in great pincer-claws that could be actuated by one's own hands inside, while the space-walker itself was moved through the void by its generated force-vibrations being shot out from a small ray-opening in the cylinder's bottom.

Standing inside the hollow, ball-like polyhedron of the flier, therefore, its mechanisms and equipment extended all about and above and beneath one, attached rigidly in every case to the flier's inner surface. That equipment, those mechanisms, indeed, had taxed all the powers of the great World Government laboratories to provide in the short time that was ours, but by a miracle of effort it had been done. And now, as we four gazed up toward the great gleaming faceted thing, resting beside us there in its framework of metal girders, we knew that there remained only the last of the four great generators to be completed, and that in two days more, as Randall had said, that too would be completed and installed and the space-flier would be ready for its final tests and for the start of our great trip. Looking up at the great thing towering there beside us in the waning afternoon sunlight, I was struck with a sudden realization of the stupendousness of the task that we had set ourselves; of the thing that lay before us.

"To go out in that from Earth to Neptune—to Neptune!—it seems impossible," I said.

Marlin nodded, his hand on my shoulder, "It seems strange enough," he assented, "but to Neptune in three more days we're going, Hunt. For no other chance is there to save Earth from the doom marching upon it."

"But can we save it?" I exclaimed. "Can we four really hope to contend against beings who, whatever their nature, have power enough to reach across the solar system and speed our spinning sun on to its doom and ours?"

Marlin looked gravely at me, and at Whitely and Randall beside me. "A chance there is—must be," he said solemnly, "even though little time now remains to us. And with that chance—with Earth's chance—in our hands, we must strike out to the last with all our power for Earth!"

Those words of Marlin, I think, steadied us all in the whirling rush of activities that was ours during the next, the last, three days. For in those three days, as the last generator approached completion and was completed and installed, we four were ceaselessly busy with the last preparations for our start, Whitely, who had designed and was to have complete charge of the space-flier's great generators, was busy inspecting and testing those generators. Randall and I were familiarizing ourselves with the flier's controls, for we two were to alternate in controlling its flight through the void. Marlin, who would not only command our little party but would have charge of the astronomical equipment in it, and would chart our course out through the trackless gulf, was occupied beside numberless other tasks in plotting, with the assistance of some of the world's foremost astronomers, that course that we must follow now. So that as there came upon us the last day of June 16th, that day upon whose night we were to start our momentous journey, it found us working still upon our last preparations.

By the time that day and night had come, too, it found the excited expectation of the world keyed up to an agonized point. For days, indeed, great crowds had swirled about the base of the huge World Government building, on whose roof we worked, and, as the last hours approached, it seemed that all the world's thoughts, indeed, were concentrated upon that roof, upon the great gleaming space-flier on it. For all knew that upon that flier and upon the mission which we four were attempting in it depended the one chance of escape for Earth. For steadily, remorselessly, the sun was spinning still ever faster, the great pushing force-ray from Neptune still stabbing across the solar system to spin the sun on and on with greater and greater rotatory speed, until it divided and doomed Earth and its sister planets. So that those last days, those last hours, seemed to all the world as to ourselves to pass with nerve-tearing slowness.

There came at last, however, the night of the 16th, the night of our start, with the space-flier complete and ready in its framework at last. The last work of Marlin and Whitely had been to check over the construction-plans of the flier, which were to be left behind so that a great fleet of space-fliers, as the World President had said, could be constructed. Were we to return from Neptune with knowledge of the position and nature of the great doom-ray's source there, that fleet of space-fliers would be ready to sally out and attempt to bring an end to the great ray. But that knowledge, if we gained it, we must bring back ourselves, since there was no method of communication from our space-flier to Earth, the well-known "Heaviside layer" surrounding Earth being impenetrable to all radio and communication vibrations and making such communication impossible. With this last preparation completed, however, we four stood ready upon the night of the 16th for the start of our great venture.

IT was an hour after midnight that we were to start, and it was not until some minutes past midnight that Marlin and Whitely and Randall and I left our quarters in the World Government building and ascended to its roof. As we emerged upon that roof we stopped involuntarily. For the great roof itself and all the surrounding colossal city of New York were lit now with brilliant white suspended lights, and beneath them upon the roof and in the streets far beneath were masses upon masses of waiting men and women. Those upon the roof were the twelve hundred members of the great World Congress, assembled there to see our start out into the void on our desperate venture. At their center was a clear, roped-off space on the roof in which there towered the framework that held our great space-flier, gleaming in the brilliance of the lights about it, and just inside that clear space stood the World President, a half-dozen officials beside him.

As we paused there for that moment, Marlin's face grave and intent with purpose, Whitely coolly looking about him, and Randall and I endeavoring to conceal the excitement that pounded at our hearts, the whole scene was imprinted indelibly upon my brain. The crowds and brilliant lights about and beneath us, the great space-flier's faceted bulk looming into the darkness, the colossal buildings of the great world capital that stretched away in the darkness in all directions, a great mass of shining lights among which swirled a packed sea of humanity gazing up toward our flier—these formed a mighty panorama about us, but in that moment we turned our gaze up from them, up toward the great constellations of summer stars that gleamed in the black skies overhead. Away in the southern skies, not high above the horizon, burned the equatorial constellations, Scorpio and Sagittarius and Capricorn, with the calm white light-globule of Jupiter moving in

Scorpio and the bright red dot of Mars and yellow spark of Saturn in Capricorn. But it was toward Sagittarius that we were gazing, for among that constellation's stars there shone also Neptune, invisible to our unaided eyes but almost seen by us, it seemed, in that tense moment.

Then we four were moving across the roof toward the looming framework that upheld the space-flier, pausing inside its clear space to face the World President. It was a moment of cosmic drama, that moment in which Earth and the silent peoples of Earth, that had gathered in millions there to watch us, were sending forth four of themselves into the trackless void for the first time, sending them forth with Earth's one chance for life in their hands. The World President, facing us, did not speak, though; did not break the thick silence that seemed to lie over all the mighty city. He reached forth, gripped our hands with his own, grasped them tightly, silently, his steady eyes upon ours, and then stepped back. And then Marlin leading, we were clambering up the framework to the flier's screw-door, passing silently inside and then screwing that great door hermetically shut behind us. That done, we passed across the little vestibule-chamber and through the second screw-door, closing it likewise behind us.

Then, clambering up to the four suspended chairs in front of the control-panels, we took our places in them; Marlin in the right chair, his telescope and astronomical equipment before him, I in the next one, with the six controls of the space-flier's movements before me, Randall in the third chair, the recording dials and minor controls of the flier before him, and Whitely in the fourth or left chair, the dials and switches of the generators before him. Seated there, the constellation of Sagittarius and the other southern stars were full before us in our big window, for our space-flier was so supported in its framework that by turning on its great force-ray from the lower ray-opening we would be shot out by the terrific repulsive force straight toward Sagittarius, toward Neptune, slanting out tangent-wise from Earth's surface. And now Marlin was peering through the short, strange-looking tube of the telescope, was touching its focusing wheels lightly, peering again, and then turning to me.

"Neptune," he said quietly. "We'll start when it reaches the center of this telescope's field of view—when the flier is pointed directly toward it."

"But we can maneuver the flier in any direction in space, could head out from Earth and then toward Neptune," Randall commented, as I applied my own eye to the telescope, and Marlin nodded.

"We can, but by starting straight toward Neptune we'll use less of our generators' power."

While he spoke I was gazing through the telescope, and though I had gazed upon Neptune many times before it was never with such feelings as gripped me now. Like a little pale green spot of calm light it was, floating there in the darkness of the great void, its single moon not visible to me even through the powerful telescope. Then as I straightened from the telescope's eye-piece Marlin had taken it again, gazing intently into it now, to call out to me the moment when the planet reached the center of its field of view, when our space-flier would be headed straight toward it. For it was then, as Marlin had said, that we planned to hurtle out toward the planet with all the power of our great force-rays, not only reacting but pushing against Earth as light pushes. But since we must necessarily change our course once in space, to allow for Neptune's own movement among other things, we would use less power by making our first start straight toward it.

Now, as we sat tensely there, I had turned, nodded to Whitely, and he had thrown open the switches before him that controlled the great generators, their throbbing suddenly sounding behind us as they went into operation, generating the force-vibrations that in a moment would be released backward from our flier as mighty force-rays. As Whitely moved the switches, the throb of the generators died to a thin hum, then rose to a tremendous drone, and then slowly sank to a smooth throbbing beat at which he rested the switches. And now Marlin, beside me, was calling out to us the divisions of the specially-designed telescope's field, as Neptune passed across them to the zero mark at which we would hurtle outward.

"—45—40—35—30—"

As his steady voice sounded periodically beside me I sat as though a poised statue, my hand upon that lever among the six lever-switches before me that would send the power of our throbbing generators stabbing out with colossal force from the flier's ray-opening behind us, that would send that flier hurtling outward. "—25—20—15—." As the calm voice of Marlin broke the silence beside me I felt my heart racing with excitement, saw that Randall, and even Whitely, beside me, had hunched tensely forward as the moment approached. I glanced out a moment through the flier's windows, seeing in a blurred impression the breathless, watching crowds, the brilliant lights. "—10—5—zero!" And as that last word sounded I threw open in one swift motion the lever-switch in my grasp!

The next instant there was a colossal roaring about us, we seemed pressed down in our chairs with titanic, crushing force, and saw crowds and lights and great buildings vanishing from about our flier with lightning-like swiftness as a great pale ray of light, of colossal force, stabbed down and backward from the flier's ray-opening behind us! In a split-second all about us was blackness and then the great roaring sound about us had ceased, marking our passage out past the limits of Earth's atmosphere! Now through the windows before and about us, as we clung there, we saw the heavens around us brilliant with the fierce light of undimmed hosts of stars, while as our great flier reeled on at mounting speed into the great gulf, we saw behind and beneath us a great gray cloudy ball that was each moment contracting in size. Earth was receding and diminishing behind us as we flashed out through the void toward distant Neptune, to save that Earth from doom!

CHAPTER FOUR
Through Planetary Perils

"MARS ahead and to the left—we ought to pass it in three more hours!"

At my words Marlin nodded. "We won't be bothered much by the pull of Mars," he said.

We sat again in our chairs before the control-panel, Whitely to my left, gazing out through the large window before us. Ahead and

Wreckers
A Tale of Neptune

We sat again in our chairs before the control-panel, Whitely to my left, gazing through the big window before us . . . soaring past the limits of earth's atmosphere.

above and all around us there stretched a great panorama, stunning in its brilliance, the vast panorama of the starry heavens as seen from the airless interplanetary void. Blazing in their true brilliant colors on all sides of us, the hosts of stars were like jewels of light set in the black firmament. And as our flier throbbed on through the great gulf of empty space at terrific speed, its acceleration still pressing us down somewhat in our chairs, we could see now amid the flaming stars dead ahead the far green spot of light that was Neptune, our goal, visible now to our unaided eyes in the clearness of empty space. Nearer toward us and to the right Jupiter was like a brilliant little disk of white light, now, the four white points of its greater moons visible about it. To the left, too, yellow Saturn shone much brighter, while nearer toward us on the left, almost beside us, hung the dull-red little shield, white-capped at its poles, that was Mars.

Behind us, by this time, Earth had dwindled to a steady spot of bluish light that was like a tiny moon, the smaller spot that was Earth's moon gleaming near it. Hardly visible as Earth was in the blinding glare of the great sun that beat upon us from behind, its great corona and mighty prominences appalling in their splendor, yet it was visible enough to show how far from it out into the void our flier had already flashed. For forty-eight hours indeed, our great space-flier had rushed outward at a speed that had already reached over a million miles an hour, and that was steadily mounting still beneath the terrific reaction of our great force-ray, that great pale ray only visible at its ray-opening source, that was stabbing back with colossal power and by the reaction of that push sending us hurtling on at greater and greater speed. Out and out we had flashed, Randall and I relieving each other every four hours at the controls, and already now had almost reached the orbit of Mars, more than fifty million miles outward. Now, as Marlin and Whitely and I gazed out toward it, the red disk of Mars itself was but several million miles from us, to the left and ahead.

Gazing toward it, we could see clearly the great ice caps of the poles of Mars, brilliant white upon its dull red sphere, and could see clearly also the long straight markings upon it, a network of inter-connecting lines, that for long had been the subject of discussion and disputation among Earth's astronomers. It was with fascinated eyes that we gazed toward the red planet as we drew nearer to it, and now Randall had joined us, moving with great efforts against the acceleration-pressure inside the flier. Marlin, though, had turned the telescope by that time toward the crimson planet, was gazing intently toward it. Minutes he gazed before he straightened, shaking his head.

"There can be no doubt that those canals—those lines—are the work of intelligent creatures," he said. "I saw great geometrical forms that seemed structures of some sort, but our space-flier is moving at such tremendous speed that it's all but impossible to get a clear focus on the planet in the telescope."

We stared toward the red disk and its dark markings. "If we could but stop there—who knows what wonders Mars may hold, what science—,"Whitely mused.

Marlin nodded thoughtfully. "Neptune's our goal, and we can't stop for Mars now, whatever may be there. But if we succeed in our great task, if Earth is saved from this doom that Neptune's beings are loosing on the solar system, we'll come yet to Mars—and to all the others."

"In the meantime," I told them, "Mars is pulling our flier out of its course more and more. I thought our speed would take us by it, but it seems we'll have to use another ray."

For even as we had gazed toward the red planet, I had noted from the dials before Randall that the gravitational pull of Mars upon our space-flier from the left was becoming more and more powerful as we approached it to pass it, and that it was pulling us slowly toward it out of our course toward Neptune. Our deviation to the left was not great as yet, but even the slightest deviation we could not permit, since not only must we head as straight toward Neptune as possible to save time, but it was necessary that we avoid also the colossal force-ray which was stabbing from Neptune across the solar system toward the sun's edge, which was turning that sun ever faster. That great force-ray, invisible to us, but lying away to our left, we knew, would mean death for us if we blundered into it, would drive our flier with titanic force and speed straight into the sun!

So that now, as our space-flier moved nearer and nearer toward the distant red shield of Mars, pulled farther and farther out of its

path toward Neptune, I swiftly manipulated the ray-direction dials on the control-panel, then grasped and threw open another of the six ray-opening switches. At once there leaped from our racing flier's side, from one of its ray-openings there, a second great force-ray like that which stabbed from the flier's rear toward Earth. This second ray, though, vaguely visible like the first at its source, but fading into invisibility in space, shot out toward the red sphere of Mars, away to our left. And in a moment more, as that light swift ray reached Mars and pressed against the red planet with all its force, our flier was being pushed away from it, was being pushed back to the right, back into its original line of flight! Thus we hurtled on, the great rear ray of the flier pushing back with terrific force and sending us hurtling on
through space, while the side-ray, striking Mars with lesser force, was sufficient to keep us out of the red planet's grip as we flashed onward.

Within a few hours more Mars was behind us, its red sphere fading rapidly into a crimson spot of light to the left and behind. The planet's two tiny moons, Phobos and Deimos, we had not yet seen despite our nearness to it, but it was with something of regret that we saw the crimson world and all the strange mysteries that we felt existed upon it, dropping behind us. Neptune alone, as Marlin had said, was our goal, and on toward its calm green light-dot we were rushing. I turned off our side-ray, therefore, which was no longer needed to counteract Mars's pull, and we gave all our attention to the panorama ahead. Save for Neptune's distant green dot, the only planets now visible amid the brilliant hosts of stars before us were Jupiter and Saturn. Saturn was shining ever more brightly to the left, its strange ring formation already becoming visible to our eyes. But it was Jupiter that now dominated all the scene before us, his mighty sphere, its oblateness plainly visible, moving in majestic white splendor at the center of his four great moons.

It was not the planets ahead that held my attention now, though, as our throbbing flier raced onward, Mars and its orbit dropping behind. "The asteroids!" I exclaimed. "We're almost into their region now—will be among them soon!"

"And they're one of the greatest perils we'll encounter," Marlin said. "Hold ready to the controls, Hunt, for if we crash into one it means our end—the end of Earth's chance!"

I DID not need his admonition, though, to make me tense my hands upon the control-switches, gazing intently forward. I knew we were now passing into one of the most dangerous regions of all the solar system—that great belt of whirling asteroids that lies between the orbits of Mars and Jupiter. More than a thousand in number, ranging from the great sphere of Ceres, 480 miles in diameter, down to the smallest asteroids of a few miles diameter only, they whirled there around the sun between the four inner and four outer planets, their orbits a maze of interwoven circles and ellipses. The greater part of them were so small, indeed, that at the tremendous speed with which our space-flier was flashing on they could be seen only in the moment that we rushed upon them. And yet in that moment we must whirl aside from any before us, since otherwise, pulled closer by the asteroid's own gravitational power, we would infallibly crash into it and meet our doom.

Steadily, therefore, we watched now, as hour followed hour, as our flier rushed on with speed still slowly mounting, traveling finally at more than two million miles an hour. The throb of its four great generators was as steady as ever, and the pressure of its decreasing acceleration still weighed upon us, but already we had become accustomed to that pressure. So now while I gazed forth with Marlin ahead, Randall was at one of the right windows and Whitely at one of the left, keeping a similar watch. And it was Randall, a few hours later, who sighted the first of the asteroids. He uttered a swift exclamation, pointing to the right and ahead, and as we looked there we saw a small bright point in the blackness of space, a point that with the swiftness of lightning was expanding into a great, dull-gleaming sphere, rushing toward us and drawing our space-flier toward itself! A moment we saw it rushing thus toward us, a great sphere of barren, jagged rock, airless and waterless, turning slowly in space; and then it was looming gigantic just beside us!

In that moment, though, my hand had jerked open one of the six levers before me, and instantaneously had shot from our flier's side a great force-ray toward that looming asteroid beside us. The next instant the asteroid's giant rock sphere seemed to flash away from us and disappear with immense speed, but in reality it was our flier that had been pushed away from the asteroid with colossal force by the force-ray I had shot toward it! Instantly I snapped off that ray, the space-flier flashing on in its straight course as formerly. And as I did so Marlin turned for a moment from his watch at the window toward me, gestured to the right toward the asteroid from which we had so narrowly escaped. In the moment we had seen it, I had estimated that one to be a hundred miles or more in diameter.

"That would be Vesta," he said, "one of the largest. It's the only one of that size in this part of their region now."

"Large or small, I want to see no more of them that close," I said. "Especially when—"

"Hunt!—look—to the left!"

It was Whitely who had cried out to me, and as I whirled to gaze in the direction in which he pointed, I noticed another swift-expanding sphere of rock, another gleaming asteroid rushing obliquely toward us! Not as great in size as the first one, but it was approaching us with terrific speed, and even as I jerked open one of the switches before me, sent a force-ray stabbing from the flier toward the rushing asteroid, it seemed that that asteroid was touching us, its great rocky surface shutting out all the firmament as it towered there beside us! My ray, though, had been shot forth just in time, had whirled us aside from the onrushing monster's path at the last moment, and as we reeled on, it too had vanished behind us. But now I had glimpsed two larger ones ahead and to the left, and was jerking the flier away from them also. Still we were racing onward, our great space-flier hurtling on and on through that asteroid-filled region, escaping those great rushing spheres of death, sometimes by the narrowest of margins. Hour upon hour, keeping our sleepless watch at the flier's windows, we flashed on, its colossal speed still mounting as more and more of our generators' power was turned into the great rear force-ray that pressed back towards Earth and that shot us outward. By that time Earth had become but a bright white star behind us, the sun's size and brilliance decreased by a third or more already. But it was not backward we were gazing; it was ahead. We were striving with all our powers to avoid the asteroids that hurtled about us. We saw, once or twice, families or groups of those asteroids moving together, sometimes dozens together, and strove to give these a wide berth. On we raced, veering now to this side and now to that, with Jupiter looming ever greater ahead and to the right as we approached the end of the asteroidal belt. But it was as we approached its end, at last, that our greatest peril came suddenly upon us. For I had shot the space-flier sidewise with terrific speed to avoid an onrushing small asteroid, and the next moment when it slowed its sidewise rush, found that I had unwittingly shot it into the very heart of a great family of full two-score of the little planets!

All about us in that moment it seemed were asteroids, gleaming spheres at the very center of whose swarm our flier flashed, and into which by some miracle our sidewise rush had projected us, unharmed! I heard the hoarse cries of Marlin and Randall beside me, in that moment, the shout of Whitely, and knew that only another miracle could ever take us out of that swarm unharmed. Already, in that split-second, three of them were looming great to our right, another one ahead and to the left, and to escape one was to crash upon another. There was no time for thought, no time for aught save a lightning-like decision, and in that fractional instant I had made that decision, and as our flier hurtled through the great swarm of asteroids, had shot out its great force-rays to right and left and above and beneath us, driving out in all directions from our flier as it flashed through the great swarm!

There was an instant in which the space-flier seemed to be jerking and flashing in wild aimless flight amid that swarm, as its striking force-rays pushed it now to one side and now to another, away from the asteroids about us. Were two of those rays to strike asteroids in opposite directions, balancing each other, the space-flier, instead of being pushed aside, would be crumpled to instant annihilation between the push of the two great rays, I knew, and we expected nothing but annihilation in that mad moment as we shot on. But after reeling to right and left with dizzy speed for a crazy instant, the asteroids of the swarm had vanished suddenly from about us as we shot out of that swarm! We had escaped, had escaped a death that for the moment had seemed certain to all of

THE UNIVERSE WRECKERS

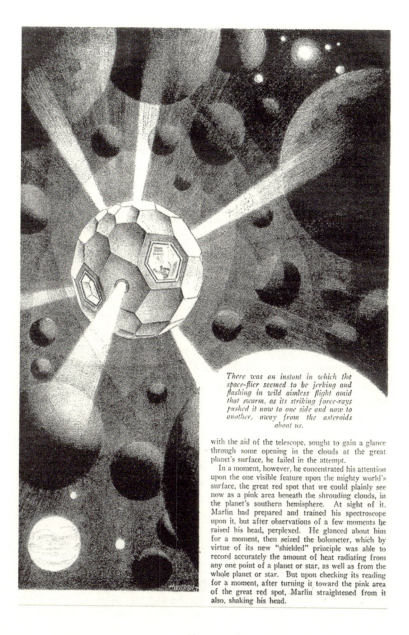

There was an instant in which the space-flier seemed to be jerking and flashing in wild aimless flight amid that swarm, as its striking force-rays pushed it now to one side and now to another, away from the asteroids about us.

with the aid of the telescope, sought to gain a glance through some opening in the clouds at the great planet's surface, he failed in the attempt.

In a moment, however, he concentrated his attention upon the one visible feature upon the mighty world's surface, the great red spot that we could plainly see now as a pink area beneath the shrouding clouds, in the planet's southern hemisphere. At sight of it, Marlin had prepared and trained his spectroscope upon it, but after observations of a few moments he raised his head, perplexed. He glanced about him for a moment, then seized the bolometer, which by virtue of its new "shielded" principle was able to record accurately the amount of heat radiating from any one point of a planet or star, as well as from the whole planet or star. But upon checking its reading for a moment, after turning it toward the pink area of the great red spot, Marlin straightened from it also, shaking his head.

us, and that I had managed to evade by instinct and luck rather than by reason.

"Close enough—that!" I exclaimed as we raced forward through the void on our straight course once more. "If we meet many more swarms like that, our chances of getting to Neptune are small!"

Marlin shook his head. "We seemed gone that time," he admitted. "However, I think we're almost out of the asteroidal region now—we should be crossing Jupiter's orbit in another twenty-four hours."

"The space-flier's doing four million miles an hour now," I said, glancing over at the space-speed dial. "We're beginning to feel Jupiter's pull a little already."

We were, indeed, already deviating a little to the right from our straight course in answer to the gravitational pull of the tremendous mass of Jupiter, looming ever greater now ahead and to the right. We were to pass it by some fifteen million miles, more than twice the distance at which we had passed Mars, but the colossal planet, larger than all the other planets of the sun together, was already attracting us strongly despite our terrific speed and momentum. For the time being, though, we gave it but scant attention, concentrating our attention, as we did, upon the watch for farther asteroids, since we had not yet emerged from their great belt between the orbits of Mars and Jupiter. Sleepy and weary as we were from our hours upon the watch, we dared not relax from that watch, and so Whitely and Marlin and Randall still kept up their constant survey of the surrounding void, while I held the flashing space-flier's controls, turning more and more of our generators' power into the great force-ray that was hurtling us on. We had not dared to use the generators' power too swiftly upon our start, lest the too great acceleration kill us, despite our shock-absorbing apparatus. But steadily our speed, already colossal, was mounting, and we were racing on through the gulf toward the distant green spot of light that was Neptune.

ON and on in those hours we shot, until it seemed to me, seated there at the controls, that always we had flashed thus through endless realms of tenantless space. For now but a few asteroids were sighted by our watching eyes, and the eventlessness and strange tension of our rush onward through space made it seem like a strange flight in some unending dream. On and on, with Marlin and Randall and Whitely watching ceaselessly about me, on with the throbbing of our generators beating in my ears in unhalting rhythm. Behind us Earth's bright white star was steadily growing smaller, but still our great force-ray, stabbing ceaselessly back from our flier with colossal power, was sending us racing on faster and faster with its huge reacting force. But our start from Earth, days, hours, before, the great mission upon which we were speeding outward to Neptune, these things I had forgotten, almost, as the dream-like quality of our onward flight gripped me.

But as we raced still onward, as Jupiter's mighty sphere loomed greater and greater to the right ahead of us, my bemused faculties were shaken into wakefulness by the necessities of our situation. By that time we had passed out of the dangerous asteroidal region, and with their watch no longer necessary Whitely and Randall, after preparing for us all a quick hot meal from the thermoscans in which all our food supplies were packed, had taken to their bunks for some much-needed sleep. Marlin sat beside me as we rushed on, his astronomical preoccupation holding him to a contemplation of the great planet, despite his own weariness. And weary enough he was, and I too, since for almost forty-eight hours we had been flashing through the perils of the asteroidal belt. It was now the beginning of the fifth day since our start from Earth, and already for a hundred hours we had been flashing at tremendous and mounting speed through the airless void. Like Marlin, though, I forgot my weariness in the spectacle of giant Jupiter, to the right and ahead.

For it was a spectacle of magnificence, indeed. Swinging like a giant disk of soft white light in the blackness of space to our right, Jupiter spun amid its four greater moons, the smaller moons being of diameter too small to be seen with unaided eyes even this close. But of the giant sphere of Jupiter, of that great sphere's surface, nothing was to be seen. For all the mighty planet's surface was covered by the colossal masses of great clouds that enclosed it, floating in its dense atmosphere and encircling it in great belts, the mighty cloud-belts that for long have been to astronomers the most characteristic feature of Jupiter's surface. So that, though Marlin with the aid of the telescope, sought to gain a glance through some opening in the clouds at the great planet's surface, he failed in the attempt.

In a moment, however, he concentrated his attention upon the one visible feature upon the mighty world's surface, the great red spot that we could plainly see now as a pink area beneath the shrouding clouds, in the planet's southern hemisphere. At sight of it, Marlin had prepared and trained his spectroscope upon it, but after observations of a few moments he raised his head, perplexed. He glanced about him for a moment, then seized the bolometer, which by virtue of its new "shielded" principle was able to record accurately the amount of heat radiating from any one point of a planet or star, as well as from the whole planet or star. But upon checking its reading for a moment, after turning it toward the pink area of the great red spot, Marlin straightened from it also, shaking his head.

"It's strange, Hunt," he said, turning toward me. "It's always been believed that the great red spot is a part of Jupiter's surface still molten and flaming, but the spectroscope and bolometer show that it can't be."

"Strange enough," I admitted, gazing myself toward that glowing pink area on the mighty planet. If we could but stop and explore the planet—but we must keep on toward Neptune."

"We must keep on," Marlin repeated, "but some day it may be, if we can save the solar system from the doom that hangs over it now, we'll come back here to Jupiter, will see for ourselves its surface."

By this time the great planet was almost directly to our right, its giant cloudy white sphere seeming to fill all space, despite the fact that it was more than fifteen million miles from us, and its four big, greater moons revolving around it. Hours before I had shot a force-ray toward the great planet from our flier's side, to counteract its growing pull upon us, but now as we came level with it, were passing it, that pull upon us was so enormous that it was only with a force-ray of immense power that I was managing to keep the space-flier from being drawn inward. Passing thus close, Jupiter's stupendous cloud-belted sphere was an awe-inspiring sight, whirling at immense speed also, since the great planet, more than a thousand times greater than Earth, rotates upon its axis at hardly more than a third of Earth's rotatory period or day, its day being less than ten hours. And passing it thus, too, the great red spot upon its lower half was an even greater enigma, for that gigantic pink oval was, we knew, fully thirty thousand miles in length, greater by far than all our Earth.

It was with awe that Marlin and I, and Whitely and Randall who had awakened now to relieve us, stared toward the gigantic monarch of the sun's planets as it dropped slowly behind on our right. A side-ray of colossal power it had taken, indeed, to hold us out from the great world's pull, and only slowly could we decrease that ray's power as we moved farther out from it. But now at well over four million miles an hour, we were flashing out beyond Jupiter's orbit, and ahead there was gleaming brighter to the left the yellow spot of light that was Saturn, the last planet that we must yet pass before reaching Neptune, since Uranus was in conjunction in regard to Neptune, being far on the other side of the solar system from us. And as Randall now took my place at the controls, I pointed toward the little yellow-glowing, ring-circled disk of Saturn ahead and to the left.

"Keep the flier heading straight toward Neptune, Randall," I told him. "We're going to pass Saturn uncomfortably close as it is, and we don't want to take any chances with it."

Randall nodded, his gaze shifting from the steady green spark of Neptune far ahead to the growing yellow disk of Saturn. "I'll try to keep her straight," he said, grinning, "though I'm beginning to wish that, if there's to be trouble, it had come back on Mars or Jupiter."

I smiled a little as I swung back from the control-panel along the flier's inside wall. I went from handhold to handhold with the pressure of its acceleration still upon me, until I had thrown myself into my metal bunk to fall almost instantly asleep, and to dream nightmare dreams of rushing on through endless space toward a goal that ever receded from us. And in the hours that followed, in the next three days that our space-flier shot on and on with Saturn growing ever greater ahead, the nightmare quality of my experience persisted. It seemed impossible, at times, that we four were in reality doing that which men had never done before; that we were flinging ourselves out into the great void, out through the solar system toward the planet that was its last outpost. We were watching and eating and sleeping, indeed, like men in a dream, so strange and utterly unreal seemed to us this unending rush through unending space.

BUT though we slept, and ate, and watched at the control-panel like men in a dream, there were times in those hours when realization of our position, of our great mission, came sharply home to us. Those were the times that Marlin trained his instruments upon the sun, which had by then dwindled to a tiny blazing disk behind us. And with those instruments Marlin found that the sun was still spinning ever faster and faster, its rotator period decreasing still by the same amount each day, its day of division and doom steadily approaching. And with his own recorders Whitely found that the colossal force-ray from Neptune still was stabbing toward the sun, still turning it faster and faster toward its doom and that of its universe. That great force-ray, we found, was stabbing toward the sun on a line between our flier's course and Saturn, but was on a somewhat higher level, so that in reality the great ray did not lie between our flier and Saturn but above both.

The consciousness we had of that great ray's existence and the knowledge we had of the doom it was loosing upon the peoples of our world served to prevent the dream-like lassitude of our conditions from overpowering us, and we were further awakened by the swift expansion of Saturn, ahead, as our flier neared it. For by then the great faceted ball of our flier was hurtling on through the void at five million miles an hour, slowly approaching the limits of its speed as our mighty rear force-ray drove us forward with tremendous power. And at that speed, in the next three days, Saturn loomed larger and larger ahead, until we saw at last that upon the fourth day's beginning we would pass the mighty planet. And at that our interest rose to excitement, because we would pass closer by Saturn than any of the planets in our straight flight out to Neptune, passing it indeed by no more than a million miles. So that as the last hours of those three days passed, we observed the big, yellow-glowing disk of Saturn ahead with intense interest.

And a strange sight indeed was great Saturn as it loomed greater before us and to the left, for strangest of all the sun's planets to the eye is this one. Greatest of all the planets save for mighty Jupiter, its huge sphere seemed even greater than Jupiter by reason of the colossal rings that encircled it, and by its nine greater moons that revolved about it. A solar system in itself seemed Saturn, indeed, its huge rings tilted somewhat, those great rings themselves tens of thousands of miles in width and thousands of miles from the planet they encircled. We could see, as we drew nearer toward the great planet, that those rings were in fact what had long been known by Earth's astronomers—gigantic flat swarms of meteorites and meteoric material revolving about the great planet at immense speed. Of the surface of Saturn, though, no more could be seen than of that of Jupiter, since like Jupiter the great planet was wreathed in colossal cloud belts.

Marlin shook his head as he gazed toward the great ring-girdled planet, almost filling the heavens beside us. "It is well for us that Saturn is not our goal," he said. "Those titanic meteoric masses that are the rings—to blunder into them would mean instant annihilation."

Whitely nodded. "As it is," he said, "there must be many meteors in this region about Saturn—many that have broken loose from the rings or are flying toward those rings."

"Let's hope that you're wrong on that, at least," I told him. "We'll soon be passing within a million miles of those rings, and I want to meet no meteorites—not after our experience with the asteroids."

By then, indeed, we had drawn almost level with Saturn, its huge sphere and colossal rings almost directly to the left, the edge of those rings, but a half hundred miles or less in thickness, being a scant million miles or more from our racing space-flier. The great maze of the planet's nine greater moons seemed crowded now upon its other side from us, Titan, largest of those moons shining brilliantly as a small white disk near the huge yellow bulk of Saturn and its colossal rings. Before then indeed, I had been forced to shoot out from the flier's side a force-ray toward Saturn, to counteract the great planet's pull upon us, but though it loomed beside us now almost as immense as great Jupiter itself, its recorded pull upon us was many times less. This was due, I knew, to the comparatively small mass of Saturn, since though of immense size and possessing a vast atmosphere, it is known to be the least dense of all the planets, being of less than 0.7 the density of water.

Even so, however, it was requiring a force-ray of great power to hold our rushing flier out from the huge planet. Though lesser than Jupiter's, its pull upon us was great, nevertheless. And now that we were passing the huge world so closely, it seemed to us with its vast rings and great family of whirling moons to be of universe-size itself, so mighty did it loom beside us. The great rings, of small thickness compared to their huge width and circle, were edge-on to us now, a million miles to the left, and we could see that they were in reality but vast swarms of countless meteors, great and small, whirling at great speed about Saturn and forming by their division three rings, the innermost a darker one. Yet despite their strange appearance and colossal size, it was not the great rings that held our interest so much in that moment as the cloud-hidden surface of Saturn itself. For even as in passing Mars and Jupiter, we were gripped with desire to veer in toward the planet and explore the strange wonders that might exist upon it, or upon its greater moons. But none suggested that thought now. All four of us knew that only the growing green spot of light, that was distant Neptune ahead, must be our goal.

AS the flier raced on, almost passing the huge planet now, Randall uttered a swift exclamation, pointing ahead and to the left a little. At the same moment, though, I had seen the thing that had caught his eye—a small dark point growing with lightning swiftness as it rushed toward us; a great dark meteor, perhaps five hundred feet in diameter, rushing toward our flier, whirling far out from Saturn's rings in the same direction as those rings! Instantly, upon seeing it, I had turned more power into the ray that held us out from Saturn, and as we were pushed sidewise in the next moment by that increased power, the big meteor had flashed past us far to the left! And a moment later, I had caught sight of two similar meteors, one smaller than the other, rushing toward us in the same direction from ahead. But these I had seen soon enough to avoid collision.

It was evident that, as Whitely had suggested, we were encountering some of the stray meteors that might be expected to whirl here far out from the meteor-swarms of the great rings. And as we watched tensely now for more meteors, it was with something of awe that we gazed toward the huge rings, that we knew to be rushing swarms of countless similar meteors. It was well, as Marlin had said, that we were not called upon to penetrate through or around those great rings, since in their awful whirling swarms of meteors no craft would be able to live even for a moment. But our space-flier was passing the midmost point of those rings; already huge Saturn was beginning to drop a little behind us; and we breathed more freely. And, ironically enough, it was at that very moment of our relief that catastrophe came upon us. There was a wild shout from Marlin, and simultaneously I saw a huge round dark mass looming dead ahead and whirling toward us. Just as I snapped open the control-levers, that great dark meteor's mass had struck our onrushing flier with a tremendous stunning shock!

For an instant, as the flier reeled and spun there crazily in the gulf of space, it seemed the end to me, but in a moment more I realized that the great faceted walls had not been penetrated, for the air in the flier was unchanged. Had those walls been pierced, the result would have been the instant freezing to death of all of us. But that death had not as yet come upon us, and as I struggled forward in my chair I saw that the space-flier was still whirling crazily around from the shock and that the throbbing of its great generators had ceased. Beside me Marlin and Whitely and Randall were coming back to realization of their surroundings after that colossal shock, Whitely bearing a nasty cut upon his temple. And as Marlin sprang to the flier's side-window, gazed obliquely from it, he uttered an exclamation.

"That meteor just grazed us!" he exclaimed. "If you hadn't jerked the controls over at the last moment, Hunt, it would have hit us head-on! As it is, it smashed through the flier's outer wall, but didn't pierce the inner wall!"

"But the generators!" cried Whitely, who had been fumbling at their switches. "They've stopped! When the meteor crashed through the outer wall it must have broken some of our generator-connections between the two walls!"

"And the flier's falling!" I cried in turn. "It's falling toward Saturn now, with its force-rays dead—we're falling into the great rings!"

For as I glanced outward I had seen that was what was happening. The halting of the generators by the breaking of their connections between the flier's double walls had halted also the force-rays that had been pushing us out toward Neptune and that had been holding us out from Saturn's pull. With the halting of those rays the pull of the mighty planet had at once gripped our space-flier and now we were moving at swiftly-accelerating speed toward that planet's mighty bulk, toward the great rings but a million miles to our left! Were falling helplessly, faster and faster each moment, toward those mighty rings, toward their vast swarms of whirling meteors in which our space-flier and all within it could meet only an annihilating death!

CHAPTER FIVE
At The Solar System's Edge

"OUT of the flier!" Marlin cried to us. "Our one chance is to get out and repair those broken connections from the outside."

"But how——" Randall began, when the astronomer broke in on him. "The space-walkers! In them we can get outside, can try to repair those connections before we fall into the great rings!"

A moment we stared toward him in sheer surprise, and then as one we were leaping toward the four big space-walkers, suspended from the flier's wall. For though we had not dreamed in taking them with us, of any such emergency as now confronted us, we saw that, even as Marlin had said, our one chance to escape the annihilation that soon would be ours otherwise lay in their use. Swiftly, therefore, we unhooked the great cylindrical spacewalkers, neither they nor aught else in the flier having any but small weight now, that weight being the result of the pull of great Saturn, toward which we were falling. Quickly swinging open the section near the cylinder's base that was its door, therefore, I pulled myself up into the cylinder, then closed its hermetically-sealing door with the small inside lever provided for the purpose.

I was standing, therefore, in a metal cylinder seven feet in height and three in diameter, its top tapering into a rounded little dome in which were small windows from which I could look outward. My arms I had thrust into the great hollow jointed arms of metal that projected from the cylinder's sides, and had at my fingers' ends inside those arms the controls of the great pincer-hands in which those arms ended outside, and the control also of the small generator inside the cylinder whose little force-ray was shot down from the cylinder's bottom. This could be shot straight down, sending the space-walker upward by pushing against some larger body, or could be shot out obliquely sending the space-walker horizontally in any direction. Once inside the space-walker therefore, with its tiny generator throbbing and the equally small air-renovator and heater functioning, I was ready to venture out into the airless void.

Glancing out through the vision-windows I saw that Marlin and Whitely and Randall had struggled into their space-walkers also, and were signaling their readiness. We grasped therefore the tools and materials we had hastily assembled for our task, these being spare plates to repair the flier's outer wall and a small molecular-diffusion welder, and then with those in the grasp of our great pincer-hands were pulling ourselves toward the flier's screw-door. In a moment we had that open, and were crowding into the little vestibule-chamber which lay between the outer and inner doors. Closing the inner one tightly behind us, we swiftly screwed open the outer door. As it opened there was a rush of air from about us as the air of the little vestibule-chamber rushed out into the great airless void outside, and then Marlin was leading the way out of that door, out into sheer space outside our falling space-flier!

I saw Marlin drawing himself in his space-walker through the door and then floating gently out that door, floating in space a few feet from our flier and failing at the same rate as it toward mighty Saturn! In a moment more I was following him, Whitely and Randall behind me, and as I too propelled myself with a slight push through the door, my cylindrical space-walker floated outward, I found myself, therefore, cased within that space-walker's cylinder, and floating in it in the sheer empty void of interplanetary space! Beside me was the great gleaming faceted ball of our flier, falling at the same rate as ourselves toward the huge rings of mighty Saturn, to the left. Beneath and before and on all other sides of me, though, was only space, the tremendous gulf, gleaming with the great hosts of stars on all sides, with the sun's brilliant little disk shining far behind us. For the moment our position was so strange, so utterly alien and unprecedented, as we four floated there beside the falling space-flier in our four great metal cylinders, that we could only gaze about us in sheer awe and wonder. Then Marlin, with one of the great metal jointed arms of his space-walker, motioned to us and toward the flier, and we realized that we had but little time left in which to accomplish the task now before us.

For with every moment the flier and our four space-walkers were falling at greater speed toward the colossal rings of huge Saturn, to the left, and the whirling titanic meteor-swarms of those rings were growing larger and larger. But a few hours remained before, with the growing acceleration of our free-falling flier, it would be meeting its end in those clashing, crashing meteors of the great swarm, so that if we were to repair the damage to it, and get its generators functioning again before it met its doom, we must work fast. Our four space-walkers were falling toward Saturn at the same rate as the great flier beside us, so that we hung just beside that flier in space without need to use the propelling force-rays of our four cylinders. And now Marlin, grasping with his great metal pincer hands one of the projecting joints of the flier's great faceted walls, was pulling himself around it even as he fell with it through space, was pulling himself around to its other side, where the meteor that had struck us a glancing blow had done its damage.

In a moment Whitely and Randall and I had followed, moving clumsily in our great cylinders as we fell with the flier on toward Saturn's rings, and as we reached the other side where Marlin was hovering now in his space-walker we saw that the meteor that had grazed us had demolished two of the great facets of the flier's outer wall, and had shattered and crumpled a third. Save for a slight denting, though, the inner wall seemed unharmed, a fact that alone had saved us, but the black cable-connections between the walls were broken in a half-score places, we saw. It was that severing of the connections that had halted our great generators, we knew, so now our first task was to repair those connections, and it was upon that task that we began at once to work. Surely never had men worked under stranger circumstances than those, was my thought as we began the work of re-matching the severed connections. For we four, cased in our four great cylindrical metal space-walkers, were falling through space at a tremendous and ever-increasing rate, even as we worked upon our great flier falling with us, we were falling through the mighty void toward the whirling rings of Saturn, looming immense in space beside us. It meant annihilation for us, if we could not complete our repairs in time to escape them!

And as we toiled there at the connections, it seemed to me that never could we complete them in time to escape the great rings. For not only were there a half-score breaks in the intricate cables, but each cable held within itself a dozen smaller connections or strands that in each break must be exactly rematched. And working as we were with the great pincer-claws of the space-walker our progress was terribly slow. Minutes passed into an hour and another hour, as we labored furiously there outside the flier with those connections, and by then it seemed to us that the colossal rings of Saturn, a huge whirling storm of meteors, were but a few minutes from us, so vastly did they loom before us, and so swiftly were we and our flier falling. With the energy of utter despair we labored on there at the seemingly endless task of rejoining the intricate connections, our tools and materials that we were not using at the moment being simply released by us beside us, since they fell with us and our flier at the same rate toward Saturn and thus were within our grasp, our tools floated there beside us!

NOW we were approaching the last of the connections, but now too we saw that it was only a matter of minutes before our space-flier and we would be whirling into the edge of the mighty rings of Saturn, that loomed now gigantic in their spinning meteor-masses before us! Already meteors were driving about us in space more thickly, and only by a miracle had our helplessly falling flier escaped them so far. It seemed impossible that we could complete our task before the flier and ourselves were shot into the crashing death of those colossal whirling meteor-swarms, but we were working with the mad energy of a forlorn hope, and now too, Marlin was leaning toward us with his space-walker to shout something to us. For when one space-walker touched another, their two occupants could hear each other's shouts, the sound vibrations carried through the touching metal sides. Marlin was crying to us that but minutes were left us, and was ordering Randall to return back inside the flier and stand ready there to shoot it away from the great looming rings the instant that the connections were repaired!

In a moment Randall had obeyed, pulling himself around the falling flier to its door and inside, while Marlin and Whitely and I worked tensely upon the last of the connections, matching and joining them with the greatest speed of which we were capable. Now it seemed that greater meteors were all about us, and now the huger, denser masses of the mighty rings were towering vastly beside us, as at plummet-like speed our flier and ourselves whirled toward them and toward death! Hanging there in sheer space at the falling flier's side, working madly upon those last connections, with all about us the glittering hosts of the stars and with beside us the titanic bulk of great Saturn and its colossal rings, we seemed caught in some unreal and torturing nightmare. Then as the huge meteor-masses of the mighty rings loomed just beside us, as I reached with the pincer-hands of my space-walker toward the last of the connections, I heard from Marlin in the space-walker touching mine a hoarse cry of despair. But at that last moment my claw-hands were swiftly joining the last connection and in the next instant came the steady throbbing of the great generators inside the flier! In that instant we had grasped our tools with one metal arm and with the other each of us had gripped the edge of the flier's shattered outer wall. And then, just as the flier and ourselves seemed hurtling straight into the mighty wall of whirling meteors that was the great rings beside us, the space-flier, with us three hanging desperately to it, was hurtling away from those rings as its great force-ray shot from inside toward them, was flashing at terrific mounting speed out from them into space!

For an instant, so terrific was the accelerating speed of the flier beneath Randall's control inside, that we three, hanging to the broken outer wall in our space-walkers, seemed on the point of being torn away from our grip on it, of falling back to Saturn once more. But in a moment more, with a great distance already between the flier and the huge rings that had almost been our doom, Randall had halted it, was holding it motionless in space by means of a steady force-ray. Then we were swiftly repairing the break in its outer wall, by means of the plates and tools to which we had clung, setting those great plates in place to replace the three shattered ones, and then welding them swiftly into the flier's outer wall integrally by means of the molecular-diffusion instrument. That done we pulled ourselves around the flier's faceted surface to its outer door, opening that door and closing it again once inside the vestibule-chamber. Then as Marlin touched a stud the vestibule-chamber was filling with air, and in another moment we were inside the flier once more, were pulling ourselves out of the great space-walkers, with Randall already out of his and at the controls.

"That was almost our trip's end!" cried Marlin as he emerged from his space-walker. "Another few minutes and we'd have been inside the rings—would have been pounded into instant annihilation by the meteors there!"

I passed a hand over my brow. "Never again do I want to find myself in a situation like that," I said. "As it was, it was the space walkers alone that saved us."

Marlin nodded, gazing out toward great Saturn looming gigantic still to our left. "If ever we come back," he said, "if ever we try to reach Saturn and explore it as we may someday, we'll certainly have our work cut out for us. Those mighty meteor-masses—those rings—"

"Well, at present the farther we get from Saturn the better I'll feel," Whitely told us. "And I'm glad enough that there's no other planet between us and Neptune, at least, for Uranus is far way."

Now, recovering from the first shakiness of the reaction from our awful peril, we turned with Randall to the consideration of our position. Our great ray that had shot back from the flier, and had pushed us by its force out through the solar system, had been snapped out by the halting of the generators, and we had now only the side-ray that was holding us out from Saturn. I suggested, therefore, that for the remainder of our trip out to Neptune we turn the space-flier's rear force-ray upon Saturn instead of Earth, since Earth by now had dwindled to a small bluish-white star far behind. To train our rear force-ray upon Earth and to adjust the mechanism that kept the ray trained automatically afterwards upon the object suggested, would take more time than if we were simply to push the rear force-ray against great Saturn.

Marlin approved the suggestion, so after sending the flier out farther from Saturn and ahead of it by oblique applications of the side-ray, we held it carefully in space until it was headed toward the far green spot of Neptune, and then turned on the rear force-ray with half its full power at the start. At once, with terrific acceleration, we were flashing on toward Neptune, the giant power of the ray pushing against Saturn and driving our flier ever outward. So tremendous was that acceleration, indeed, that despite the shock-absorbing apparatus of our chairs we came near to being overcome by the awful pressure upon us. Yet it was necessary that we use the highest possible speed and acceleration, now, for our former speed and acceleration had been completely lost when the halting of the generators had allowed Saturn to pull us inward. And though we were now flashing out past Saturn's orbit, with only the orbit of Uranus between us and our goal of Neptune, we had still two-thirds of our journey before us! So colossal are the distances between the great outer planets, distances beside which the gaps between Mars and Earth and Venus and Mercury seem tiny.

With the utmost acceleration of speed that we could stand, though, our space-flier was now hurtling outward, its great force-ray pushing against Saturn with more and more power and sending us flashing forward with greater and greater velocity. In the next dozen hours of our flight we had reached again to the speed of five million miles an hour that had been ours before we had met with our misadventure at Saturn. And as we hurtled on Neptune was slowly largening before our eyes, its distant, tiny little spot of calm green light becoming bigger, brighter, though very slowly. But the eyes of Marlin and Whitely and Randall and myself were always upon that green light-spot as we hurtled on, hour following hour and day following day in our eventless onward flight through the solar system's outer immensities of space. And still our speed was steadily growing until at last, by the time we approached Uranus' orbit, we were flying through the great void at the space-flier's utmost velocity, more than eight million miles an hour.

That was a speed colossal, yet so accustomed had we four become to the space-flier's tremendous velocities that it seemed not unusual to us. Flashing through the void as we were, the only objects by which one could measure speed were the planets before and behind us, and these changed in size so slowly as to make our speed seem small. The greatest change to us in the attaining of the space-flier's immense utmost speed was the change of conditions inside the flier itself. Formerly the pressure of our constant acceleration had replaced to some degree the effects of gravitation, that pressure forcing us always towards the flier's rear, as we turned more and more power into our giant pushing ray, as we shot out with greater and greater speed. But now, with our utmost speed attained and that acceleration's pressure missing, we floated inside the flier as though entirely weightless, being attracted only very slightly toward the walls by the slight gravitational attraction of the flier's mass itself. So that now the straps across chairs and bunks and the handholds here and there on the walls that we had provided proved indispensable to us, indeed.

IT was upon the fifteenth day after our start from Earth, the first day of July as I noted by Earth-reckoning, that we crossed the orbit of Uranus. As we approached that orbit, only our recording distance-dials, of course, marking the fact that we were nearing the path of Uranus, I stood or rather floated with Marlin and Whitely at the flier's rear windows, gazing backward. Behind us gleamed in the star-swept heavens the planets past which we had come, and those others beyond them. Great Saturn with his vast rings that had almost been our deaths was already dwindling fast, as our flier shot out from it with its force-ray pressing with ceaseless power against it. Already the huge ringed planet was but a tiny yellow disk of light to our eyes, so far out from it we were.

To the left, too, shone the white star of giant Jupiter, small but intensely brilliant still, while farther distant and infinitely fainter was the red spark that was Mars. Our eyes shifted from these to the bluish light-point that was Earth, and then beyond it to the little disk of brilliant fire that was the sun, its light and heat reaching us now in the smallest of quantities as we fled on into the chill immensities of the outer reaches of the solar system. There close beside that fiery little sun-disk we could also make out the silvery little light-point that was Venus, and by making use of a small hand-glass could also discern closer even beside the sun the tiny point of rosy light that we knew to be Mercury, smallest and inmost of all the planets. But as we watched there, as our space-flier hurtled on at unvarying, colossal speed over the orbit of Uranus, it was toward Uranus itself we were gazing. Far back from us on the solar system's other side hung the green spot of light that was Uranus, booming onward in its vast path around the sun, but though we watched steadily through the hand-glass toward it we were unable to make out the four small moons that accompany the great green planet, which shone with a deeper green even than the greenish spot of Neptune, ahead.

"Uranus—Venus—Mercury—," said Marlin, as he gazed musingly backward, "Those three we have not passed, yet they're no greater mysteries to us than those that we have passed. But someday—"

"Someday—," I repeated, staring back, lost in thought myself, not completing, any more than Marlin, the thought that I had started to express.

Nor did I need to complete it, for as Marlin and Whitely and I stared back to where the sun's disk sent its light bravely out across the unthinkable reaches of space that separated us from it, our thoughts were all on those three planets, on Uranus and Venus and Mercury, and on those others, Mars and Jupiter and Saturn, that we had passed. What wonders, unknown to us, might not exist upon any of those worlds? But they were wonders barred to us for the time, since time was the one thing of which we had the least, in our great rush outward to the sun's outermost planet, in our desperate race outward to attempt to save our own Earth from the doom that hovered over it. For still that doom cast its shadowing wing darkly over Earth, still Whitely's instruments informed us that the giant force-ray from Neptune was stabbing back toward the sun, turning the sun ever faster at the same remorseless rate. So that it was toward Neptune, after minutes, that we turned, taking our places in our chairs beside Randall, at the controls, and gazing with him toward the planet far ahead that was our goal.

And now that we had crossed the orbit of Uranus, some two-thirds of our colossal journey's length lay behind us, and Neptune was becoming ever brighter ahead, its pale green spot of light having become almost as brilliant to our eyes as Saturn, behind us. As we viewed it through our telescope, too, we could make out the tiny light-point of Triton, the single moon of Neptune. Somewhat larger than our own moon was Triton, we knew, and we could see through our glass what had long been known by Earth's astronomers, that this single moon of Neptune's revolved about it in a plane sharply slanted or inclined to the plane of Neptune's equator, to the general plane of the ecliptic or solar system. And close indeed seemed the light-point of this single moon to Neptune, since we knew that it was at almost the same distance from the great planet as our own moon is from Earth.

It was toward Neptune and its little moon that our eyes turned now and in the hours and days that followed, while gradually our excitement became tense as the great planet loomed ahead of us. Soon it had become a perceptible pale green disk, widening out as we shot on and on toward it. We would reach it, we calculated, upon the twenty-first day of our journey, twenty-one days after starting from Earth. An eternity it seemed, that period of three weeks, such vast realms of space we had come through, such tremendous perils we had dared and passed. But now all those perils and worlds we had passed, Mars and the deadly asteroidal belt, great Jupiter and Saturn and the doom that had almost been ours there, all these things faded from our minds as we found ourselves with our thoughts concentrated wholly upon the far planet that from the first had been our goal, that planet which we must reach if Earth was to be saved. For ever, ever, the great force-ray of Neptune was turning the sun faster, and now less than a hundred days remained before that turning sun would be no longer able to hold together, would be dividing and releasing fiery doom upon Earth and almost all its other planets.

What was awaiting us at Neptune? That was the question that was foremost in all our minds as we shot on in those last tense days. What manner of beings there would they be who, we had assumed, were stabbing this ray of doom toward the sun? What manner of beings could they be who could exist at all, if exist they did, upon such a planet as Neptune, a planet moving about the sun at the unthinkable distance of almost three billion miles? Upon a planet that could receive but a minute fraction only of the sun's light and heat compared to that received on Earth? Upon a planet which astronomers had always believed to be of far lesser density than Earth, of a density little more than that of liquids rather than of solids. Was it possible that upon this farthest of all the sun's circling worlds there could exist life of any kind, not to speak of life intelligent enough to stab across the solar system and spin the sun itself faster to its division and its universe's doom?

THOSE were the questions that throbbed through our brains now as our hurtling space-flier shot on and on, Neptune growing with each hour before us. By the nineteenth day its disk had expanded to such a degree that we were able to discern upon it the cloud-belts that had already long been seen upon it by Earth's astronomers. By the twentieth those great vapor-belts were plainly perceptible, and also Triton, its moon, had become visible to our unaided eyes, revolving close about the great planet in its sharp-slanted plane, being now behind the planet but so much above it as to be completely visible to us. By the twentieth, too, the sun behind us had become hardly more than a super-brilliant star, its tiny fiery disk bathing us still with a certain amount of light, although long before this we had ceased to rely upon its heat on our flier's sunward side and had had recourse to our own heating-mechanism. By this time too, of all the planets, only Jupiter and Saturn were visible behind us; the rest were invisible to us at the colossal distances which now separated us from them.

It was not behind but ahead, though, that we were gazing, as our space-flier flashed over the last portion of its great trip, as Neptune apparently grew in size before us. Seated in my control-chair, with Whitely and Marlin and Randall in their chairs beside me, I watched the mighty planet fascinated, as we hurtled on toward it in the early hours of the twenty-first day, that day that we had calculated would bring us to our goal. And truly, now, Neptune was looming in something of its true greatness before us. Only a tiny point of light in a telescope on Earth, hardly more than that on the long days of our journey outward, we saw it now in some size and splendor, a huge cloud-belted world as large almost exactly as Uranus, outrivaled in the solar system only by it and by the two giants of Jupiter and Saturn. Over sixty times larger than our own Earth it was, a huge world spinning far out here at the solar system's very edge, the last outpost of that solar system with beyond it only the awful emptiness of interstellar space.

Silently we gazed toward its great, green disk, its small gleaming moon, as our space-flier throbbed on toward it. Whitely, as usual, was checking from time to time the performance of the never-ceasing generators whose great force-ray, pressing against Saturn still, was hurling us forward. Randall was gazing forward with me, helping me now and then to ascertain from our speed and distance dials our distance from the great planet, Marlin had applied himself to the telescope, was gazing ahead through it toward the big world's cloud-wreathed surface, touching a focusing wheel now and then. For minutes we throbbed on thus, the beat of the generators the only sound in the hurtling space-flier's interior, but at last Marlin drew back from the telescope's eyepiece and frowned as he gazed toward the great green planet ahead.

"I can make out nothing through those cloud-belts," he said. "Those belts show, as astronomers have always believed, that Neptune has a great atmosphere. But what lies beneath them we'll not know until we penetrate through them to the planet's surface."

"That won't be long," I told him. "We're already only fifty million miles from Neptune-should reach it in seven or eight hours more."

"You'll be slowing the flier's speed before long then?" asked Whitely, and I nodded.

"We'll wait until we're ten million miles from it and then cut out our rear-ray that's pushing us on, and send out a front force-ray toward Neptune to break our progress."

Those next several hours, however, seemed to us in passing to be drawn out to infinite length, so great had become our suspense. At last, however, as we stared tensely ahead, Randall gave the word beside me that marked our place as within ten million miles of the great planet, which had now grown to a vast pale-green cloudy disk in the heavens before us. And as he gave that word I snapped shut one of the six switches before me, turning off the great rear force-ray of the flier, and at the same moment snapped open another switch that sent a great force-ray stabbing straight out from the ray-opening in the flier's front, stabbing straight out toward the great disk of Neptune ahead!

Almost at once our mad flight toward that huge world began to diminish in speed. Minute by minute the figures on the speed-dial crept backward, so that from eight million miles an hour our speed dropped quickly to six million, and then to four and to three and to two million.

With this swift decreasing of our speed we were experiencing now the reverse of that pressure that had been ours upon our acceleration, since now we were straining upward and forward against the straps of our chairs, the pneumatic shock-absorbing apparatus of those chairs functioning now as it had done then. But though we felt again the dizziness and slight nausea attendant upon these tremendous changes of speed, we forgot that in our intent contemplation of the huge world that loomed but a million miles ahead, its tremendous pale-green sphere, belted with great cloud-masses, seeming to fill the heavens before us. Already Marlin, with his instruments, had found as we neared Neptune that the giant world's rotatory speed was a little more than twenty Earth-hours, solving a problem that long had defied Earth's astronomers by the discovery that the great planet turned on its axis each score of hours.

An involuntary thrill of pride ran through me even as we shot in toward those great cloud-masses that encircled Neptune. Neptune! The sun's farthest world, and we four had reached it, had shot across the awful gulf that none had ever thought to span! Marlin, beside me, was gazing forward into the great cloud-layers now with the astronomical curiosity of his entire career gleaming in his gray eyes, as we approached this farthest of our solar system's worlds.

Whitely was contemplating it with his usual cool detachment, but thoughtfully. Randall's face was as eager with interest as my own must have been, and when, a little later, there came a low mounting roar of sound around our flashing space-flier, the roar of an atmosphere through which we were rushing, he uttered a low exclamation, swiftly manipulated our outside air-tester, and then turned to us.

"An atmosphere to Neptune, surely enough!" he exclaimed. "About twice the pressure of Earth's, even this far out, and the air-tester shows a large percentage of water-vapor and rather larger amount of oxygen. Otherwise it seems much the same as Earth's."

Marlin nodded. "We should be able to move in that," he said, "but the greater gravitation of Neptune will probably be such as to make it necessary to keep inside the space-walkers."

But now the space-flier was hurtling into the outer vapor-layers, that swirled about us in white mist-masses in the pale light that came to us from the tiny, distant sun. Onward and downward through those vapor-layers, through the cloud-belts about the great planet, our space-flier shot, while we four gazed ahead and downward, now with excitement keyed to an utter tenseness. Then with sudden stunning surprise, for we had thought those cloud-layers of immense thickness, our space-flier shot out and down from them, shot down into clear air, clear atmosphere. And as it did so, from the four of us came simultaneous cries. For there in the pale, dim unearthly light there stretched far away beneath us the surface of the planet that for so long had been our goal on our great race to save Earth from doom, the surface of great Neptune!

CHAPTER SIX
Into Neptune's Mysteries

"METAL, over all Neptune's surface!"

"A metal-covered world!"

Our stunned, astounded exclamation sounded together there as we gazed downward from our flier, whose drop I had instinctively halted. For it was metal indeed that lay beneath us, a gigantic surface of smooth dark metal or metallic substance that glinted dully in the pale light that fell on it, and that stretched away in all directions to the horizons, completely covering the giant planet Neptune as far as we could see! A metal-covered world! In amazement, in awe, we stared down upon it in that moment. For we had expected many things, many aspects which the surface of Neptune might have had, frozen ice-fields or flaming craters or even a liquid world, but never had we expected what we now saw beneath us. Never had we expected to find the huge planet thus sheathed in a dark metal covering that apparently extended over all its gigantic surface! And in all its vast smooth expanse, we saw, there was no higher structure of any sort, nothing but the level plain of smooth dark metal, sweeping far away to the flat horizons.

"Neptune a metal-covered world! And I think I see why, now," said Marlin quickly as we gazed down. "I think that I can understand why the beings of Neptune have covered their world with this shield—"

"But what lies beneath it?" Randall asked. "Do you mean that these beings of Neptune—"

"I mean that beneath this great shield they have built must lie the real world of the beings of Neptune—must lie the source of the giant force-ray that they're stabbing toward the sun!"

"But how to get down inside?" said Whitely. "There seems no opening in this gigantic metal shield—"

"We must go on, then," Marlin told us. "Must go on until we find some way of getting beneath, since beneath that shield there lies our goal!"

A moment we stared toward each other, and then I had snapped open one of the switches before me, turning the ray-direction dial, sending down slantwise toward the metal surface a force-ray, instead of the vertical ray that had upheld our flier. The pressure of this slanting ray at once sent our ball-like space-flier moving forward across Neptune's surface, across the smooth vast dark metal plain whose presence was so astounding to us. I glanced at the outside-temperature dial as we shot forward, saw that the atmosphere through which we moved though dense was cold indeed, hardly above zero in temperature. Then with Marlin and Whitely and Randall I turned my attention to the smooth great metal surface over which we were driving. On and on we shot, though, without finding any slightest change or opening or structure in that unending dark metal surface, that swept away in its vast, bare curve to the horizons, which were very far from us, so great was the radius of curvature of Neptune's mighty sphere. But after tense moments of this fruitless watch from our racing flier, Whitely uttered a low exclamation and pointed ahead, toward a round lighter circle in the dark metal plain far to the left, a circular opening in the giant metal shield!

None other of us spoke as we gazed toward that opening, but at once I had sent the space-flier rushing toward it. As we raced nearer to it we saw that that opening's circle was a full five hundred feet in diameter, and that we could see down through it a great, bright-lit space beneath! Tensely we watched, until in another moment I had sent the space-flier directly above the great opening, so that it hovered motionless above the circular opening's center. And as it hung there we four, forgetful for the moment of all else, were gazing down through the space-flier's window through that opening, down into the great more brightly-lit space that we could see beneath, beneath the huge metal shield that covered all this world!

The first thing that I noted, gazing downward, was that the space beneath the giant metal roof of Neptune was a great one, since it was a full mile from the opening in that roof to the surface of the world far below. Gazing down toward that surface, seeing at last the true surface of Neptune lying in the brighter light that existed in some strange way beneath the gigantic metal roof, we gasped. For upon that surface there loomed countless strange structures such as we had never seen before. Rectangular in shape were those structures, with straight black walls, of great size but seeming rather low in height, and they were without exception roofless! In them we could dimly make out from our great height the gleaming shapes of what seemed huge machines of one sort or another, but could not at that height see whether living beings of any sort moved among the structures. The great circle of the world beneath that we could see, hanging above the opening, was completely covered with these structures, the black walls of one roofless building being surrounded on all sides by the walls of others, there being no streets or open spaces whatever between them! It was as though, indeed, all the surface of the great world beneath had been divided into great compartments by a great checker-board arrangement of intersecting black walls!

Marlin's eyes were gleaming with excitement as he gazed down. "The city of the creatures of Neptune!" he breathed, as in awe we four stared down. "The city of Neptune that lies beneath the colossal roof, and that must hold somewhere that which we have come to seek!"

"You're going to venture down into this city—down under the great roof?" I asked, and he nodded.

"We must hunt to find the giant force-ray's source. But stand ready to flash the space-flier back upward—for if we're discovered by whatever beings inhabit this strange world, I think we'll get short shrift!"

A moment we paused there, and then as my hands moved upon the switch-controls, decreasing the power of the force-ray that held us upward the space-flier was sinking smoothly and slowly downward, down through the great opening! Tensely and with fascinated interest we gazed about now as we sank into the great space that lay beneath the huge metal roof. That space was brighter-lit than above the roof, we saw, and as we turned a moment to glance upward we saw that looking upwards, the roof was perfectly transparent! Dark, opaque metal when seen from above, it was almost invisible in its transparency when seen from below! And, seeing that, we understood the great roof's purpose. It had been constructed and placed above all Neptune, encircling the great planet and enclosing it, to retain that planet's heat as much as possible. For it was apparent that heat and light radiations or vibrations could not pass up through the metal of the roof from beneath, making it appear black and perfectly opaque from above, but could pass freely down through it from above, making it appear almost perfectly transparent from below!

EVEN as we grasped the wonder of that, though, we had forgotten it, in the greater wonder of the things that lay now before our eyes. For as we sank down in our space flier into the great space beneath that roof we could see the surface of great Neptune itself, stretching far away beneath that mighty enclosing shield above it, and covered to the horizons by the strange rectangular and roofless structures such as we had already seen. These were formed, indeed, by smooth black walls of some two hundred feet in height that ran in straight lines in checker-board arrangement across all the surface of this huge planet, apparently, forming upon all its surface, without streets or parks or openings of any kind, a vast city of rectangular compartments, large and small! A titanic streetless city that covered apparently all the surface of giant Neptune!

But most wonderful of all the things that lay before us in that moment was the fact that nowhere about us could we see any sign of supporting pillars or piers for the giant roof that stretched far above us! For though we could gaze far away to the distant horizons of this great world, we could find no single support for that huge metal roof that apparently covered all the great planet, and whose weight must have been incalculable! And another feature of the giant roof puzzled us. It puzzled us to see the great openings in it like that down which we had come, great circular openings which we could see in it here and there at great distances from each other. Those openings were provided on their underside with great sliding shutters for closing them tightly, yet all were open! Why should they be open, we silently asked ourselves, if the purpose of the roof was to retain Neptune's heat within that roof? For the existence of those great and unclosed openings in the roof must surely be defeating that purpose, for our outside-temperature dial recorded the same zero temperature as prevailed above the roof.

Yet even these strange things could not wholly draw our interest and attention from the strange compartment-city beneath, as our space-flier sank toward it. We were within a few hundred feet of it, now, and as we dropped nearer, Marlin and Whitely and Randall staring eagerly down beside me, my hands were tense upon the switch-controls, ready to send our flier leaping instantly upward. For if the beings of the city beneath, whatever their nature, caught sight of us, we could expect nothing but instant attack. So that a tenseness held all of us as our great flier's faceted polyhedron dropped on through the pale light beneath the great roof toward the black-walled, checker-board like city that stretched across the surface of the great world beneath us. And now, as we sank lower, our eyes were making out ever more clearly the details of that amazing city.

The rectangular black-walled compartments held, as we had half-realized from above, various strange-shaped mechanisms and objects which we could even now only vaguely discern. We could see clearly, though, that here and there across all the vast city's compartmented surface there stood giant metal globes, each a hundred feet in diameter and each occupying a square compartment of its own. There seemed hundreds of these great gleaming globes, scattered here and there in compartments across the city's surface as far as we could see, though their purpose was then quite incomprehensible to us. But as we sank lower still, ever more cautiously, it was not the globes or the compartments' contents that held our attention so much as the astounding, stupefying fact that now was thrust upon us—namely that in all the gigantic compartmented city, in all its strange great black-walled rectangular and roofless enclosures, there moved no living being!

"Dead!" Randall's cry expressed in that instant the stupefaction of all of us. "A dead world!"

"Neptune—a dead world!"

A dead world! For truly it seemed a dead world that lay there in the dim pale light beneath us! A world whose strange contiguous compartments stretched away from horizon to horizon to form the colossal city above which we hovered, but a world, a city, in which was no single discernible thing of life! The endless black-walled compartments, the strange-shaped structures and mechanisms, the great enigmatic globes—all these things lay beneath us in a silence and a death that were stunning to our senses! Lay beneath us as though death had reached out of the unknown to annihilate suddenly all living things upon this alien world, leaving in it only the cold and the silence and the death that enwrapped it now! Neptune—we had flown across the awful void toward it for week upon week, prepared to find within it any strange beings, any alien and terrible form of life, but never had we been prepared to find it without any life whatever—an utterly lifeless world!

As we stared down toward it in utter silence it seemed to me that my brain was spinning from the stupefying shock of amazement that was ours. For if the world beneath us was truly a dead one, if Neptune lay now without life, its colossal compartmented city entirely lifeless, whence came that giant force-ray that was stabbing across the solar system from Neptune to turn the sun ever faster toward its division? Whence came that doom which was being loosed upon our Earth and upon all the solar system, almost, by that gigantic ray? Was that great ray, after all, only some incomprehensible freak of natural forces, impossible to withstand, and had Neptune, once the home of some alien, mighty civilization, lain for eons in silence and death? Had our desperate mission which alone held a chance for Earth, our terrific race out through the unthinkable reaches of the solar system's spaces toward its outermost planet, been in vain?

Marlin must have felt something of the same despair in that moment, but his strong face betrayed no trace of it as he turned to us. "It's evident that this vast compartment-city, this whole world, perhaps, is deserted," he said. "But where does the great ray come from?"

Whitely shook his head, glancing at his instruments, "Impossible to say," he said. "The recording-instruments here show only that we are close to the great ray's source, that that source is in the region around Neptune. But the emanations or reflections from it striking the instruments are so powerful as to make it impossible to determine the ray's source exactly."

"But the city beneath!" I cried. "Even if it is dead, deserted, we might be able to find in it some clue to what has happened here, some idea of what manner of creatures the Neptunians were, and perhaps some clue to the great ray's source!"

Marlin pondered, then nodded. "Hunt's right," he said. "If we explore this deserted compartment-city beneath we may find some suggestion that will lead us to the great ray's source. And we *must* find out soon, for only eighty-five days are left before the sun divides into a double star and dooms Earth!"

"But we shouldn't risk all of us on this venture," I said. "The safest way would be to keep the space-flier, with two of us inside, hovering here above the city while the other two go down to it and explore it in their space-walkers."

This we finally agreed to do, and Marlin and I insisted upon being the two to make the venture, Whitely and Randall reluctantly agreeing at last to remain within the space-flier, watching and waiting for us. So, bringing the space-flier down to a height of a thousand feet above the compartmented city, I set the force-ray to hold it motionless there, Randall taking my place at its controls. Then Marlin and I were quickly getting into our two cylindrical space-walkers. Once inside them, we each gripped in a great pincer-hand the pointed bars of steel that we were to take with us, and then unscrewed the inner door and passed into the vestibule-chamber. Another moment and with the inner door closed, the outer one was swinging open, and the denser and colder air from without was rushing into the vestibule-chamber. We did not feel its cold, however, snug in the insulated and heated cylinders of the space-walkers, but drew ourselves to the outer door, turning on the force-rays from the bottoms of our cylinders. Then as we drew ourselves out through the door and into empty air, we were both sinking gently downward, our fall slowed to a mere floating drop by the down-pressing power of our force-rays.

DOWN through the dim pale light of Neptune's day we sank, down until just beneath us lay one of the intersecting black walls. As I saw this I shot my supporting force-ray outward at a slant, and as this sent me down obliquely, I floated down past that wall, Marlin doing the same beside me, and in another moment we had come gently to rest just above the black smooth floor of one of the great compartments, the force-rays from the bottoms of our space-walkers holding us a foot or so above the floor. Resting there, Marlin and I looked up first. Beside us towered the black two-hundred foot wall of the compartment, and far above we could make out the hovering space-flier, its great gleaming polyhedron hanging motionless and watchful above. We waved the great metal arms of our space-walkers toward it, toward Whitely and Randall inside it, and then turned to examine the place in which we stood.

It was an oblong compartment some four hundred feet in length, and half that in width, its great black walls towering on all sides of us. Ranged around the compartment against those walls were rows of strange squat mechanisms of a roughly pear-like form, that loomed each a score of feet in height. Marlin and I shot our space-walkers toward the nearest of these mechanisms, to examine it. We saw that in the top of it was an odd cone-like opening, and that there ran out of the gleaming metal cover of the thing a thick pipe or tube that connected with a larger pipe that encircled the compartment, connected to each of the mechanisms. Then as we reached forward, swung aside the metal cover of the mechanism, exposing an intricate system of sections inside it through which ran slender tubes acted upon by what seemed projectors of electro-magnetic force about them, Marlin pointed toward them, leaned toward me until his space-walker touched mine and spoke to me through the touching metal.

"A water-making mechanism this seems to be, Hunt," he said. "In some way it must draw down ceaseless supplies of hydrogen and oxygen atoms from the great vapor-masses above the roof, and then recombine them here into water."

I nodded, gazing intently at the thing. "But it hasn't been used for years—for centuries, perhaps," I said. "Look—that dust upon it—"

For upon the pear-shaped mechanism before us, and on all those others and all other things about us, there rested a coating of fine dust that was inches thick, a dust-coating that we knew only a great period of time could have deposited there. A moment we stared at that, two grotesque figures there in the great cylinders of our space-walkers, and then were moving on, along the wall. That black smooth wall, we saw now, was composed of a material that looked much like a black seamless stone, but one that seemed diamond-hard. For our pointed steel bars could make not the slightest impression upon it, and it was evident, from the monolithic construction of the great walls about us and of the smooth black paving upon which we walked, that this diamond-like smooth stone had been artificially made. Later we were to learn that it was constructed by a building up of molecules into a deliberate crystalline formation that far exceeded the strength and stability of any other material's crystalline structure, and thus gave to the black artificial stone a diamond-like hardness and a tensile strength exceeding that of steel.

Around the great compartment we walked, our eyes ranging over the great pear-shaped mechanisms and the great pipes connecting them, and then Marlin and I stopped short. For there in the black wall before us was a door, an opening that connected with the adjoining compartment on that side. It was by means of doors like that, it was plain, that the necessity of streets in this compartment-city had been obviated, making it possible to pass across the city through the compartments themselves if needed. Yet it was in stupefying surprise that Marlin and I now gazed toward that door. For it was all of six feet in width, but hardly more than four feet in height! Its opening stretched there in the black wall as though an ordinary door-opening of one of Earth's buildings had been set in that wall sidewise! And as we looked stunnedly about we saw that all the doors set in the compartment's four walls were of the same size and shape!

"Those doors!" I cried to Marlin, leaning beside me, "Those were never made for human beings or for near-human beings!"

"Then these Neptunians that once were here—" Marlin began, and then stopped; we gazed in silence at each other through the vision-windows of our space-walkers.

And silence seemed oppressive all about us then, a silence that lay as thickly over the deserted compartment-city as the thick dust of un-guessable years that covered it. A chill seemed to have struck home to us in some strange fashion with the discovery of those grotesque door-openings and their significance. I glanced upward, saw that the faceted ball of the space-flier was still hanging motionless high above, and then as I turned back saw that Marlin had moved toward the low door toward which we had been gazing. A moment he contemplated it, then motioned to me with the big metal arm of his space-walker, and as I came to his side, grasped that door's edge with his great arms and lowered his space-walker's big cylinder until it lay on its side on the smooth black paving. Then he was drawing it through the door, aiding himself with a force-ray shot from the opening in its bottom toward the compartment's opposite wall behind us. When he was through, he drew himself erect, and in a moment I had followed him and was standing with him in the next compartment.

That second compartment, we found, was a replica of the first, being of the same size and holding within it several dozen more of the pear-shaped water-manufacturing mechanisms. We passed through it, therefore, over the dust-strewn paving and through the low similar door on its opposite side, to find ourselves in still another compartment of water-manufacturers. Pressing on, rapidly becoming able to pass through the low strange doors easily in our cumbrous space-walkers, we passed through a half-score more of similar compartments all holding only the dust-covered, pear-shaped water-mechanisms, and then at last we passed into a different compartment, one that held a strange shelving that covered all its walls, at which we stared in perplexity for some time.

This shelving consisted of horizontal and perpendicular shelves of smooth black stone like that of the walls themselves, running along and up and down those walls and forming thus a continuous series of box-like openings, each some four feet in length and two in height. There were hundreds of these shelves in the compartment, we could see, yet all of them were quite empty, and in the compartment there seemed to be no other object. They suggested the equipment of a store-room, yet there was no faintest clue as to what had been stored in those shelf-tiers of openings, ranged one above the other all around the walls. Had Marlin and I been able to guess the astounding truth as to those tiers of compartments as to their significance and purpose, much would have been clear to us right then. As it was, after vainly endeavoring to fathom the purpose of the things, we gave it up and moved on out of the compartment, and through similar shelf-tiered compartments beyond it.

BY this time we had passed some distance from beneath our hovering space-flier, but still could see its gleaming polyhedron hanging high in the air behind us. Reassured by the sight of it, we passed on, and in the next half-hour progressed through many more compartments. Some of these contained water-manufacturing mechanisms or tiers of strange shelf-openings such as we had already seen. But many others held mechanisms or objects strange to our eyes, before which Marlin and I stood entranced. We almost forgot, in the over-powering interest of the things that we found in those compartments, the object of our exploring search through the strange compartment-city, our search for clues as to the beings of Neptune and as to the great force-ray that was turning the sun ever faster.

Compartments we found in which were structures that puzzled us as completely as had the tiers of shelf-openings. These structures were great flat metal containers, each scores of feet in length and width but hardly more than a foot or two in depth. They were ranged one above the other in great supporting frameworks, and each container was filled with black fine soil. The compartments that held these had set in their walls great white disks which were connected to intricate apparatus that seemed generators of some kind of force, but more than that we could not ascertain from our inspection of them. The whole arrangement, the great shallow containers of soil, the disks in the walls, the generators connected to them—all was utterly enigmatic and perplexing to us, and we were forced to give up the riddles and pass on into other compartments, in which were other things almost as mysterious.

Some held giant globes of burnished metal, now dust-covered, which occupied almost a whole compartment each. These great gleaming globes were among the most puzzling things we had found, since there was, in the compartment of each one, no other object or indication of their purpose, save for a few switches mounted upon a panel, the combination of which we could not discover, opening and closing them in vain. We had seen these great globes from above, dotting the vast compartment-city here and there in great numbers, but we could learn no more of their purpose standing there beside them than we had been able to guess from above. And near these there were strange looming machines, many-cogged and with a great hopper above whose purpose we guessed, at least, guessing that these were the mechanisms that produced from some raw materials the artificial diamond-hard black stone-material that made up all the intersecting walls of this strange huge city-world.

Each of these machines had before it a very low, round metal seat, with in front of that seat the controls of the machine, a half-dozen burnished metal levers. As we saw them Marlin and I exchanged startled glances. Had the being who operated that machine, who sat before it, held and operated all those control levers of the mechanism? Back to our minds flashed the strange low openings of the doors through which we had come, and for a moment the same strange sense of dread chilled me. But I shook off the feeling, followed Marlin on into another compartment, glancing back through to where our space-flier poised in the air now far across the city behind us.

It was into another long rectangular compartment that we passed, one that held, like that out of which we had just come, rows of strange many-cogged mechanisms. But one feature of that compartment caught our attention instantly, held us motionless and staring. And that was that those rows of great mechanisms were not complete! Here and there in those rows were gaps, as though machines had been removed from the compartment, and where those gaps were, where the missing machines had stood, were squares on the floor where their bases had rested, *squares that were entirely free of the inch-thick dust that lay over all else!* And even as we stared, as we comprehended the astounding significance of that, we saw that upon the dust-coated floor before us were many tracks, small round and strange tracks in the thick dust that were of great number and that had been made, it was apparent from their dust-free condition, but days or hours before!

"Marlin!" I whispered, grasping my companion's space-walker with the great metal arm of my own and touching head casing to head casing. "Marlin—those tracks-someone, something has been here—and but recently!"

"It can't be!" he exclaimed, his voice hushed strangely like my own. "Neptune—all this great compartment-city—it's all dead, deserted—"

"But those tracks!" I insisted. "Those squares in the dust-something's been here and has taken a half-dozen of these great machines away with them! And we know that something on Neptune is sending the great force-ray out to the sun!"

"It can't be," Marlin repeated. "We found no source of the great ray on Neptune's sunward side, and, too, how can that ray shoot always toward the sun from some spot on Neptune when Neptune itself is constantly turning? No, Hunt, I think that this means—but look up there!"

As he cried out he was gazing suddenly upward, his space-walker's great arms pointing up, and at that horror-stricken cry, I glanced up to see a sight that froze me motionless there in astonishment. For there, high above us and above the great compartment-city, a dozen strange great shapes were dropping down through the air toward us, were dropping down through one of the openings in the great roof! Long great cylinders of gleaming metal those shapes seemed, dropping silently and smoothly down from the opening, toward the compartment-city, but even as we looked in amazement and terror up toward them, they had halted in mid-air, as though seeing the faceted ball of our hovering space-flier hanging above the city far behind us. Then the next instant all the dozen great cylinders were flashing with unbelievable speed toward our space-flier, a half-score narrow, pencil-like rays of pale, almost invisible light or force stabbing ahead of them toward the space-flier!

Marlin and I cried out in the same instant as those great cylinders whirled through the air toward the space-flier, and in that moment it seemed to us that our wild cries had been heard, for we saw the space-flier whirl itself to one side suddenly, as though Randall and Whitely in it had caught sight suddenly of that onrushing menace. The pale, almost unseen stabbing little rays of force or light shot past them as they swerved thus, and then the next moment cylinders and space-flier seemed to be whirling in a wild mélange of geometrical metal forms there in the pale dim light above the great compartment-city. We saw the slender, pencil-like shafts of force stabbing this way and that, saw one cylinder, struck by the shafts of its fellows, riven asunder by those shafts as though by swords of steel and then suddenly the gleaming polyhedron of the space-flier had plunged up out of the wild melee and was rocketing up toward one of the great openings in the vast roof above!

As Whitely and Randall thus whirled the space-flier up in an effort to escape their outnumbering, unknown attackers, we saw three of the great cylinders rushing up after them. In another moment the space-flier, closely followed by its three pursuers, had rushed up through the opening and disappeared above, and as they did so we saw that the remaining eight cylinders were dropping now again toward the compartment-city! Watching stupefied still in our amazement, Marlin and I saw that four of the cylinders were heading down toward a point in the great city somewhat to the right of us, while the other four were slanting down now almost straight toward the compartment in which we stood! And as I saw that, as I saw and understood the significance of the tracks and missing mechanisms in this compartment, I grasped Marlin's great metal arm with one of my own, again touching head-armors.

"They're coming down to this compartment!" I cried. "It was they who took the missing mechanisms from here—they've come for more!"

"Out of the compartment, then!" Marlin shouted. "They're after Whitely and Randall in the flier, and if they find us here—!"

With the words we were throwing ourselves, prisoned in our great cumbrous space-walkers as we were, toward the low door through which we had come. In a moment we were through that door, were in the adjoining compartment, but hardly had we gained it than there swept through the pale light from high above four great cylindrical shapes, slanting smoothly down toward the compartment we had just left! From above they could see us easily, whatever beings were inside those descending cylinders, so that as they shot down over our roofless great compartment, Marlin and I poised motionless, praying that our great gleaming space-walkers might be mistaken for mechanisms. Far across the compartment-city we could glimpse the four other cylinders dropping down toward a different point, also, and then in the next moment the four above us had shot down over us and with a throbbing sound coming clearly to us from those cylinders' interiors, were coming to rest in the compartment we had just left!

GLANCING for a moment at each other through the vision-windows of our space-walkers, Marlin and I then softly moved in them toward the low door through which we had just come. For though our fear was great, our curiosity, our realization of the mission that had brought us out here to Neptune, was greater. In a moment we were at the door, were lowering ourselves awkwardly and silently to a position from which we could gaze through it into the adjoining compartment. In that compartment, we saw now, the four great cylinders had landed, and were resting upon the floor at its center. Each cylinder was of forty feet diameter and twice that in height, and their gleaming metal sides were broken here and there by small windows. They were broken too, we saw with a start, by ray-openings like those of our own space-flier, and it was evident from those that the cylinders were propelled through space by the same force-rays that moved our flier!

Before we could fully comprehend the meaning of that fact, though, there came a low clanking of metal and before our eyes a section in each of the curving sides of the cylinders, near the base of each, was abruptly sliding aside, leaving in the metal wall of each cylinder a low oblong door-opening like those of the compartments about us. Now we heard from inside that opening a stir of movement, and saw vaguely a shape or shapes that moved in the cylinder's dark interior. Then, as we gazed with tense nerves toward that opening, there moved out of the cylinder's dark interior through that opening, into the pale dim light of the Neptunian day, a creature at which Marlin and I stared in that moment with horror-stunned minds! A being so grotesque and so awful in appearance that for the moment it seemed to me that it needs must be a creation only of our overstrained nerves and brains!

It was a creature that bore no conceivable resemblance to the human form or to any other in our knowledge. The body was a great flat disk of pale-green flesh, five feet in diameter and hardly a foot in thickness. It was supported in a flat or horizontal position above the ground by seven short thick limbs of muscle or flesh, which were each three feet in length and which projected down from the big disk-body at equal intervals around its circle. The only visible features of the creature were the eyes and mouth. The eyes were two in number, and were set close together in the *edge* of the disk-body. They were like the eyes of some insect, being each inches across and bulging outward, being composed each of a myriad smaller glistening lens-divisions, like the eye of a fly! And as I saw with shuddering horror those two bulging strange eyes gazing about, it came to me that it was only by means of such great, powerful eyes and their many lenses that any creature here in the dim light of Neptune could see clearly all things about it!

The mouth was a white-lipped circular opening, and was set at the very center of the horizontal disk-body's upper surface! No stranger combination can be imagined than that which presented itself thus in the appearance of that creature before us, with the two bulging glassy eyes staring forth from the edge of the great disk-body, and the round mouth gaping there in that disk-body's flat upper surface. Slung around the disk-body the creature wore a flexible armor or dress of connected straps of flexible metal. In a loop of this rested a metal tube formed by the joining together of two tubes of dissimilar thickness. And attached to the flexible straps in another position, at the disk-body's edge, was one of the strangest features of its appearance, a small metal ball that seemed glowing with unceasing radiant light!

The creature gazed about him, unaware of our awe-stricken gaze, and then half-turned and seemed to call to others in the cylinder from which he had emerged, a strange sound issuing from his mouth-opening. That sound was like a swift succession of staccato snaps of sound, as clear and sharp as the snap of metal on metal. From the variation in their utterance, though they were in a single pitch only, it was evident that they formed the speech of the strange creature, and as he gave utterance to them, others like him, other similar disk-bodied green beings, were emerging from the cylinder behind him and from the other cylinders. In a moment a score or more were gathered there, moving toward the great cogged mechanisms beside them, and as they did so the staccato snapping of their strange speech came loud to our ears. And as they did so, too, we saw that the seven strange limbs of each of them served him as arms as well as supporting legs, since some used some of those limbs to carry tools, holding them tightly in fingerless, muscled grasp!

"Neptunians!" whispered Marlin beside me. "Neptunians, Hunt—those squat, flat disk-bodies—those great eyes—!"

Neptunians! Yet I had seen myself that they must be so, that only on a great planet like Neptune, with far greater gravitational power than Earth, could those squat, flat bodies have evolved. For the greater the power of a planet's gravitation, the lower and the more squat will be the forms of life that evolve upon it. And just as these Neptunians had evolved in their strange disk-form here on the great planet, due to its greater gravitational power so had their great light-gathering eyes been evolved by the dimness that reigned here always. And it was these beings, it was clear, who had built the vast compartment-city that covered all of the great planet's surface about us, since it was only beings like these who would have built such strange, low doors in it for their own flat disk-bodies, only such beings as these who, with their seven great limbs, could manipulate the controls of the mechanisms we had seen!

"Neptunians!" I whispered it, myself. "But if it's beings like these who inhabit Neptune, who have sent the great force-ray stabbing toward the sun to divide it, where are they all? Why have they left all this city, all this world, dead and deserted?"

Marlin, inside his space-walker, shook his head. "God knows, Hunt! If all these Neptunians have deserted their world, where have they gone? I know no more than you. But it's clear that they've come back for more of those great mechanisms."

It was, indeed, evident that that was the object of the Neptunians' visit to the compartment-city, for now the score or more in the adjoining compartment were busily working with their tools upon three or four of the great cogged mechanisms that loomed there. Swiftly they were taking down those mechanisms, were dissembling them into a myriad intricate parts which were stowed away in the four great cylinders. More than once some of them passed close to the low door through which Marlin and I were gazing, but none ventured through it into the compartment in which we hid, seeming all to be intent upon the business at hand. And as they worked on we began to understand some of the features about them that had puzzled us in our first horrorstricken sight of them.

We had been puzzled, indeed, that they were able thus to move about unheedingly without protection of any sort in the zero-cold that reigned about us. But now as one or two of them passed close to the door by which we crouched, I gazed closely at the glowing little ball that each had attached to his metal armor, and guessed then what I was later to learn was the truth, that that ball was glowing with radiant heat and had the power of heating to comfortable temperature the atmosphere for a few feet directly around its wearer. Thus the wearer of it moved always in a little volume of warm air, though the air outside that area might be at zero temperature. And thus it was that the Neptunians were able to withstand the bitter cold about us, from which we were protected by our space-walkers.

As we gazed toward the Neptunians, they were completing the process of disassembling and stowing away the great mechanisms, and now I moved closer to Marlin, my thoughts being on retreat from the dangerous position in which we were. Not only might we be discovered at any moment by the Neptunians before us, but somewhere in the compartment-city behind us were others, we knew, who had landed in their four cylinders at another point. Whatever had happened to Whitely and Randall in the space-flier, Marlin and myself were in the most perilous of positions. Even were we to escape the Neptunians we could not exist for long in our space-walkers in this dead and deserted city, in the cold of this strange and terrible world of death. Yet to escape from them was our first consideration, and I whispered as much to Marlin through our touching space-walkers.

"We've got to get clear of these Neptunians," I whispered to him. "Back farther in the city we can hide until they go."

He was gazing toward the strange creatures and their tools and mechanisms with intense scientific interest, but turned toward me at my whisper. "We'll get back, then," he whispered. "It may be that Whitely and Randall—"

It was a sentence that he never finished. For we had hardly turned to cross the compartment in which we crouched than we had to stop short in our space-walkers. There behind us a dozen or more great disk-creatures had been standing—a dozen or more great Neptunians! Even as we faced them there in that stunned moment, their bulging glassy eyes upon us, I saw the tracks in the thick dust at our feet, realized that these creatures were of the others who had landed in the compartment-city, and that finding our space-walkers' tracks here and there in the thick dust, they had followed them, had trailed us and stolen behind us while we watched their fellows! Then in the next moment had come a staccato cry from the foremost of the Neptunians, and in the instant following, they had flung themselves straight forward upon us!

For in this atmosphere sound penetrated our cylinders.

CHAPTER SEVEN
The Giant Ray

THE minute that followed was a grotesque whirl of swift action, a desperate reeling struggle between Marlin and me cased in our great space-walkers, and the great disk-bodied Neptunians. Even as they had leaped upon us, we had shot to one side, had brought down upon the foremost of them the great steel bars carried in our pincer-like metal hands, and had sent two of them crumpling to the black paving with a thick green liquid oozing from their shattered bodies. The remainder, though, were upon us before we could strike again, and then as they gripped us I could see the Neptunians who had been working in the adjoining compartment come running toward the combat, to assist their fellows. So that though Marlin and I struck out with desperate fury at the monstrous creatures with the great metal jointed arms of our space-walkers, they had in a moment more with their numberless limbs fettered our arms and torn the bars from our grasp, holding us then motionless and helpless.

Thus held, part of the creatures stepped back from us, and then we heard one of them, who bore a single, crimson-circle device upon his metal dress or armor, utter a staccato order to the others. At once four of them drew from their armor the long tubes we had noted there, and trained them upon us. I knew, instinctively, that those tubes held some deadly force like that with which the cylinders had attacked our space-flier in the battle in mid-air. Later I was to learn that the tubes could release a force-ray similar to that used for propulsion by our space-flier and by the cylinders—a force-ray so concentrated into a pencil-like beam that, instead of merely pressing against whatever it struck, it pierced whatever it touched with terrific force, riving it asunder. Knowing the deadliness of the tubes, I looked for instant annihilation.

But it was evident in a moment that it was only as a precaution that the tubes were held upon us. For now, while a half-score of the Neptunians held Marlin and me firmly by the arms of our space-walkers, the one who had given the order came closer to us, clambered with his powerful multiple limbs upon the top of my space-walker, and gazed in through its vision-windows at me. To see those bulging, glassy and insect-like eyes outside the window so close to my own struck me through with a chilling horror greater than anything I had yet felt. I saw that the creature had discerned me inside the space-walker, had assured himself that creatures of life yet different from himself occupied the two cylinders. For in a moment he had clambered back down to the ground, and then as he uttered another sharp order, the creatures that held us were dragging us forward, toward the door of the compartment into which we had looked before.

Through that low door they dragged us in our space-walkers, and across the adjoining compartment toward one of the great upright cylinders resting there. In another moment the Neptunians had pulled us inside the door of that cylinder into its dark opening, and I saw the one who had given the orders following, with a half-dozen of his fellows. The others were dispersing to the other cylinders, and in a moment the door of our own slid clanging shut behind us. Then there was a hissing and throbbing of strange machinery in the dark interior of the cylinder about us, and at the same moment the leader of the Neptunians motioned to us to emerge from our space-walkers, having removed their own glowing ball-heaters.

I think that both Marlin and I hesitated for a long moment before complying with that command, yet we saw that upon us still were trained the tubes of the four Neptunians who guarded us, so reluctantly we threw open the lower doors of the spacewalkers and emerged from them. As we did so, forgetful for the moment of the strange creatures about us, we gazed in amazed interest around us. The huge cylinder's interior, we saw, was divided into a half-dozen compartments by metal floors or ceilings set at intervals of ten or twelve feet from its bottom to its top. A light metal ladder ran up through openings in all of those floors or divisions, and up that ladder now a few of the many-limbed Neptunians were hurrying toward the upper compartments. We ourselves were standing, with the Neptunian leader of the red circle-insignia, in the lowest or bottom compartment of the cylinder, his four tube-armed guards and a half-dozen green disk-bodied monsters about us.

That lowest compartment held great gleaming-cased mechanisms, from which came the throbbing that we had already heard, and that was so exactly similar to the throb of our space-flier's generators as to remove all doubt but that these were the similar generators of the cylinder. As our eyes roved about them, the Neptunian leader uttered a staccato command, at the same time pointing with one of his seven limbs, up toward the ladder. His meaning was unmistakable, and at once Marlin and I stepped toward the ladder and began to climb upward on it, the tubes of the four watchful guards just beneath us as they followed. As we passed up that ladder, through the upper sections of the cylinder's interior, I saw vaguely the things within those sections.

One of them held the disassembled parts of the great cogged mechanisms we had seen them taking down and storing inside the cylinders. Another two or three sections held similar disassembled parts of differing machines that had evidently been taken from another part of the dead vast compartment-city beneath. We passed up through sections that held supplies and strange tank-like affairs, that seemed not unlike the batteries of our own space-flier, and then were climbing up into the topmost section of the cylinder. This was a section whose top and walls were set with so many windows as to make its sides seem quite transparent. And this topmost section, in which a pair of Neptunians already were standing, was quite apparently the control-section.

For at its center rose from its floor a thick metal pillar or standard, upon the top and sides of which were set a battery of dozens of small green studs, and around this were strange seats in which the two waiting Neptunians were now taking their places. As Marlin and I climbed into that uppermost section, the guards and the leader of the disk-bodied Neptunians behind us, we gazed wonderingly about, at the central control-standard and at the strange graduated scales with moving dots of light upon them, that were set here and there in the walls and that seemed recording instruments of one kind or another. Then the crimson-marked leader had given utterance to another sharp succession of snapping sounds, a swift command, at the same time motioning us to the side of the circular room, where were similar low, strange seats. In these we seated ourselves, the four Neptunians who watched us taking places on either side of us, and then as the leader took the remaining seat at the control-standard, we saw one of the other two seated there reach forth with strange quick limbs and touch a number of the studs in swift succession.

At once the great throbbing of the generators or mechanisms in the cylinder's lowest section intensified, and as Marlin and I gazed quickly outward through the windows about us we saw that now the other cylinders in the compartment were all closed and throbbing like this one. Then, as one of the Neptunians at the control-standard touched another stud, the cylinder in which we were rose swiftly upward and out of the great black-walled compartment, rose up smoothly over the dead compartment-city into the pale light of the Neptunian day, followed at once by the three other cylinders. The dim day about us was already waning, fading, as night crept across this huge world of silence and death, with its ceaseless rotation, but there remained still enough light for us to see far across the mighty maze of compartments that was the deserted and dead city. And now across that city the four cylinders were rushing, racing over it in horizontal position, the strange seats upon which we and the Neptunians were seated swinging in gimbal-like frameworks as the cylinder swung thus from vertical to horizontal.

OVER the huge compartment-city our four cylinders flashed, then slowed and halted, as up from another point in it rose four more cylinders, the four that we had seen land in a different part of it, and whose occupants had discovered and captured us. Then all of the eight great cylinders, our own in the lead, were rising sharply upward, up toward the opening in the vast roof above, through which we had seen them come. As they shot up toward it, Marlin and I, glancing down and backward, could see, even as we had seen from our space-flier, the vast extent of the dead and deserted compartment-city, with its mechanisms and huge globes and high black intersecting walls lying now in such dusty silence and death. Yet it was only for a moment that we glanced back toward it, for now our eight cylinders were flashing up through the round opening in the huge roof, and out over that vast roof, seeming solid metal from above, that covered all of mighty Neptune. And as we flashed over it, now, I found for the first time opportunity to whisper to Marlin, beside me.

"They're leaving Neptune!" I whispered. "Where can they be going, Marlin? And what has happened to Whitely and Randall?"

He shook his head, answered in the same low tones. "Whitely and Randall have escaped, I hope. They had a small start on their pursuers—they may have eluded them here above Neptune—"

We were abruptly silent as the guards glanced suspiciously toward us with their bulging multiple eyes. And as the great cylinder and those behind shot on, the huge metal roof of Neptune below and the vast vapor-masses of its dense atmosphere stretched above us, I wondered if ever men had found themselves in the position that now was ours. Captured by monstrous disk-bodied beings of horror unutterable, flashing with them above the vast roof that sheathed Neptune and its dead, deserted and colossal compartment-city, to a destination of which we could not dream! And as that thought passed, another came, and I remembered the great mission that had brought us out here to the terrors of mighty Neptune, our great flight outward to find and put an end to the huge force-ray that was stabbing across the solar system and turning the sun ever faster, with every day bringing it nearer to the division that meant doom for almost all its universe. What chance was ours to accomplish that mission now, separated and captured as we were, not knowing even from what source the great ray was issuing, from what strange place these disk-bodied beings had come and to which they were now returning?

I was aroused from my silent despair, though, by a low exclamation from Marlin, and looked up to see that the cylinders of which our own was foremost had now halted, hanging midway between metal roof beneath and great vapor-masses above. Then down from above I saw, dropping quickly toward us, three other cylinders similar to the eight, three cylinders at sight of which my heart beat suddenly faster. For it had been three cylinders that had pursued Whitely and Randall in the space-flier! Tensely I watched as the three drove down among our eight, and then one of them had shot suddenly close to the cylinder in which we were, hanging beside it so that its low door-opening was directly touching the door-opening of our own. There was a clang of metal beneath as the doors of both cylinders slid aside. They fitted so closely against each other that no colder air from without could enter into the warmed interior of the two cylinders. Then from the other were coming into our own cylinder three Neptunians who climbed swiftly up into the top-section in which we were, while Marlin and I watched them in indescribable suspense.

As they came up into the uppermost section they spoke in their sharp, staccato talk to the Neptunian leader of the crimson-circle insignia, making report to him, it was apparent. But it was not to their snapping speech that Marlin and I gave our attention, but to the things they carried in their grip, and which they were showing to the leader. Those things, I saw with a start of horror, were some shattered and crumpled plates of metal, great flat metal plates that I recognized immediately as being of our space-flier's faceted sides! And they also held a broken, twisted metal thing that I recognized instantly as one of the space-flier's smaller liquid-oxygen tanks! I needed not to understand the strange speech of the Neptunians in that moment to understand what the three were reporting. For those shattered fragments of the space-flier told the tale with terrible clearness.

"Whitely and Randall!" It was Marlin's whisper of horror beside me. "They were caught by those pursuing cylinders—were annihilated by their rays—!"

"Whitely and Randall—" I felt my voice choke then, as I gazed at those last fragments of the space-flier's wreckage, mutely testifying to the end which our friends had met with beneath the shattering rays in their space-flier somewhere in the cold, vast vapor-masses above us.

Whitely—cool and detached and steady, stirred to passion by nothing save some unprecedented physical phenomenon, considering with curious, impersonal eyes each new peril that had confronted us; and Randall—with his sunny hair and eager young courage and unfailing sense of fun; it was as though they had risen before me in that moment, when we saw at last what death had overtaken them and our space-flier there in the chill clouds of mighty Neptune. I felt Marlin's steadying hand on my shoulder and knew that he was sounding similar depths of despair. For with Whitely and Randall gone, with our space-flier and with ourselves captured and held by these monstrous disk-bodied Neptunians who yet seemed not of Neptune, our chance to halt the great doom-ray that was radiating toward the sun, our chance even to return to Earth with word of the position and nature of that ray's source, was gone also!

Through the despair that had sunken upon me I was aware, in a moment, that the throbbing of the cylinder's great generators had waxed again in intensity. Already the three Neptunians, who had reported the destruction of the space-flier, had returned to their own cylinder, which had separated from ours, and now the whole eleven cylinders, our own in the lead, were racing forward once more, were shooting forward between the great vapor-masses above and the vast metal roof below. At immense and mounting speed they shot forward, a dull roar of whistling air coming to us from without, and in a moment the pale, dim light about us had begun to change to dusk, to darkness, as we shot on. For the eleven cylinders were racing around the surface of Neptune toward the side of it away from the sun at the moment, and as they entered the shade of that side they were plunging through the eternal night. But as the cylinders shot on they seemed to need no light or star to guide them through the deep darkness, though all that was visible was an occasional glinting of the great metal roof below.

On we shot through that deep darkness and there rose in me a sudden thought that roused me a little from the despair that held Marlin and me. Could it be that upon that other side there still remained a remnant of their race? A remnant of the race, that once had built the mighty compartment-city that covered all Neptune and the vast roof that shielded it, but that now occupied but a small part of the huge city? Was it from Neptune's other side, then, that the giant force-ray had stabbed toward the sun? Yet how could that be so, how could that great ray be shot out from any point of Neptune unceasingly as it was, when each twenty hours the great planet turned on its axis, when for half of that twenty hours whatever point that was the ray's source would be turned away from the sun instead of toward it?

WITH tense interest Marlin and I gazed ahead into the darkness through which our cylinders were rushing, while at the control-standard the leader and the other two Neptunians manipulated the force-rays that were propelling onward the cylinder in which we were. At last, after some minutes of this rushing flight of immense velocity, the cylinders seemed to slow down, to pause. Looking out I could discern the surface of the gigantic metal roof below us, just showing itself to us by a little glint of light here and there from it, and in that moment Marlin and I waited in suspense for the cylinders to sink down toward and through it, to whatever place upon Neptune's other side it was that held the remainder of their strange races, since by then, we knew, we were at that side of Neptune almost exactly opposite the sun. Only a moment the cylinders slowed and paused, and then were leaping through the air again at mounting speed. But instead of flashing downward toward the great roof, they were flashing upward!

Upward they were shooting, up through the dense air and straight into the great vapor-masses that loomed above us! Through those great clouds they were racing then, driving upward through them as through a darker darkness, and then suddenly had shot up and out from them, up and out into the clear and thinner air of Neptune's atmosphere's outermost limits. Behind our cylinders thus lay the huge, vapor-wreathed planet, shutting out by its vast bulk all sight of the sun's distant little disk of fire, or of the greater planets. But before us there stretched once more the black vault of space, unfolding itself to our eyes for the first time since we had ventured down through those shrouding vapors to Neptune's surface.

Brightest in that black void there shone, before and somewhat above us, Triton, the moon of Neptune. It was almost white in color, tinged with the pale green of great Neptune, about which it moved, and seeming of the same size to our eyes as Earth's own moon. Beyond and all about it, though, there flamed the great stars, seeming the same to our eyes here at the solar system's outermost limits as they had seemed to us when far within it, at Earth. The great field of stars and star-clusters that was Sagittarius, straight ahead and upward, the irregular parallelogram of Capricorn's stars, to the left, the throbbing crimson heart and jeweled menacing claws of Scorpio, to the right-all seemed to our eyes as they had seemed when we had started—how long ago it seemed!—out from Earth toward great Neptune, that lay now behind us. Yet now, with Neptune behind us, our eleven cylinders were flashing forward with greater and greater speed, were flashing out apparently from the solar system's last outpost into the vast void of interstellar space!

"They're going on—going out from Neptune into outer space!" I exclaimed to Marlin, as we gazed ahead, transfixed.

But suddenly he shook his head, pointing ahead and upward, for now the cylinders were flashing upward as well as forward. "It's Triton they're heading toward!" he said. "Triton—Neptune's single moon!"

"Triton!" I exclaimed, thunderstruck with amazement. "Then—then—it must be on Triton that the remaining Neptunians now are!"

Triton! For it was up toward it, up toward the white, green-tinged moon of Neptune that shone dully in the black vault above and ahead of us, that the eleven cylinders, our own in the lead, were heading! And as they shot out of the last limits of the atmosphere of Neptune, as they flashed forward at swiftly mounting speed still toward the moon, I could but stare at it in amazement. Triton! It was from it, then, that there had come these strange disk-bodied Neptunians who had captured us, who had annihilated our space-flier and our friends. It was on Triton, then, that there must remain whatever Neptunians still were left of those who had built the vast compartment-city that covered all the surface of Neptune itself, who had shielded it with that gigantic floating roof that enclosed all the mighty planet. Yet why had they deserted their vast compartment-city, their great world of Neptune? Why had they left that world for the single moon of Neptune, so much smaller in size? And the giant force-ray that was shooting across space to the sun, turning it ever faster, was it from Neptune then or Triton that that colossal ray was radiating?

It seemed to me that these questions were spinning in my head in a kaleidoscopic whirl of enigmas, as our throbbing cylinder and the ten behind it shot on and upward at a great slant toward the dull-gleaming sphere of Triton. Marlin, beside me, was staring ahead obviously as much mystified as I was, while the four Neptunians ranged on either side of us kept their ceaseless watch upon us. The other three sat still at the central control-standard, directing the cylinder on its rush out from Neptune toward its moon. And now, that moon grew larger ahead of us and above us, a strangely-gleaming sphere that seemed still very small, in comparison with the huge pale green disk of mighty Neptune that loomed behind us.

I knew, though, that Triton was of the same approximate size as Earth's own moon, and revolved around the great planet at the same approximate distance as Earth's own moon, roughly a quarter of a million miles. As we had noted from our space-flier in flashing out toward Neptune, its moon was now behind the great planet, that is on the other side of it from the sun, but due to the sharp inclination of the plane of Triton's orbit around Neptune, it was so much higher than its great planet in space as to make it possible to see the single moon, even from Neptune's sunward side. And now as our eleven cylinders shot toward it, it was spreading out across the black vault of the heavens before and above us, until at last we were within a few thousand miles of it and the speed of the cylinder was perceptibly decreasing beneath the controls of the three at the central standard.

Smoothly the cylinder, and the ten behind it, slowed, until they were racing forward at a comparatively low velocity. Triton's dull-gleaming sphere filled the heavens before us. Behind and a little below the great green disk of Neptune, belted with the vast cloud-masses of its immense atmosphere, loomed almost as great as ever to our eyes. And far beyond it there burned the sun's bright little disk, just above the huge sphere of Neptune, and visible to us through the thinner vapors of Neptune's uppermost atmosphere. We turned back toward the nearer world of Triton. As the cylinders rushed on toward it, all the suspense of expectation and mystery that had been ours since our first arrival at the strange dead world of Neptune gripped us now with renewed power. And as Marlin and I stared ahead we were aware that the cylinders were dropping, swinging about our pivoted seats and dropping toward the surface of Triton that seemed now to gleam beneath us.

Toward it we smoothly shot, and as Marlin and I gazed intently down we saw that there were below none of the great cloud-masses that wreathed the surface of mighty Neptune. Instead was only a smooth and strangely gleaming surface that we could but vaguely glimpse, and the sight of which made my heart pound in sudden anticipation. Could the thing be—could it be that here upon Triton as upon Neptune—? But my wondering speculations were cut abruptly short by reality as we shot lower toward the surface of Triton, as that surface came clearly at last to the eyes of Marlin and myself, bringing involuntary exclamations of amazement from us. For that surface was metal! Triton was shielded on all sides by a giant metal roof similar to that which enclosed great Neptune itself!

DOWN toward that mighty roof our eleven cylinders were rushing. When they seemed just above it, they halted their drop and raced along above it, around Triton's vastly curving surface. As they did so, Marlin and I, gazing downward, saw that the vast roof that shielded Triton appeared to be, from above, of the same dark metal as that which protected Neptune, and that it extended away without break or seam as far as we could see over the big moon's surface. And as our cylinders flashed above it, around the world's surface, we were aware that Triton had an atmosphere even as had its great parent world, since from outside was coming the dull roar of air against the speeding cylinder. It was a fact startling enough, but at that moment it was driven from our minds by a thing more startling still.

For as we flashed thus around Triton's sunward side, Marlin suddenly uttered a hoarse exclamation, pointed ahead and to the left. I gazed in that direction instantly and for a moment saw nothing unusual, but then as the cylinders flashed on I saw that in that direction was what seemed a great round opening in the smooth, dark metal, a titanic circular opening that must be miles across. Up out of that opening was rising what seemed at first glance a vast cylinder of pale light that sprang straight up and outward from the gigantic opening, and that was only visible for a short distance above that opening, fading swiftly into invisibility as it shot out into the gulf of space from Triton. Instinctively my eyes followed the fading length of that mighty beam outward, and then as they did so I felt sudden, awed understanding descending upon me and stared with Marlin toward the giant pit and its great ray in stunned silence. For that giant ray was pointing straight into the great gulf of space, toward the tiny, fiery disk of the distant sun!

"The giant force-ray!" Marlin whispered. "The great force-ray that's turning the sun ever faster—and that we came out here to find!"

"And pointing straight toward the sun!" I exclaimed. "Pointing through Neptune's upper atmosphere toward the sun!"

For we could see now that the giant ray, visible only there at its source, must indeed be cleaving through the upper limits of great Neptune's atmosphere as it reached across the great gulf toward the sun. For since Triton was on the other side of Neptune from the sun, was on its outward side, the great green sphere of Neptune lay almost between the sun and Triton, the big moon being high enough above the great planet, though, due to the inclination of its orbital plane, to make the sun visible to it through the upper reaches of Neptune's vast atmosphere. Through that atmosphere, therefore, we knew, the giant force-ray must be driving on its path across the solar system toward the sun, hurtling across the gulf to strike against that spinning sun's edge with terrific pressure and to spin it ever faster toward that day of division and doom that was marching relentlessly upon it!

But as our cylinders now swept nearer toward the giant force-ray and the pit from which it stabbed up and outward, Marlin and I were staring obliquely down into that vast pit. Seen from the side as we saw it, the tremendous opening seemed only like a mighty well of metal, from which the colossal pale force-ray, almost as great in diameter as the huge pit, stabbed. We could see, however, that set near the great pit's top at regular intervals around its curving wall were what seemed metal cube-like rooms, which were set on the pit's smooth curving wall. They were a score in number, those out-jutting metal cubes, and from slits in their walls came light from within, and glimpses of stud-covered walls and Neptunians moving about them. We knew, without doubt, that those twenty cubes held within them the unthinkably complex controls of this mighty force-ray that was destroying the solar system!

But now our cylinder and the ten that drove close behind it were passing the vast pit, the huge force-ray. I noted that they took extreme care to pass pit and mighty ray at a respectable distance, and knew, too, the reason for it, knew that any luckless cylinder that blundered into that colossal out-stabbing ray would be driven instantly at terrific speed and force out through the solar system and into the sun that the ray was striking! So that it did not surprise us that the cylinders veered far to the side of the huge ray, picking up speed once more when they had passed it, and racing on around Triton's metal-shielded surface and through the cold, dense atmosphere outside it. But as the cylinders drove on the eyes of Marlin and myself now were turned backward, back toward that gigantic pale ray of awful force that shot ceaselessly up and out from that vast pit in Triton's metal side.

"We've found it—the great ray we came out here to find—the source of that ray," I exclaimed to Marlin, "but we've found it too late! Whitely and Randall and the space-flier annihilated—we captured—"

He bent toward me. "Keep your courage up, Hunt," he said. "We may have a chance yet to get free—to get away from this world of Triton before they take us down inside it."

"But what—?" I began, when with a gesture he cut me short. "No more now, Hunt—the guards are watching. But be ready to act if a chance shows itself, for once down in Triton, we'll probably have no chance."

I saw that the four disk-bodied Neptunians who sat about us and guarded us were indeed watching us closely now with their strange bulging eyes, so gave over for the moment our whispered conversation, though with a slight gleam of hope. Glancing back again toward the great force-ray that was almost invisible behind us as the eleven cylinders raced on around Triton's metal surface, I was aware that Marlin was staring back toward it also, intently, shaking his head a little, as though puzzled by something concerning that giant beam of force. In a moment he turned his attention ahead. Our cylinders now were flashing around Triton from its sunward side to its dark side, and as we rushed on Marlin and I could see that to all appearances Triton was not rotating, or at least not above a low rate of speed. Then as we entered into the deeper shadow of the dark side, the sun's little disk vanishing behind us as we shot around Triton's curving surface into the shadow, Marlin uttered a low exclamation once more, and as I turned to look in the same direction I saw that far ahead there was stabbing out and upward into the black void of outer space a second giant force-ray like that one we had already seen shooting toward the sun!

Stupefied, I gazed toward it. For the first giant force-ray, amazing as it was, had yet been expected by us, more or less, since we had known from the first that such a colossal force-beam was stabbing from the region of Neptune toward the sun. But this second mighty force-ray, which seemed exactly the same in size and appearance and which rose from a giant pit or well in the vast metal roof even as did the first, was not directed toward the sun. For it was on the other side of Triton from the first ray, was exactly half around Triton from the first and was going out into space in an exactly opposite direction! Thus while the first colossal force-ray, springing out from Triton's sunward side, shot straight toward the sun, this second huge force-ray, on Triton's dark or outer side, was radiating straight out into the vast void of interstellar space, was radiating straight out, to all appearances, toward the unthinkably distant stars of Sagittarius that burned in that mighty void!

What could be the meaning of this other colossal force-ray, of equal size and power, going out into the vast void outside the solar system? The first great ray that was shooting toward the sun and turning the sun ever faster—its purpose was at least comprehensible, but what purpose could there be in sending an opposite and equal ray out into the mighty void from Triton's other side? That was the question that whirled in my astounded brain in that moment as the eleven cylinders shot on toward that second great ray, over Triton's metal surface. Marlin, though, on seeing that second great ray, seemed to be less puzzled than before. It seemed to have solved for him some problem which the sight of the first huge ray had suggested. To me it was utterly incomprehensible, and perplexed and awed I watched that huge pale ray and the vast pit from which it sprang as we raced toward them. I saw that on that pit's curving walls there jutted forth a score of cube-like projections or control-rooms similar to those in the pit of the first ray. Then I forgot pit and rays alike as the cylinder in which we were and all those behind it slowed suddenly in mid-air and then dipped sharply downward.

DOWN and down they shot, toward the vast gleaming metal roof of great Triton; down, until we saw that just beneath us there was outlined in that roof a great circle, slightly sunken. Toward this the cylinders dropped, and then as they came to a pause just above it I saw that set beside that circle in the roof was a transparent section beneath which was a small cage-like room, brightly lit. In this were a half-dozen Neptunians, and as they saw the eleven cylinders dropping and pausing above the circle in the roof they turned swiftly, pressed what seemed a series of knobs in their cage-room, and at once the great sunken circle beneath us was sliding along beneath the roof to one side, sliding smoothly away and leaving thus beneath us a great circular opening in the roof.

Instantly up from that opening around our cylinders was rushing a torrent of air, a torrent of uprushing air that I understood well was caused by the warmer air beneath the roof rushing up into the colder outside atmosphere. But now down through that opening and through the air-currents the cylinders were swiftly dropping, and we could see far below in dim light a great compartment-city like the one we had found upon Neptune! In a moment more we would be below the roof, the opening closed above us, prisoned hopelessly in Triton to meet whatever fate our captors decreed. Already two of our four guards, and two of the Neptunians at the control-standard, had left the cylinder's upmost section and had clambered down the ladder to the lowest section in preparation for emerging. There was left with us in the upmost section of the cylinder only two guards and the Neptunian leader of the crimson-circle insignia at the control-standard. And as I saw that, I was leaning quietly toward Marlin.

"Now's our chance, Marlin!" I whispered tensely. "If we could overpower these three Neptunians and the rest beneath afterward we might yet get back to Earth!"

He glanced calmly around, then nodded. "We'll take it!" he whispered, "Once beneath this roof of Triton, there'll be no chance."

"Go for the guard beside you, then, when I cough as signal," I told him. "If we can dispose of them and the leader there we can hold the rest below for a time."

He met my eyes with his own, then turned and as though merely shifting a little in his seat moved nearer toward the guard on his side. I had already done the same toward the disk-bodied monster beside myself, both guards having slightly relaxed their first watchfulness. I glanced out, saw that even at that moment our cylinder was sinking with the others toward the great opening in the roof and knew that no moment was to be lost. So, with heart beating rapidly now, even as our cylinder prepared to sink down through the opening with the rest, I coughed slightly. In the next moment I had flung myself with a single motion upon the Neptunian guard beside me and had seen Marlin in the same instant throwing himself on the monster at his own side!

The moment following was of such swift action as to defy the memory. In my leap upon the Neptunian beside me it had been my first object to knock his tube from his grasp before he could loose its rays upon me, and so swift and sudden was my attack that I did so, as did Marlin with the other guard. With the same motion, even as the guard's seven great limbs reached toward me, I had grasped his big disk-body and then with a super-human effort had raised it in my arms and had cast him from me, down through the opening in the section's floor to crumple against the floor of one of the sections below! I whirled, saw that the other guard had gripped Marlin and was bearing him down, and then even as there came from beneath and from the Neptunian leader at the controls staccato cries of alarm, I had gripped that other guard likewise and hurled him across the cylinder to strike with stunning force against its wall! Then Marlin and I were whirling toward the Neptunian leader at the control-standard, but in the moment that we turned toward him we stopped short. For that Neptunian had leaped aside from the controls of the cylinder and had swiftly drawn his own ray-tube!

CHAPTER EIGHT
Prisoned On Triton

NOTHING, I know now, of our own doing could ever have saved us from the death that in that moment loomed dark and close above us. For, as the Neptunian leader raised the tube toward us, I knew that before ever a leap could take us across the cylinder to him, the pencil-like rays of force from his tube would be tearing through us. For that split-second, therefore, escape seemed impossible, and then before we could fully realize the situation there came an interruption. The currents of warmer air from the opening just beneath, down through which the cylinder had been dropping with the others, were sweeping still upward with great force around the cylinder. Only the Neptunian's grasp on the controls had kept the cylinder heading down through those currents, and now, as he leaped away from the controls for the moment and drew his tube, those currents immediately seized upon the unguided cylinder and in the next moment had whirled it over and sidewise with immense speed and power! And as it whirled thus over, Marlin and myself and the Neptunian before us were thrown instantly and indiscriminately to the cylinder's side!

For a moment we rolled helplessly about the whirling cylinder's interior, about the upmost section, and in that moment all thought of battle had left us. Then, as I felt Marlin and the Neptunian leader and the stunned guard rolling with me indiscriminately, I was aware, too, of cries from the cylinder's other sections and of Neptunians drawing themselves up to the upmost section on the ladder. Abruptly, in a moment more the cylinder steadied, hung poised and upright as before, and then as Marlin and I scrambled to our feet we saw that a trio of the Neptunians beneath had made their way up to the upmost section, despite the cylinder's whirling, by means of their multiple limbs, and that while one now held the controls the other two had their tubes trained once more full upon us!

Our wild attempt at escape had failed, it was evident, for now, as the Neptunian leader of the crimson-circle rose, he was addressing to the others a sharp, snapping order, and at the same time motioning Marlin and me peremptorily to the seats we had formerly occupied. We took them with no further resistance, for we knew that our desperate outbreak had put the Neptunians upon their guard and that the slightest suspicious motion on our part might well mean instant death. And as we seated ourselves once more with the guards on either side, one from beneath replacing the one I had killed, the despair that formerly had filled us seemed immeasurably intensified. For now the cylinder was sinking down after the others, through the great opening in Triton's roof, and even as Marlin and I looked outward we saw the great opening in that roof closing again above us with a clang that to our ears was like the clang of doom.

Above our sinking cylinders now there stretched the great roof, and, even as Neptune's enclosing roof, this one was almost entirely transparent from below, though opaque from above. And here as on Neptune we could see no supporting pillars whatever for this vast spherical roof that enclosed all Triton. This world seemed, indeed, but a smaller replica of mighty Neptune. For, as our cylinders sank down through the shadows of its darker side and then leveled out and began to race back around its curving surface toward the sunward side once more, we saw that all of Triton's surface was covered, even like Neptune, with a great compartment-city whose intersecting black walls stretched in their vast checker-board arrangement over all the great moon's surface. But as our cylinders shot over these, over the darkened portion of the surface of Triton and toward the sunward side, we saw that the compartment-city beneath was different, in some features, from that of Neptune.

For one thing, there were moving to and fro above it a number of great cylinders like that in which we were, and in the compartments of the darkened side moved, too, a few Neptunians here and there. And the great globes of metal that dotted this compartment-city of Triton, even as that of Neptune, were here glowing with radiant light; glowing, I knew, with radiant heat. For this was the secret of the Neptunians' existence on Triton, this heat that glowed from the numberless giant globes set in compartments here and there. Those great glowing globes kept the air beneath

Triton's great roof warm and comfortable, the great roof itself preventing that warmer air from escaping into the moon's colder outer atmosphere. As we shot on over the darkened side of Triton, the side turned away from the sun, I could not but think that the remnants of the Neptunian race must be few indeed, so few of them moved in the shadowy compartments beneath.

At last, as Marlin and I gazed ahead, we could make out a brighter crescent of light at the edge of the strange moon-world, and as we shot on we saw that we were approaching the edge of the sunward or sunlit side. A moment more and we could see it clearly and as we did so Marlin and I gasped in utter amazement. For that part of the great compartment-city that lay on Triton's sunward side, in the pale sunlight, was swarming with incalculable millions upon tens of millions of Neptunians! Crowding, seething, pressing together, they were pouring to and fro through the compartments in the pale light of day, busy with the mechanisms that scarce had room in those compartments, so great were their crowds! And over this sunward side hundreds upon hundreds of cylinders swarmed, rushing to and fro!

"Neptunians! Neptunians in countless millions here on the sunward side of Triton! But why then are there so few upon the dark side?"

Marlin shook his head at my exclamation. "I can't guess," he said. "And I never dreamed that—"

Before he could finish the sentence there came an amazing interruption from beneath. As we gazed downward from our speeding cylinder we saw a giant band of intensely brilliant white light spring suddenly into being at the very line that marked where dark side and sunlit side of Triton met. A mile in width, that great brilliant band of light seemed to extend clear from Triton's north pole to its south, as far north and south of us as our eyes could reach. And then, even as we stared, astounded at it, that brilliant and immense band of light was moving around Triton's surface over the dark side! Swiftly it moved, like a great wave of brilliant light sweeping around Triton's surface, and in a moment had disappeared from view far around the horizon from us on the dark side!

And as that dazzling light-band moved around the big moon-world's dark side, around the almost empty compartment-city that covered that dark side, we saw emerging into that compartment-city of the dark side, as though from its walls themselves, millions on millions of disk-bodied Neptunians that matched in number the vast swarms on the sunlit side! And as we gazed down in utter amazement we saw from whence they came. There were in the dark compartment-city's extent many compartments like those we had seen upon Neptune, with nothing in them save shelving, which formed in their walls myriads of shelfed openings a few feet in height and some four feet in width, one above the other. And in these narrow, flat shelf-openings countless Neptunians had been sleeping! Their disk-bodies, with the flexible legs drawn up, fitted snugly into those flat, strange openings in the walls, and vast hordes of them, countless millions of them, had been sleeping in the shelf-compartments on Triton's dark side!

As that band of brilliant light swept swiftly across the dark side, though, they had awakened, were pouring forth in all their hordes into and through the compartments, all streaming toward the sunward side, while the more remote of them were heading toward the same side in flashing cylinders above. Then, as we gazed toward that sunward side, we saw the brilliant band of light reappearing there, moving swiftly still around Triton's surface, through the pale dim light of its sunward side, having in those moments moved completely around Triton! It moved on until in a moment more it had stopped where first it had formed, at the junction of the dark and sunward sides. There it hung for a moment, dazzling, and then had suddenly snapped out of being. And now we saw that all the crowding millions of Neptunians that had been busy upon the sunlit side were streaming through the compartments toward the dark side!

"The Neptunians' day and night!" Marlin exclaimed, as we gazed downward. "Triton must keep one face always toward the sun and one dark, so these Neptunians spend their day on the sunlit side and sleep their night on the dark side!"

"And that great band of light that traveled around Triton was their signal, then!" I added.

IT was plain now that that was the astounding truth. These countless millions of Neptunians, coming here to Triton for some reason, had been accustomed upon their own great turning planet to a day and night of ten hours each, much like those of Earth. Triton, though, as we had already guessed, kept the same face always toward the sun, it was evident, turning at just such a rate of rotation as compensated for its revolutions around Neptune and its slower movements with Neptune around the sun. Thus, with one face always toward the sun and the other always in darkness, the Neptunians had been forced to establish arbitrary day and night periods, dividing their millions into two great bodies, apparently. While half of them worked on the sunlit side for ten hours, in their day, the other half were sleeping upon the dark side. Then, when the ten hours ended, the great band of light went around Triton as a signal, and the two bodies of them changed places, the millions who had worked upon the sunward side taking their places for an equal period of sleep on the dark side, while those who had slept on the dark side streamed to the sunlit side for ten hours!

Even as we watched from our speeding cylinder we saw that great change taking place, millions upon millions of the Neptunians streaming from one side to the other in great throngs through the compartment-city, while, from farther around Triton's two sides, rushed countless cylinders, in which hosts of others were changing sides. Within a few minutes, it seemed, that change had taken place, and beneath us on Triton's sunward side there thronged in the pale light of its day the vast hordes that so lately had been sleeping, while on the dark side the other masses of the Neptunians had disappeared into the countless shelf-like openings of the sleep-compartments, to lie in sleep for another ten hours. In marveling wonder Marlin and I stared, and then woke suddenly to a realization of our own position.

Beneath us there lay the very edge or dividing line between the dark and sunlit sides, a belt of twilight dusk that was very narrow. Squarely across that belt, we saw, there lay beneath us a great compartment that was largest by far of all that we had yet seen, and that was unique among them in that, instead of being rectangular, it was circular in shape. Down, over and past this mighty circular compartment our cylinders were speeding, and we could but vaguely note some circular object inside it, when we were past it, were speeding low over the thronged and busy compartments of the sunward side. Rapidly the speed of the cylinders decreased, and then they had paused in mid-air, were beginning to descend. And in a moment more they had come smoothly to rest in a great rectangular compartment which seemed reserved as a landing-place, since on it there rested scores of other cylinders, others constantly arriving or departing. Later we were to learn that these landing-compartments were scattered in large number over Triton's surface, on the sunlit and dark sides both.

For the present moment, though, Marlin and I were gazing only at our immediate surroundings. As we landed the guards on either side of us gripped us tightly, the others keeping their tubes pointed toward us, and then, as the throbbing of the cylinder's generators ceased, the Neptunian leader of the crimson-circle insignia uttered a staccato order. At once our guards were thrusting us toward the ladder that led downward, and, holding us above and beneath, were descending that ladder with us into the cylinder's lowest compartment. There the Neptunian leader followed us in a moment, and as the cylinder's door was slid open a flood of warm, heavy air and a babel of sound from about us rolled inside. Before emerging, though, the Neptunians performed an action that for the moment puzzled me completely.

This was to take from the cabinets in the cylinder's side a number of small metal objects that seemed to be disks of gray metal a few inches across with flexible metal straps attached to them. These the Neptunians attached to the bottom or ends of their round, short limbs, as though little round sandals of metal. Then at the order of their leader they took other disks and attached them to the feet of Marlin and myself, one to each foot, binding them to our soles by passing the flexible straps up around our ankles. The thing was as puzzling to Marlin as to myself, for the moment, nor could we understand its object until, a moment later, the Neptunians began to pass out of the cylinder to the paving of the compartment outside. For as they did so I had reached toward one of the unused disks to examine it and had uttered an exclamation to find that, though so small in size and thickness, it was of many pounds weight! Yet as Marlin and I, in answer to the leader's order and gesture, passed out of the cylinder to the landing-compartment's floor, we could not feel at all that weight of dozens of pounds which had been fastened to our feet!

Abruptly, though, light came to my perplexed mind, "Triton!" I exclaimed. "It's of about the same size as Earth's moon and hasn't much more gravitational power. And these Neptunians, used to the far greater gravitational power of Neptune, have to use these weights to add to their weight here on Triton to make it possible for them to move as always!"

Marlin's eyes widened, and then he nodded. "It must be so," he said, "I wondered when I saw them from above how these creatures of Neptune could move so freely on its smaller moon."

It was, indeed, a simple, yet ingenious device which the Neptunians had adopted. Accustomed as they had been to the great gravitational power of Neptune, seventeen times that of Earth, their squat, strange bodies owing their form to that great gravitational power, their muscles would have sent them through the air of Triton in immense and uncontrollable leaps at each step, so much smaller was the moon-world's gravitational power. So they had devised these small disks which fitted to the end of their strange limbs, and which, though so small and thin, yet had great weight, no doubt because the atoms of their substance had been compressed closely together for the purpose. The Neptunians had used disks of some thickness for themselves, and had used thinner ones for Marlin and myself, their smaller weight just sufficing to counteract the difference in gravitational power between Earth and Triton. And now, as we stepped out into the landing-compartment with our guards, it seemed as though we were walking with lead-weighted shoes at the ocean's bottom.

The landing-compartment about us held scores of resting cylinders like our own, and even as we looked about we saw throngs of Neptunians hastening forward and removing from our own and the other ten that had just landed, the disassembled mechanisms which they had brought from Neptune. The leader, however, motioned to our guards to follow with us, and set off quickly across the landing-compartment toward one of its doors. Following him, our four tube-armed guards watchful now about us, we saw him pass through the low, broad door before us, and though his strange disk-body passed easily through that door, Marlin and I were forced to stoop low to get through it. Then, our guards never relaxing their cautious watch over us, we were moving on through the next compartment, and the next, and the next, on through compartment after compartment, all thronging with Neptunians, moving across the great compartment-city toward the twilight band that divided Triton's dark and sunlit sides.

And as Marlin and I moved with our guards and their leader thus through the pale daylight of Triton, through the compartments crowded with masses upon masses of Neptunians, we forgot almost the uncertain fate that hung over us, in the interest and wonder of what we saw. For though we had explored the greater compartment-city that covered all the surface of mighty Neptune, had seen its marvels also, it had been a city dead, a city of lifeless and unused mechanisms whose purposes we had not been able to guess. But here on Triton, in the compartments that covered its surface, we saw a Neptunian city bursting with crowding life, saw it as the giant city of Neptune itself must once have been, before some unguessed purpose of the Neptunians had brought them here to Triton. And, seeing it thus, we were able to comprehend many things that had puzzled us in our venture through the city on Neptune's lifeless surface.

WE passed through compartments in which throngs of Neptunians moved about great rows of looming, pear-shaped mechanisms such as we had seen on Neptune, great water-making mechanisms that were beating here with a slow, rhythmic sound of power, and from which there pulsed into the great connecting pipes a ceaseless gush of water. That water, we knew, was made synthetically in the mechanisms by the combination of hydrogen and oxygen atoms, but whether those atoms were derived, as on Neptune, from the break-down of Neptune's great vapor masses, or whether they were formed themselves from the primal electricity, we could not guess. Through many compartments of these we passed, and through other compartments that held great pumps that evidently forced the water supplies thus manufactured to every part of Triton's surface.

And we went through compartments, too, in which were other great objects that had puzzled us so completely on Neptune, but whose purpose we saw now. These were the great flat metal containers stacked one upon the other, each a foot or so in depth, and each filled with black, green-shot soil. About them, as on Neptune, were set in the walls great white disks connected to generating apparatus of some kind, but here those generating mechanisms were humming with power, tended by many Neptunians, and there shot from the disks, over and through those great containers of soil, a ceaseless flood of pale violet light or force. And, even as we passed through those compartments, we saw strange and stocky pale-green plants bursting up from the soil of the containers, growing at incredible speed before our eyes, attaining a height of inches in but a minute or so! As these strange pale-green plants reached a height of a foot or so, there formed upon them masses of fruits or vegetables dead white in color, some being long and pod-like and others ball-shaped. And as these formed, the attendant Neptunians were swiftly turning off the violet force, pulling the fruit-laden little plants from the fine soil, and depositing them in low-wheeled containers, which were wheeled instantly away. Then from the framework that held the great soil-containers there sprayed out upon them fine whitish-green particles that I recognized as seed of some sort, that fell upon the soil and then were turned under it as some reversing mechanism turned over the soil in each container. Then the violet force from the wall-disks was turned on again, and in a moment another crop of pale-green plants was shooting up out of the containers!

It was then that I saw the astounding purpose of those projectors of violet force that were set in the walls around the soil containers. For it was evident that they shot forth upon the containers a force or vibration which held in it the ultra-violet and other radiations which, in sunlight stimulate the growth of plant-life. These vibrations were projected artificially through the containers of soil with immeasurably greater intensity than in sunlight, and so stimulated the growth of plant-life in those containers immeasurably more. Also I could see that tubes ran from the framework through the soil of the containers, flooding that soil with moisture, and as that water used thus came through special cubical tanks and mixers, it was apparent that it was impregnated with the chemical elements needed by the plant-life in its swift, astounding growth. Thus, stimulated to an intense degree by those influences, the plant-life in those containers could germinate and shoot up and ripen with unbelievable speed. When it was removed, the containers were ready at once for another crop. The whole operation was swift and almost automatic, and as we saw great masses of the white fruits or vegetables being wheeled away from the plant-compartments, we realized at last how the Neptunians, in their great compartment-cities, obtained a ceaseless and inexhaustible food and water supply.

As we passed on, marveling, we saw other great mechanisms at work. Some were huge and cogged, operated by seated Neptunians before them, turning out ceaseless great blocks of smooth, black stone-like material that composed the intersecting compartment-walls, which poured out as a thick liquid and hardened in molds into that diamond-hard substance. Others were strange-appearing machines like none we had seen on Neptune, whose purpose we could not guess. Here and there, there glowed in its square compartment one of the great heat-radiating globes, sending currents of intensely warm air rushing out from about it, all the mechanisms of those globes seeming to be cased inside themselves. Yet even these things were no more wonderful to us than the throngs of Neptunians that swirled and pressed in their millions in the great compartment-city about us.

Numberless, indeed, were the hordes of those Neptunians, their masses swarming about us in great crowds of disk-bodied, pale-green monsters, busy upon the clanking, beating, hissing mechanisms around them, busy in providing the heat and food and water of their strange world. It seemed impossible, almost, that so many countless millions of them could thus have crowded together on Triton's surface. All wore the strange armor or dress of flexible metal around their disk-bodies, some carrying ray-tubes slung in that armor and others various tools or instruments. Here and there we saw one with the same crimson-circle insignia as our leader's upon his metal armor, and it was apparent from the silent deference shown these circle-marked Neptunians that they were officials of some kind. As we marched on behind our leader, our guards close about us, we saw that, despite our strange appearance to them, the Neptunians paid no great attention to us—so busy were they. We saw, too, that here on Triton's sunward side there were no shelf-like sleep-compartments at all, all such being upon the dark side. In silent awe and wonder Marlin and I moved on through the thronging compartments, countless Neptunians crowding busily all about us, and countless cylinders throbbing through the air above, with the vast roof far above them. Then I sensed that we were approaching our destination.

For before us now, as we crossed a last compartment, there lay that twilight band of dusk which marked the division of Triton's dark and sunlit sides, and as we passed out of the pale, dim light of the sunlit side into the twilight of that band, we saw that before us lay a compartment wall that was curving instead of straight, the wall of the great single circular compartment we had noticed from above. The compartment that lay between us and that wall was empty save for a file of Neptunian guards who stood motionless along the curving wall with their force-ray tubes ready in their grasp. As our leader reached them he halted, spoke with them for a moment in staccato speech, and then as their snapping voices ceased the guards stood aside to right and left and permitted us to pass through the low, broad door in that curving wall. Through it we went, our circle-marked leader first and then Marlin and I, our four guards still close about us, and then as we halted inside that door, we two were gazing with a deepened awe and wonder about us.

We were standing just at the edge of that great circular compartment that we had glimpsed from above, hundreds of feet in diameter, the twilight about it dispelled somewhat in it by soft glowing disks in its walls. In this great compartment there stood what seemed an immense circular table of metal, only a few feet in height, ring-like in form and with a clear circular space at its center. This great ring-table's edge was not more than a dozen or so feet from the compartment's circular wall, and ranged around it, on low seats between the ring-like table and the wall, were thirty disk-bodied Neptunians. Silent and almost motionless they sat there around the great ring-table, and I saw that upon the metal armor of each was a crimson circle like that of our leader, except that there was a crimson dot at its center, a symbol we had noted on no other Neptunian so far. And from each of the thirty there ran in toward the clear space at the ring-table's center a slender black wire-connection, attached by diverging connections to the body of each of the thirty.

These thirty connections ended at the space at the ring-table's center, running there into a strange object or mechanism that stood in that space. It was composed of a great metal pedestal with straight sides, like an upright pillar, into which the thirty connections ran, while upon the pillar's top was supported a globe of metal somewhat greater in diameter than the pillar, being some five feet across. In this globe's side was a round opening, while set at two other points at opposite sides of it were what seemed inset diaphragms. From the supported globe came a fine hum, scarcely audible, and that was the only sound in the great compartment. The whole scene was strange—the towering black walls of the great circular compartment about us, the great ring-table in it and the thirty silent, motionless disk-bodied Neptunians seated around that table, and the giant globe on its pedestal at the table's central space.

AS we stood there the Neptunian leader before us spoke in sharp snaps, as though explaining our presence, but not to the thirty around the table; it spoke to the great central globe of metal! In amazement we watched him, and then we saw that the globe was turning upon its pedestal, turning toward us a small circle of clear glass set in its opposite side, that surveyed us for the moment exactly like a single calm eye. Then the globe turned again, the opening in its side again facing us, and then from that opening came a staccato answer to our leader, a swift question, apparently, in the snapping speech-sounds of the Neptunians! The globe was hearing our captor's report, was questioning him concerning that report, while the thirty around the table uttered no sound, and turned not toward us!

"Good God!" I muttered at that astounding spectacle. "That globe of metal, Marlin—it hears him, answers him! The thing must be alive!"

"Not alive, Hunt," Marlin said swiftly, his own eyes startled, though. "Those connections that run from the thirty to the globe—they center in that globe's mechanism in some way the minds, the intelligence, of all the thirty!"

Swift light flashed upon me at Marlin's words, and as I gazed astonished toward the thirty Neptunians and the central globe I knew that Marlin's explanation was the only logical one. These thirty Neptunians, it was apparent, were the supreme rulers, the highest council, of all the Neptunian race. And since it was necessary that they use all of their differing minds as one in directing the destinies of their strange race, they had in some way devised a mechanism for that purpose, which synthesized the intelligence, the minds, of the thirty into one single mind by means of that strange mechanism. So that it was literally as one mind that the thirty perceived and thought, when gathered here together, the central globe speaking out the synthesized thoughts and questions of all the thirty!

As Marlin and I stared in amazement toward it, our leader was answering to the globe's questions concerning us, the snapping speech of the Neptunian indistinguishable from that of the mechanism. Then when he had finished, the globe was speaking briefly to him again, a short order, and in answer to that order the Neptunian leader turned at once toward us. I think that both Marlin and myself would not have been surprised to meet then the death that we knew hung over us, but, instead, the leader gestured to us and to our guards and led the way out of the great circular Council Compartment, through a different door from that by which we had entered. As we passed through that door I glanced back and saw the thirty Neptunians of the great Council still sitting motionless and silent around their weird globe-mechanism, which was listening now to the report of three other Neptunians who had entered behind us.

Once out of the great circular compartment, we found ourselves with our guards in an irregular-shaped compartment, filled with Neptunian guards who parted to allow us to pass. Through that and through another rectangular compartment we went, and then into a long oblong compartment in which we could see, despite the twilight that reigned here, were many smaller compartments or divisions along the walls. These were very like cell-compartments, and the low door of each of these was closed by a black slab that slid down across it from above. Before these doors there were patrolling in the long compartment a half-dozen of Neptunian guards, and, after being challenged by these, our own leader and four guards marched us to one of these little cell-compartments, reaching forth to grasp or touch something on its outside wall.

As the Neptunian leader did so, the door of the cell-compartment slid smoothly and silently upward, leaving its opening clear. Without ceremony, then, Marlin and I were motioned to pass inside, and with the four ray-tubes of the guards full upon us we had no choice in the matter. Stepping inside, therefore, we found ourselves in a compartment some ten feet square, whose walls, like all the black walls of the compartment-city, towered for two hundred feet upward around us, the only light the square of dusky sky far above. Then, as Marlin and I stared about us, the door shot smoothly down across the opening, and we heard the soft, shuffling steps of the Neptunian leader and our four guards retreating, outside, leaving us gazing at each other's white faces in silence. Our great mission out to Neptune, our great attempt to save Earth and prevent the wrecking of the solar system, had come to an end at last, with our two friends gone and with Marlin and myself imprisoned here beyond all hope of escape on Neptune's peopled moon!

CHAPTER NINE
Before The Council

"PRISONED here on Triton—and Whitely and Randall dead! It's the end, Hunt—for us, and for the Earth!"

Marlin's voice was but echoing my own thoughts in that moment, and darkly I nodded. "The end—yes. And less than twelve weeks before that end comes, before the sun's rotatory speed reaches its critical point, before it divides into a double star, we've found the source of the great ray from Neptune, and we're helpless."

"Yet the World President—the World Congress—" Marlin seemed to be thinking aloud. "They sent us out to dare all for Earth, and until Earth is destroyed or we are dead we can't give up hope."

"But what hope is there?" I asked. "These Neptunians have only reprieved us for the moment from death, for their own purposes. Death will be ours before long, and in the meantime who could escape from this place?"

I swept my arm around the cell-compartment, and Marlin considered the place with me as silently and almost as hopelessly as myself. For it was, truly, a prison inescapable into which we had been thrust. The square little compartment's walls were diamond-hard, of that impenetrable black stone-like substance, and they towered two hundred feet above us. There were in them no windows, the only light that reached us being the dusky illumination that came down to us from the compartment's roofless top, far above. That illumination was but small indeed, for the cell-compartment lay in the same twilight band as the great Council Compartment, that band of twilight lying between Triton's dark and sunward sides. By it we could see, however, that the black walls about us were quite vertical and smooth, and that the only break in them was that of the low door-opening, closed now by the smooth, black slab across it.

It was, indeed, a prison from which no efforts of ours, it seemed, could win us free. For even were we to escape from it, we knew, we would but find ourselves in the great compartment-city that covered all Triton, thronged with the Neptunians' countless millions. And even that city, in turn, was held beneath the giant metal roof that shielded and enclosed all Triton, so that never, indeed, it seemed, could we hope to be clear of the big moon-world and escape back across the solar system to Earth, to tell the peoples of Earth from what strange source was coming that colossal force-ray that was spinning the sun on to division and doom. Yet, despite that, Marlin and I paced ceaselessly about the little cell in a vain endeavor to formulate some plan of escape.

Our first action was to remove from our feet the heavy-weighted little disks which the Neptunians had fastened upon them, and with those removed we found that we could jump a score of feet upward in our little cell, due to the lesser gravitational power of Triton compared to that of Earth, sailing slowly upward and falling as slowly. Yet this increased agility seemed of no avail to us in escaping, since there were no breaks in the surface of the cell's smooth, towering walls by which we might have been able to jump higher. So, after some futile attempts, we rested upon the cell's floor again, re-attaching to our feet for convenience sake the super-heavy little disks, that increased our weight to its normal Earth-figure.

"It's useless, Marlin," I said, as we sat here, resting after our efforts. "We can never get out that way—or any other, I think."

"Keep steady, Hunt," he told me. "We can't do anything now, it's clear, but a chance will come."

"It had best come soon, then," I said. "For with but eighty-odd days left before the end, I see small hope."

He did not reply to that, and I think that the gloom of utter despair that had settled upon me weighed upon him also. They were hours in which there was no change. The twilight that existed here on this band of Triton's surface never changed; its dusk never lightened or darkened. The only sounds to be heard, too, were the occasional staccato voices of the half-dozen Neptunian guards outside, or the answering snapping speech-sounds of other Neptunians, that seemed to be confined in cells like ourselves. Later we were to learn that despite their super-intelligence, perhaps because of it, the Neptunians were afflicted now and then with a brain disorder in which it seemed that a part of their mind's mechanism would cease to function for a time, during which time they were confined in these cell-compartments about us. Save for the staccato speech of these and the guards, and the dull, dim, distant roar of clanking and humming and hissing mechanisms that came to us from Triton's sunward side, there was no sound in our cell except when cylinders throbbed by overhead.

In those hours the door of our cell never opened, and we found that our food and water were supplied to us inside the cell itself. There were in its wall two metal taps, one of which yielded clear water, that tasted flat and chemical to us. The other gave forth a thick, viscous white liquid, which we recognized after a time as a liquefied preparation of the white vegetables and fruits we had seen grown so rapidly. This preparation or liquid was apparently pumped through the compartment-city like the water. Thus there was no need for the guards to enter our cell. It was a number of hours later that there came an interruption to the monotony of eventlessness of our time, which roused us somewhat from the gloomy apathy of spirit into which we had fallen.

Without warning there sprang into being all about us an intensely brilliant flood of pure white light, that bathed all things about us in its blinding glare for the moment and then swiftly moved away toward the dark side of Triton. We were stupefied by its appearance thus, and then remembered suddenly the great band of brilliant light that we had seen appear and move swiftly, completely around Triton, marking the end of a ten-hour period and the signal for the sleeping millions of Neptunians on Triton's dark side and the busy millions on its sunward side to change places upon this strange world. Surely enough, in a few moments, the brilliant band of light had swept upon us from the sunward side, having traveled completely around Triton, and dwelling for a moment again upon us, had snapped out of being. That great brilliant band of light, as we were to learn, was produced by great projectors at Triton's two poles, and whirled around it by the turning of those projectors. Now as its brilliant signal swept around the big moon-world, we could hear the countless hordes of the Neptunians shifting from dark side to sunward, and from sunlit side to dark, while overhead there throbbed and shot this way and that innumerable cylinders.

Swiftly as before that great change was accomplished, and then, as there began again the dull clamor of activity upon the sunward side, Marlin and I turned from our listening attention. But at that moment we heard a staccato rattle of speech outside our door, and an instant later the great black slab of that door slid sharply upward and three Neptunians moved inside the cell. The foremost one of these bore on the metal armor of his great green disk-body a crimson circle that marked him as one of the Neptunian officials. The other two were apparently guards brought in as a precautionary measure, their force-ray tubes unsheathed and leveled unhesitatingly upon us. The Neptunian official carried in his grasp a small octagonal object or mechanism with a simple button-control, which we gazed at curiously. He touched the button-control of it, and there sounded from it a series of swift, sharp snaps of sound exactly like those of the Neptunians' staccato speech. Then, speaking aloud himself, he motioned from himself to us, and then to the mechanism.

It was Marlin who first understood his purpose. "The Neptunian language!" he exclaimed. "This one has come to teach it to us, to make it possible for them to communicate with us."

"But the mechanism?" I said. "What is its purpose?"

MARLIN stared at it a moment, then reached forth and touched its round button-control, bringing from the mechanism an irregular succession of snaps of sound. "It's for us!" he said suddenly. "They know that with our different bodies we can't make the sharp, snapping sounds that are their speech, so have brought this mechanism to us to serve us as an artificial voice!"

The Neptunian official, as though he had understood us, motioned again to the mechanism and then from himself to us, at the same time uttering a few speech-sounds as though in explanation. It was plain, indeed, that his object was to teach us the strange Neptunian speech. Pointing to himself, and to the two guards, he uttered a succession of five sound-snaps, irregularly spaced, over and over again, until it was evident that they represented the name of the Neptunian races. Then Marlin and I attempted with the little speaking mechanism to reproduce those five snaps of sound, and after experimenting for a time with the mechanism's button-control we succeeded. That done, the Neptunian pointed to us and uttered another short succession of sounds, another word, which we then learned to utter on the mechanism also.

Thus, for hour upon hour, the Neptunian continued with us, teaching us word after word, in their strange staccato language. That language, we found, seemed very much like a communication code of dots and dashes, all its sounds or sound-snaps being of the same pitch, there being no raising or lowering of the voice, while for each word there was a certain combination of the sharp sounds. Quickly, too, after a time, we began to understand and learn that strange language, and though never could our own vocal apparatus have produced the clacking bursts of sharp sound which were their speech-sounds, we learned to manipulate easily the little mechanism that spoke to them for us. Hour followed hour and day followed day, until we became so proficient in the knowledge and expression of their words as to be able to communicate effectively, though haltingly, with the great disk-bodied Neptunian who was teaching us.

Yet we found that that ability served us nothing. For though we plied the Neptunian with innumerable questions concerning the great mysteries that we had come through and that lay about us, he would answer nothing. What great chain of events had it been that had made of mighty Neptune's colossal compartment-city a silent desert of death, and that had sent all the Neptunians crowding upon Triton? What was their purpose in directing their mighty force-ray toward the sun, turning the sun ever faster to accomplish its division into a double star? Why, too, had they sent a second great force-ray out in an opposite direction from the first, passing out into the vast void of interstellar space? These questions we put many times to the great Neptunian who taught us, but the big, green-bodied disk-monster simply contemplated us as though unhearingly with his bulging, glassy eyes, and went on with the teaching of their strange speech.

So days followed days while we slowly progressed in our learning of the Neptunian speech, days in which the despair that had gathered in our hearts grew darker and darker. For at last, when more than a score of Earth-days had passed, we realized that all was hopeless indeed, that even had we chanced to escape, even had we still our space-flier that had been destroyed with Whitely and Randall, we would hardly have time enough to return from Neptune to Earth and bring back the fleet of space-fliers that were being prepared on Earth. Not much more than a half-hundred days, indeed, remained before that last day that would see the sun splitting at last to engulf almost all its planets, for with each day, we knew, the giant force-ray of the Neptunians emanating from Triton was turning the sun faster and faster.

Twice, indeed, I almost made a wild attempt to overcome our Neptunian teacher and guards, but was held back by Marlin, who knew as well as I that instant death only could result from such an attempt. And as those days passed, as with each ten hours the great band of light went around Triton and the millions of Neptunians on dark and sunward sides interchanged, I came to look on death as a release from the agony of suspense and torture in which we were. I think that not much longer could either Marlin or I have endured the terrible torture of that imprisonment, when there came at last a break to it, on the twenty-second day of our captivity.

On that day, as we waited in the unchanging twilight for the coming of our Neptunian teacher and his two guards, we were astonished when the door slid up to find facing us outside a different Neptunian official, of the same insignia of the crimson circle, with four guards behind him instead of two. He did not speak to us, but motioned us silently to move outside, and as we did so he gestured to Marlin to take with us the small speech-mechanism by which we were able to converse with the Neptunians. Then, guarded closely before and behind, our attempted escape in the cylinder having kept the Neptunians extremely watchful of us ever since, we were marched out of the long oblong compartment of the cells and across others toward the great circular Council Compartment. Into it we were marched, and found that, as before, there sat around the great ring-table the thirty silent members of the Council, the great metal globe still on its pedestal at their center. They did not turn toward us as we entered and halted beside them, but the great globe did, turning first the single gleaming eye upon us by means of which, we knew, all the massed minds of the thirty members of the Council were receiving a visual impression of us.

Then the globe turned swiftly so that its speech-opening faced us, and it spoke to us, spoke as the assembled minds of the thirty, with all emotions removed and with all thoughts synthesized by its mechanism. "You are the two creatures captured upon our world?" it asked. "And you have been taught our language as we ordered?"

Marlin pressed the button of the little mechanism in his grasp, speaking back in the same snapping speech-sounds by means of it. "We are those two," he said simply.

The globe was silent a moment, then spoke on, the thirty whose minds spoke through it never turning. "When you two were captured upon our great world, others, no doubt like you, were discovered in a space-vehicle which, it was apparent, was operated by the same principle of force-rays which we of Neptune (it was their own word-equivalent for the name of the planet) have long used in our own space-vehicles, and in other ways. That vehicle and those inside it, it has been reported to us, were destroyed by those who discovered it, but we desire to know from whence it and you two came, and in what way you were able to reproduce the force-rays which we of Neptune have long used. From the structure of your bodies it is apparent that you come from a small planet, in all probability the second or third of the sun's worlds. But from which, and why, have you come here?"

Marlin did not answer for some moments, then spoke back through the little mechanism he held. "It is from the sun's third world, indeed, that we have come," he said. "And we have come here, have plunged out through the void to this, the sun's outermost world, to find out why you of Neptune are loosing doom on the solar system with that great force-ray of yours that spins the sun ever faster, and to use all our power to halt that doom!"

IN that tense moment a thrill of irrepressible pride shot through me, even in the dark peril in which we stood, at Marlin's words. For they were not his alone; they were the words of Earth, the words of Earth and all its races to Neptune and all its hordes! And at that bold defiance, flung across the void from world to world and issuing here from Marlin in the very face of this supreme Council of the Neptunian rulers, of this great globe-mechanism that held their gathered, synthesized minds for the time being, an order to the guards behind us for our instant death would not have surprised me. Yet here again we were given proof of the difference between the mind-workings of the Neptunians and ourselves. It was evident that the human passions of hate and anger held small place in their cold, machine-like minds, for the great globe that spoke for the minds of the assembled thirty was silent for a time, and when it did speak it seemed not to regard the passion of Marlin's words.

"When you speak of halting the doom that confronts your world," it said, "it is apparent that you do not know the necessity of that doom, the great necessity which has caused our races of

Neptunians, under the direction of the Council of Thirty, to loose that doom upon the solar system. Learn now, therefore, that it is to save our own world, our own races, that we are loosing this death upon the sun's other worlds and peoples!"

The great globe again was silent for a moment, the thirty members of the Council silent around it as their assembled minds poured their thoughts into its mechanism, to be released in a single voice. Marlin and I stood there at the great ring-table's edge, and surely no stranger scene could have been imagined than that, with the great circular compartment's towering black walls around us, the twilight that reigned above and around, the thirty silent disk-bodied Neptunians and our own disk-bodied guards, and the great, enigmatic globe-mechanism before us, that spoke and listened as a living thing, representing the massed minds of the thirty. And now that great globe was speaking to us again, in the staccato Neptunian speech.

"It is most wise, perhaps," it said, "that you two of another world learn now what colossal forces and necessities lie behind the loosing of that great doom which you come to strive vainly against. It is most wise that you learn now how useless it is for you or any of your world to oppose yourselves to the plans of us Neptunians. For we of Neptune are of an ancient power and might, beside which you of the inner planets are as newcome children. And lest you doubt that power, lest you doubt the colossal forces that we of Neptune have called into being and use for our own purposes, we of the Council tell you now what mighty past is ours.

"Oldest of all the eight worlds of this solar system, indeed, is our world of Neptune. This you must know, indeed, if your scientists know aught of the formation of the sun's planets. For those eight planets were formed unthinkable eons ago, out of the fiery sun itself. Up to that time the sun had moved through space entirely without planets, one of the countless stars of this galaxy of stars, all moving through the void in differing directions. One of these other stars chanced to be moving in the general direction of our own star, our own sun, and their mutual attraction for each other drew them closer together, until at last they passed each other closely, perhaps even touched each other, their nearness to each other causing by gravitational attraction huge masses of the flaming gaseous substance of each to break loose. Thus the space between the two passing suns was filled with those great flaming masses, and as they separated, each by its gravitational power drew a share of those fiery masses with it on its path through the void.

"Thus when the two suns receded from each other once more, each carried with it a rough half of the fiery masses that had been torn from each. As the sun moved on through space with these fiery masses about it, the greater part of them dropped back into the sun. The flaming masses that remained, however, had been thrown by the cataclysm into a swift motion, which by the sun's attraction had been converted in the case of each flaming mass into a circular or elliptical orbit around the sun. And since the speed of each flaming mass just balanced with its centrifugal force the pull of the sun inward, they continued in those orbits for age on age without perceptible change. The solar system, then, had become stable.

"Thus the sun was moving on through space with eight great flaming masses of matter revolving around it, in addition to a number of great clouds or aggregations of smaller fragments. These eight flaming masses became in time the sun's eight worlds, a solid crust forming first on one and then on another of them. The outermost of these great fiery masses was that which in time was to become the planet Neptune. It had been one of the first of the great fragments of the two suns torn loose by their encounter, and being one of the first had been hurled out to a greater distance than any of the others. And being the first, too, it had had more time to cool, its solid crust had formed earlier on it, and thus Neptune was in fact the oldest of the sun's planets to form as a solid-surfaced world. Neptune, too, is composed of much lighter materials than the denser inner planets, and the reason for that is, that it was the lighter matter of the two suns that had naturally been sent flying forth from them in their encounter; and thus the outer planets, the four great outer worlds, being of the sun's lighter matter, are all much less in density than the four smaller inner worlds, which were thrown forth later from the sun's heavier matter, and thus in smaller masses.

"So out of the great irregular-shaped outermost mass of flaming gases had been formed the great planet Neptune and its smaller moon of Triton. And as Neptune's surface solidified, as the great masses of water-vapor and air that made up its dense and immense atmosphere ensheathed it, it became a habitable world, one fit for life and the continuation of life. For though small heat came to distant Neptune across the great void of almost three billion miles that separated it from the sun, the sun giving it indeed a heat hardly perceptible, yet there was heat enough for the great world in its own fiery interior. For so great in size was Neptune that, though a solid crust had formed upon it, there still lay beneath that crust the vast raging fires of its interior, and those fires' heat was so great that they kept the surface of Neptune and the dense atmosphere above that surface warmed constantly. And Triton had an atmosphere also and interior warming fires.

"Thus great Neptune, though farthest of all planets from the sun, became habitable the earliest of all. And since, wherever a world is found on which life is possible, life sooner or later will arise, so it arose on Neptune. Race upon race of living creatures rose upon it, and race after race vanished, annihilated by changing conditions on its surface which they could not withstand. It was not until we disk-bodied Neptunians evolved upon the great world's surface, indeed, that there came a permanent form of life upon it. For we, whose disk-bodies owed their squat, flat shapes to the gravitational power of Neptune, so much greater than that of your inner worlds, had in larger measure that spark of intelligence which the other creatures had lacked. And with that gleam of mind, of intelligence, we were able to withstand the changing conditions on Neptune's surface by adapting ourselves to those conditions, growing ever in numbers and spreading out over our world's surface, until at last we swarmed in millions upon it and were rising into greater and greater comprehension of the universe about us, into greater and greater intelligence and power.

"GREAT buildings we built upon Neptune's surface, and deep we tunneled below its surface, also. Through breaks in the great cloud-screen about our world we looked forth and saw with our instruments the other planets that moved about our sun, and looked forth also into space and saw the hosts of other suns that moved at vast distances from our own. Our eyes were accustomed to the dim Neptunian day, our bodies to its great gravitational power, and it was our home-world. Yet by this time so vast had become our numbers that millions of us were crowded too closely together, and desired to migrate to Triton, our moon, and settle there. And though we had never yet been able to sally forth from the surface of our own great world of Neptune, we found the way to do so then.

"That way was given to us by the discovery by our scientists of a new force-vibration, one that lay in wave-length between the light vibrations and the higher electrical vibrations. This force vibration, they found, exerted a definite pressure or force upon any object struck by its waves, just as the light-rays themselves exert a definite, though far smaller, pressure upon whatever matter they strike. With this new force-ray, therefore, we planned to propel vehicles through space, and we constructed great cylindrical vehicles which were to hurtle out into space by generating inside them a great force-ray which would be shot back against a world and thus propel them by repulsion away from that world. These cylinders were made and tested, and since they worked perfectly, we constructed many of them, enough to take out all the millions of our surplus population to Triton. And so in those cylinders those millions of Neptunians went hurtling out to Triton.

"They found, as our observations had shown us, that Triton had a good atmosphere, and that it was swarming already with many forms of life, some of them unutterably grotesque, and none of more than the lowest intelligence. Using weapons of concentrated force-rays, which clove through all they touched, our millions of Neptunians proceeded to annihilate all life upon Triton, and with that accomplished, proceeded to build for themselves structures and cities like those on Neptune. They found that Triton was a perfectly habitable world for them save for two considerations. One of these was the lesser gravitational power of it, which made it extremely inconvenient for them to move on it with their Neptunian muscles. They solved this problem by attaching to their limbs small and unobtrusive disks of an extremely heavy metal which we could make by the artificial massing of atom-protons without electrons. These disks increased their weight to such a point that they could move as freely and conveniently on Triton as on Neptune.

"The other problem facing them on Triton was the fact that it turned one face always toward the sun. Its rotation on its axis, indeed, was of just enough speed to counteract its revolution around Neptune and Neptune's own revolution around the sun, the sum total of its movements resulting in this keeping of one side always toward the sun, with that side always palely lit by the sun and the other always in darkness. Even when Triton was behind Neptune, invisible perhaps from your own world by reason of the edge of Neptune's great atmosphere projecting up to hide it somewhat, Triton's orbit was so slanted or inclined toward the plane of the solar system that the sun was always in sight of its sunward side, though dimmed a little when the edge of Neptune's atmosphere was between them. The Neptunians who had gone to Triton were accustomed to Neptune's alternating day and night, of approximately ten hours each, and so they solved the problem by living upon the sunlit side of Triton for ten hours, for a day, and then passing to the dark side for ten hours of night.

"Thus they had conquered all the inconveniences that had faced them in settling upon Triton, and so upon Triton as upon Neptune were Neptunians and their cities. The civilization of both Neptune and its circling moon seemed secure and unchangeable, indeed; a civilization that existed upon our world and its moon when all the other planets of the solar system held only the lowest forms of life, if life they held at all. Easily could we of Neptune have ventured into the sun's other worlds had we wished, in our space-cylinders, but we had no desire to do so, having learned all that we wanted of those worlds by observation with our instruments, and being content to remain safe upon our great world of Neptune and smaller moon-world of Triton. And safe we remained there, for ages, yet, during all those ages, there was coming closer toward us a great crisis which we had long before foreseen, yet which we had considered so remote a peril as to give it no attention.

"But now that peril had become close, and great. And it was none other than the extinction of all life on both Neptune and Triton that faced us, due to their steady cooling. For all worlds, however fiery their interior, cool in time and die. And steadily, surely, the interior fires of both Neptune and its moon had been cooling and the substance solidifying. Already they had cooled so far that the surface of Neptune was much colder than ever before, and that of Triton also, and with each passing century that cold was increasing. It would be a matter of time only, it was plain, before both Neptune and its moon would lie utterly without life, a terrible frigidity reigning upon each, all life perished from them in that bitter cold. For though worlds nearer the sun might exist by means of the sun's heat, though life on them could cling to existence through the sun's warmth, Neptune and its moon were so unthinkably distant from the sun that almost no heat reached them from it, and as their interior fires cooled, they must inevitably become so cold as to annihilate all life upon them!

"It was evident that some great plan must be adopted that would prevent this condition, and such a plan was quickly decided upon. This plan was to enclose both Neptune and Triton with great roofs of metal that would hold in them the heat that was being radiated out, and that would make it possible to aid the failing heat of the two worlds by artificial means. It would be a gigantic task to place those great roofs about Neptune and Triton, but we set to work upon it and for years upon years all the energies of the Neptunians were centered upon the construction of those roofs. We had established vast workshops in which the plates of metal that were to form the great roofs were turned ceaselessly forth, and these in turn were joined together to make the great roof of giant Neptune.

"It had been decided that that great roof that was to enclose Neptune would have no supports whatever. For that roof was to be in effect a gigantic spherical shell enclosing Neptune, and as such it would float in space around Neptune without touching it at any spot, since the attraction of Neptune upon the roof would be the same in all parts; thus it would not be pulled to this side or that, and would not touch the great planet in any place. The small attraction of the sun and the other heavenly bodies on the free-floating spherical enclosure was nullified by an automatic force-ray pressing against the inside of the roof in the right direction, and thus the giant spherical shell could enclose Neptune, and could float about it, moving with it through space, without touching it at any point!

"The metal plates, that had been joined together to make the vast spherical shell, were of a strength to resist all stresses, and they had been specially treated by a crystallizing process that gave them a unique property. This was the property of admitting all heat and light vibrations from above through them, but repelling those from below. Thus when the great roof was in place around Neptune, enclosing it completely, the sun's light and heat penetrated down to it through the roof without check, making the roof seem transparent from below. But no light or heat vibrations could pass up through the roof from beneath, so that it appeared quite opaque from above. Thus what light and heat the sun furnished were not lost, and Neptune's day not darkened. But very little of that heat of Neptune itself could be radiated outward into space.

"With the great roof in place around Neptune, and with openings that could be opened and closed at will provided in it, for entrance to or exit from Neptune, a similar roof, though far smaller, was constructed around the smaller globe of Triton. With those great enclosures thus shielding Neptune and Triton, therefore, their cooling was slowed, and it seemed to all that the expedient of the great roofs had warded off the menacing cold that had threatened to extinguish all life on Neptune and Triton. Strange new cities were built on Neptune and Triton, great compartment-cities that needed not roofs with the great roof above them. New methods were found of producing vast food supplies for the crowding millions of Neptunians, by stimulating with electrical force and chemicals the growth of vegetation to an unthinkably swift rate. Thus we Neptunians, in our giant enclosed world of Neptune and in our enclosed moon, Triton, had checked the colossal peril that had threatened us and could continue to live safely upon Neptune and its moon for age upon passing age!"

CHAPTER TEN
To Split The Sun!

"WE had checked the great peril that had hung over us, but we found, as the centuries and ages passed, that we had only checked it, that we had not banished it. For nothing in the universe could halt the cooling of Neptune and Triton. As their interior fires cooled, colder and colder grew their surfaces, despite the roofs that enclosed them. It was then that we had recourse to another means of halting that oncoming cold—the use of artificial heat. We set up in the giant compartment-city of Neptune, and in that of Triton also, great globes that radiated out unceasing and intense heat. These globes held inside them their own mechanisms, mechanisms that could change etheric vibrations of electricity and light and others into heat-vibrations, by changing their wavelength. And with these radiating their ceaseless heat, and with the great enclosing roofs, the oncoming cold was again checked.

"Yet after a time we were forced to recognize that this check also was but temporary. For we were fighting the most grim and hopeless battle in the universe; we were fighting against the relentless and inevitable changes caused by the immutable physical laws of the universe. So that, aid its failing heat as we might with artificial heat-producers, the interior heat of Neptune was waning still, and more and more globe heat-radiators were required to keep the temperature of Neptune at its usual height. The Neptunians of Triton were faced with the same problem, but their situation was not so desperate as of those upon Neptune, since though Triton had cooled as quickly, its enclosed space was so much smaller than Neptune's, its great roof so close to it also, that it was possible with an effort to keep enough heat-mechanisms going there to maintain the warmth.

"On Neptune, however, the struggle became more and more desperate, our great struggle against the blind laws of nature. For as Neptune's interior heat declined farther and farther, it became more and more impossible for us to keep enough heat-mechanisms going to keep it warm enough for life. And at last, after years upon years of that awful struggle against fate, we of Neptune realized at last that it was no longer possible to keep Neptune warm enough for us to exist there, and that we must leave it at once for some other world if we were to escape extinction; since as the great planet's interior heat declined, it became more and more agonizing for us to keep enough heat for life by means of the heat-mechanisms, and it was clear to all that the end was at hand unless we left Neptune!

"But where could we go? Even if one of the other planets were suitable to receive us, we could not have transported all our masses from Neptune to another planet in time to escape the doom of cold and death that was closing down upon Neptune. To transport all those masses would have required countless trips with our limited number of cylinders. And to take refuge upon another planet, even had time been ours, was almost out of the question. For long our scientists had studied the other planets with their instruments, and though some of them were so cloud-wreathed and others so distant as to make observation difficult, it had long been known to us that none of the other planets, due to their natural conditions or to the presence of intelligent alien beings already upon them, would be possible as a world for us Neptunians. It was for those reasons, indeed, that no expeditions of cylinders had ever been sent to the other planets.

"There remained, then, but one place where we might go, but one place to which our millions might go before Neptune's cold grew too great for life. That place was Triton, our peopled moon. For peopled as that moon was with its own masses of Neptunians, struggling against the same menacing cold that had vanquished us on Neptune, it was the one refuge for our peoples. By crowding into its every corner, the countless millions of Neptune's peoples would be able to exist upon Triton. And though the cooling of Triton had menaced it with cold also, it has been found, as we have mentioned, that it was not so hard to keep Triton warm by means of the artificial globular heat-mechanisms, the space enclosed by its great spherical roof being much smaller. It was a desperate expedient, truly, to mass all the thronging millions from the compartment-city that covered all giant Neptune, to mass all those millions upon little Triton, yet that was the one expedient open, and so it was followed at once.

"Out from Neptune to Triton went all the cylinders of both worlds, loaded with as many Neptunians as they could carry, depositing those Neptunians upon Triton and racing back for more. Countless trips made those thousands of cylinders, trip after swift trip, each occupying but little time because Triton was so near. And so at last there came a day when the whole of Neptune's millions had been transported out to Triton, when there remained on Neptune itself no single one of our races, our giant world lying cold and deserted and dead, no longer a habitable world, its vast compartment-city empty of the millions that had for ages swarmed through it, while all those millions were crowded now upon little Triton.

"And so crowded were those vast hordes of the Neptunian races that for a time it seemed that they could not exist in such numbers upon Triton. This crowding was made less acute, however, by an expedient now adopted by us. As mentioned, the Neptunians who had settled upon Triton long before had found that the unchanging day on one side of it and the unchanging night on the other were inconvenient for them after the alternations of Neptune's day and night, and so had begun the custom of spending a day of ten hours upon the sunlit side of Triton and a night of equal length upon the dark side. And now we found that we could make the crowding of our races upon Triton less acute by having half of them working and active upon the sunward side for ten hours while the other half slept through their night on the dark side. Every ten hours these two halves of our people changed sides, changed from day to night, a signal having been devised to mark the hour for that change, a signal which consisted of a brilliant band of intense light, that passed swiftly around both Triton's dark and sunward sides. With this shifting of our peoples each ten hours it was possible to make use of all of Triton's surface, and thus the crowding of our peoples upon it was made less acute.

"Yet that crowding was still very great. All the thronging Neptunians that had existed upon the surface of giant Neptune had been poured out on little Triton, far, far less in size than its great parent-world. And thus, though they could exist upon it, it was existence only that was possible to the Neptunians on Triton, since this awful crowding would grow worse, we knew, rather than better. And also, and more important, here on Triton the same deadly menace that had driven us from Neptune was again confronting us. For even as Neptune had cooled, Triton had cooled, was cooling also. And though we strained every effort to keep the warmth in Triton constant, though we sent cylinders constantly back to dead and deserted Neptune to bring from it more heat-mechanisms and other needed mechanisms, we found that even as on Neptune we were fighting a losing battle with nature. For Triton was cooling, was cooling still farther, and soon would be completely cold and dead, its interior heat gone out into space. And when that happened, no number of heat-mechanisms could keep warmth upon it, even beneath the great enclosing roof, and all life on it must perish.

"The Neptunian races had come to their last stand! Crowded upon our refuge of Triton, striving with all our power to keep upon it the warmth, without which we could not live, we saw at last that some new and radically different plan must be found, or we could no longer exist. So all the greatest of our Neptunian scientists were called together by us, the Council of Thirty. Into a great conclave here on Triton they were called, and to them, without equivocation of any sort, and to the races of the Neptunians, the situation that confronted us was stated. We had been driven from Neptune by the relentless growing cold, and now that same cold was upon us here at Triton, was threatening us here also with annihilation. How were we to meet this great menace that threatened to wipe us out?

"COUNTLESS were the plans that were advanced in answer to that menace by our scientists. The first, and most obvious plan, was migration to another planet. But here we were checked by the same considerations that had made us unwilling to try that before, for we knew by observation of the other planets that upon none of them could we live as we lived upon Neptune. Some of them were greater in size than Neptune, with greater gravitational power, and that was a difficulty that could not be overcome by us since upon those planets our weight would be so increased as to make us helpless, even had those planets been fit for our life. Some planets were peopled by intelligent and powerful races which we might be able to conquer after terrible struggles. Others were too near the sun for us to ever inhabit them, who had evolved on the dim, cool world of Neptune, the outermost world. Other planets, as far as we could tell, were quite uninhabitable. Mercury, Venus, Earth, Mars, Jupiter, Saturn, Uranus—not one of them was suitable as a world for us Neptunians. And we had, also, no desire to move to another planet, in truth, since so many ages had it taken for us to build our great compartment-cities upon Neptune and Triton, to shield them with their great roofs, that it was impossible for us to leave them, even had we been able to start anew upon another world.

"We must remain with our own great world, it was plain, but how then could we continue to live? Innumerable were the suggestions that were advanced, but even those who advanced them were forced to admit them impracticable. Scores upon scores of useless plans were submitted to us, but none held even a shadow of hope for us, and it was not until we of the Council of Thirty had come to despair almost of warding off the doom that threatened us, that a plan was finally advanced by which that doom could indeed be halted.

"That plan, put forth by three of our Neptunian scientists in cooperation, was one of such colossal nature that even we Neptunians, who had rooted our worlds and had fought for so long the forces of nature, were stupefied by it. These three Neptunian scientists, in stating their plan, stated first that it was apparent to all that no escape to other planets was possible for us, and that our races must remain at Neptune and its moon, for life or death. They stated that it was equally clear that no means could be found by which even Triton could be kept heated artificially, all such means suggested requiring such vast expenditures of energy as to make them impossible for any but the shortest period of time. These premises, they said, were clear indeed, and it was equally clear that unless a new source of heat were found in some way for Neptune and its moon, we races of Neptunians must swiftly die. And so these three suggested a source of heat that never even had occurred to any of the rest of us, suggested—the sun!

"The sun as a source of heat for us! The idea seemed incredible to us—the Council of Thirty. For to us of Neptune, lying so far out in space from the sun, that sun could never mean and had never meant what it does to you of the inner planets. To you it is a source of ceaseless blazing heat, of brilliant light, warming your worlds sometimes to scorching, no doubt. But to us that sun has seemed always but a tiny little disk of fire far off in the void from us, a little sun-disk that gives to us the dim light of our pale Neptunian day, but that gives to us hardly any measurable heat whatever. We had simply never thought of the sun at all as a source of heat, any more than you would think of a star as a source of heat, since we had been accustomed always to rely upon the interior heat of Neptune for our existence. But now with that interior heat gone, with Neptune cold and dead beneath the zero temperatures that reigned there, and with Triton fast approaching the same condition, these three Neptunian scientists advanced the sun as a possible source of heat that might save us.

"The sun, they admitted, was too infinitely far from us to help us any with its heat as conditions were. But what, they asked, if the sun were to divide into a double or multiple star? Countless stars of the universe, we knew, had done so, had split into a double or triple or multiple star, and in so dividing, by reason of their rotary speed or centrifugal force growing so great as to make it impossible for them to hold together, the two or more small suns forming out of one always moved some distance apart from each other, by the first force of their division. If the sun were to divide into a double star, therefore, the two smaller suns that would be formed thus would undoubtedly follow the same course, would be pushed apart from each other by the very force of their division, some two billion miles, our astronomers had calculated.

"Pushed apart thus, the two new suns would form an ordinary double star, or binary, the two revolving around each other. And by their division almost all the planets of the solar system would without doubt be engulfed in one or the other of the two suns. The four inner planets would inevitably be annihilated when the sun split into two suns, when those two rushed apart from each other. For if they were not directly in the path of the two separating suns, they would be drawn into those separating suns almost at once by the tremendous gravitational disturbances attendant upon this tremendous cataclysm. They would have no more chance of life, indeed, than midges in a great blaze. And in the same way Jupiter and Saturn would be whirled out of their orbits, since those orbits would be fatally confused and changed by the first division of the sun, and by the loss of centrifugal force attendant upon their confused slowing they, too, would without doubt be drawn into the path of one or the other of the separating suns and perish in them. And even Uranus would meet a doom as inevitable, since with a distance of two billion miles between them the two new suns would be resting almost exactly upon Uranus' orbit, and so that world too would go to blazing death in one or the other of them.

"But Neptune would not! For Neptune, farther out than Uranus, farthest out of all the planets, would be the one planet in the solar system that would escape the tremendous cataclysm, due to its distance from the sun. When the two suns separated, Neptune's orbit would probably change a little, it would probably sweep closer in toward those suns for some distance, but except for that it would be unchanged, and would by reason of its great distance continue to circle in its curving path through space, but would circle then around these two new suns instead of around the former single sun. And with those two suns separated as they were, by a distance of two billion miles, Neptune would be near always to one of those suns, because it would undoubtedly sweep nearer to them when the cataclysm occurred, and would take up an elliptical orbit about them with the two suns as the foci of that ellipse. Thus it would always be near enough one of them to gain from it or from both a large amount of heat! For not only would Neptune in its elliptical orbit be far, far closer to them thus, but the other planets hurtling into them would tend to make them hotter. Thus Neptune, revolving close about the two suns, would gain from them the warm, life-giving heat that it had never gained from the single sun!

"That heat would thus solve the great problem that faced us; it would halt the doom that was closing down on us. For that heat would so warm Neptune, that we could go back again and take up our existence once more upon it free from all peril, could live again in that great compartment-city that covered all Neptune. And Triton, too, would be livable, then. For the great roofs that we had erected around Neptune and its moon would tend to make of both worlds great hot-houses in effect, the sun's or suns' heat being able to penetrate down through those roofs. And with those enclosing roofs about us, and with the two new suns close, we could live on in safety. For the enclosing roofs themselves would prevent any inconvenience from the fact that Neptune now and then would be farther from the two suns than at other times, those great roofs keeping a constant warmth upon Neptune and its moon.

"Thus all the great peril that confronted us would be thrust back, and we could live once more on Neptune, more warm and comfortable there than ever before; we could pour back once more to our mighty world that lay now dead and cold and deserted—could do all this, if the sun did divide into a double star. Yet what hope was there that this could happen? We knew that the reason other suns of the universe divide into double or multiple stars is because they have reached a rate of rotatory speed that makes it impossible for them longer to hold together. For when a sun is spinning its mass tends to split up by its own centrifugal force, just as a turning wheel, and the faster the sun spins the greater grows its centrifugal force, the greater its tendency to split. And then at last that rate of spin grows so great, and its centrifugal force is such that its mass can no longer hold together, and fission takes place, the sun dividing into two or three or even more stars, that push apart from each other. But what chance was there of the sun doing this? For the sun, we knew, rotated at the speed of one turn in 25 days, at its equator, and to split it would have to be rotating at a speed of one turn in an hour. That meant that it would be unthinkable eons before the sun's rotatory speed would have increased to that point. For though a sun's rotatory speed does increase as time passes, due to the shrinkage of its mass, it increases so infinitely slowly that it would be eons, indeed, before the sun's rate of spin would be so great as to cause its division. And thus there seemed small hope indeed in that plan.

"THEN it was that those scientists revealed to us the heart of their plan, and made clear to us the true colossal nature of their suggestion. What, they asked, if we ourselves increase the sun's rotatory speed? What if we of Neptune should reach across the void of almost three billion miles and set the sun to spinning faster, spinning it ever faster and faster until it had reached the critical point, until it turned once in one hour? Fission would result then, the sun would divide into a double star as they had calculated, and all the benefits mentioned would come to us, and Neptune and its moon would be warmed always by the heat of the two suns about which they would revolve. If we could do that, if we could reach across the void and set the sun to spinning ever faster, it would soon divide into two new suns, and thus we would have saved ourselves. Yet we were thunderstruck by this suggestion of the Neptunian scientists. To reach out across the infinite leagues of space that lay between our outermost planet and the sun, to turn that sun ever faster until it split into a double star-however could such a gigantic, stupefying feat as that be accomplished?

"But the Neptunians who had suggested this plan now calmly explained how that colossal deed could be accomplished. Long before, indeed, we had discovered force-vibrations, finding them a vibration that exerted tangible and definite pressure or force upon whatever matter they struck. And we had used those force-rays in some ways. We had used them to propel our cylindrical vehicles out through space from Neptune to Triton, and vice versa. We had used them also, concentrated into slender, pencil-like rays of great power, as weapons, since those concentrated rays penetrated and destroyed all that they touched. Now our scientists proposed to use them for this huge plan—to reach across the void, across the solar system, and to turn the sun ever faster, until the desired division of it had happened.

"Nor was this, as they outlined it, impracticable. The sun, turning there in space at the center of the solar system, has naturally one edge or limb turning away from us, and the other turning toward us. Now, if we constructed colossal generators of the force-vibrations, generators that could produce a gigantic ray that would have almost inconceivable power, and shot that ray across the solar system toward the edge of the sun turning away from us, what would happen? It was clear that that great ray, striking against the side of the sun's mass turning *away* from us, striking that side with titanic pressure and force, would tend to turn that side *faster* away from us, would tend in that way to make the whole sun turn faster! Such a gigantic ray, though it would increase the sun's spin thus but slowly, would continue to increase the sun's spin steadily as long as it was kept turned upon the sun's side. Slowly, but steadily, the sun would turn ever faster, until soon it would have reached that critical rotatory speed, of one turn in one hour, that would make its centrifugal force so great as to make it divide into a double star, and so save us of Neptune from the cold death that hung over us.

"Thus this mighty plan was presented to us, and it was at once accepted by us of the Council of Thirty, by all of the Neptunian races. For we saw that in it lay our one chance for life, our one chance to halt the doom of our races, our worlds, and to halt that doom we were willing to make any effort. We knew that the other planets of the solar system, that the seven other worlds of this universe and all their moons, would go to flaming death when our plan succeeded, would be annihilated when the sun divided, but we recked not of that. For the last necessity was upon us, the last closing down of the doom that we had fought against so long, and to remove the shadow of that doom from over us, we were willing to send to a more terrible doom all the other planets of the solar system.

"Only one great difficulty lay before us. That gigantic ray could be generated and shot forth by us, since it would not be difficult, by concentrating all efforts, to construct the generators and mechanisms needed, but from what place was that ray to be shot toward the sun? And how? It was evident that the giant ray could not be sent from Neptune's surface. For not only would it be almost impossible to keep its great mechanism working in the constant terrible cold that reigned there, but Neptune's rotation would make it impossible to send the ray forth from any spot on the great planet, since because of Neptune's rotation, it would follow that that spot—that great ray, would be toward the sun half the time, on Neptune's sunward side, and the other half would have turned and point away into space from its dark or outer side. It was apparent, therefore, that the great ray could not be sent forth from Neptune, since to achieve its effect that ray must play constantly upon the sun's one side or edge; and it became apparent that only from Triton could it be sent forth, since Triton kept one face always toward the sun and it would therefore be necessary only to set the great ray's mechanisms in that sunward side, when it would point unchangingly toward it.

"As far as position was involved, therefore, it was quite feasible to drive the colossal force-ray out from Triton's sunward side toward the sun. But there was another point involved, one that bid fair to ruin the whole great plan. When this gigantic force-ray reached out across the gulf, and struck the sun, it would push the sun's side with inconceivable power, as was planned, with a power great enough to turn that sun's titanic mass faster. It would be, in effect, like a solid arm reaching forth from Triton to press against the sun's edge. But the sun is gigantic, is millions of times greater in mass than Triton, and so what would be the result of that great pressure of the ray? It would, without doubt, turn the huge mass of the sun with that pressure very slowly, but it would, by that pressure and by its reaction, push back against the infinitely smaller mass of Triton itself, and push it away from the sun; it would push it back away from the sun with such colossal power that Triton would be torn loose from the grip of Neptune, its parent-world; would be torn loose almost instantly from the solar system itself, and would be hurtled straight out into the awful void of interstellar space away from the sun and all its planetary worlds!

"It was the same principle, indeed, as that of our cylindrical space-fliers. Those cylinders, generating inside themselves a powerful force-ray, shot that force-ray down against the planet upon which they were. But that force-ray striking with great pressure from the comparatively tiny cylinder to the great planet, did not move the planet, of course, with its push. It moved instead the cylinder itself, hurtling it upward from the planet because its mass was so infinitely smaller than the planet's. And it would be the same way with Triton and the sun. For Triton, sending forth the great force-ray generated upon it, toward the turning sun's edge, pressing against the sun's huge mass with colossal power, would not move the sun, would not turn it noticeably faster as we planned, but would move Triton itself out from the solar system into the void of space! Almost instantly, by that terrific push, Triton would be hurled out into the awful gulf of space, and thus by that terrific push outward would be torn loose from the attraction of the sun and its planets forever, and would by its own inertia shoot out through the interstellar void for all time! And that meant, of course, death for all the massed Neptunian races upon Triton, since in the sunless, awful void of space outside our universe, our solar system, they would at once perish!

"This seemed, indeed, the difficulty, which was to make our great plan impossible. But with only that obstacle standing between us and success, we did not despair, but sought to overcome it. And at last we found a remedy for this difficulty, found a means by which it might be overcome. Triton would be pushed out into the gulf of space away from the solar system forever, when its great force-ray struck the sun's edge. But what, it was asked, if Triton were braced against the push outward of that great ray, were braced by a great force-ray of equal colossal power shooting out from it in an opposite direction against some great mass, tending in that way to push Triton inward toward the sun even as the great ray striking the sun would tend to push it outward? The result would be obviously, that Triton would be pushed on either side by the two opposing great force-rays with equal power, and being so pushed between them it would not move either inward or outward. And thus being immovable, being braced against the pressure of the ray shot toward the sun by the pressure of the ray shot out into the void against as great a mass, Triton's ray striking the sun's edge would, as we desired, turn that sun faster and faster, spin its huge mass faster without affecting Triton itself! For, the two great rays being so exactly balanced in power, Triton would not be affected in the least in its own positions or motions.

"There was needed, then, only a second great force-ray to go out into space opposite in direction to that of the first. It meant, however, that since the first was radiating straight toward the sun from Triton's sunward side, the second must radiate straight away from the sun from Triton's dark side, which would make the second ray point out into the void toward the constellation in which it would be in reference to the sun. That is, we calculated that by the time all would be ready for us to send the force-ray in toward the sun, the constellation Sagittarius would be straight out from Neptune and the sun; then the second ray would need to be sent out toward Sagittarius. For it would be, then, against one of the great stars of Sagittarius that this second opposing force-ray would strike, to brace Triton against the other ray striking the sun, the star calculated best for that purpose being the bright star in the quadrilateral of Sagittarius. It was apparent, therefore, that when the great force-ray was shot toward the sun, the second or bracing ray should be shot out against that bright star in Sagittarius to brace Triton against the first ray's push.

"YET in reality the problem was not as simple as that. For that star in Sagittarius, we well knew, lay like all the stars infinitely farther from us than the sun. It would require but a little more than four hours for the first great force-ray, which travels as you know almost as fast as light itself, to reach the sun. But it would require a number of years for the second great force-ray, traveling at the same speed, to reach the bright star in Sagittarius and strike against it. For even the nearest of the stars, of course, lies so far from our solar system, our universe, that it requires years for light to cross that colossal distance; in consequence it would require as long or longer for the second force-ray to cross such a great distance, traveling as it would at a speed almost that of light. Thus, since that bright star in Sagittarius that had been fixed upon lay dozens of light-years from our solar system, it would require dozens of years for that second great force-ray to reach that star!

"It was evident, therefore, that the second force-ray would need to be shot out toward that star long before the first, since it was vitally necessary that the two rays strike their objects at the same moment.

"The first thing to do, therefore, was to prepare the great generators and send that second ray out toward Sagittarius. That work was begun at once, for only a short time was left us. On Triton's dark side, beneath the great roof, countless great generators were constructed, giant generators of the force-vibrations which could by their massed power produce a colossal ray of unthinkable power. Then a great pit or giant well was sunk in the roof, one whose sides sank down from the roof toward the surface of Triton. At the bottom of that great pit, on Triton's surface, was set the mighty mechanism or ray-concentrator that would send the gathered power of all the massed generators driving out into the great void in one colossal ray. That mechanism was, of course, upon Triton's surface, and was cut off from the rest of that surface by the metal walls that rose around it to the roof, since in that way it was possible to send the great ray out from Triton's surface through an opening in the great roof, the enclosing walls or sides of the pit preventing the warm air beneath the roof from escaping outward, and keeping it air-tight as ever.

"With that much done, the controls of the colossal ray and its generators were then constructed. Those controls were not single but were repeated no less than twenty times, there being a score of control-boxes for the great ray, set around the walls of the huge pit from which the ray would spring forth, and entered not from without but from within those walls, of course. A single control-box would have been enough, but our object in having a score of control-boxes was clear enough. It was a matter of life or death for all the Neptunian races that those controls should function properly. If this great second force-ray ceased but for a moment to go toward the star in Sagittarius, as mentioned, the backward pressure of the other great force-ray pressing against the sun would hurl Triton out of the solar system for all time, with all the Neptunians upon it. So those controls were not entrusted to a single control-box but were duplicated in twenty, so that if anyone control-box was destroyed or harmed in any way, or even if a half-score or more were so destroyed or harmed, the great ray would continue to go forth.

"With that done, with the great generators ready, the ray mechanism or opening ready, and the control-boxes and their intricate controls all completed, the first step was finished and there remained but to turn on the giant ray, to send it forth to that bright star in Sagittarius. So on the day that had been designated, the Neptunians to whom had been entrusted the all-important watch of the twenty controls, took their places in the control-boxes. The great ray-mechanism had been so placed in Triton's dark side, of course, that it pointed directly toward that star which the ray was to strike, and so it was needed only to turn on the giant ray. And so, at last, with all the Neptunians gathered there beneath the roof around the walls of the giant pit, staring through those walls, transparent from within, we gave the word. Then, as one, the twenty controls were opened, and from the gathered throbbing generators from the great ray-mechanism at the huge pit's bottom, there drove upward and outward into the great void of space the colossal force-ray, visible only near its source as pale light, flashing out at almost the speed of light itself, on its stupendous journey across the void toward that bright star in Sagittarius that was its goal!

"There was no push against Triton, of course, when that colossal ray went forth, for there could be no push against Triton until that ray struck a solid body, struck the star that was its goal, and then it would push back against Triton. Just as if you reach forth to push yourself away from a wall, there is no push on your body until your hand reaches the wall. Not until dozens of years had passed, we knew, would that great ray strike the star in Sagittarius that was its goal, and not until then would come the back-push against Triton, the bracing back-push that was its purpose. And in those dozens of years, with the great ray shot ceaselessly forth to that star, of course, Neptune and Triton themselves would be moving somewhat, would be moving as Neptune followed its slow orbit around the sun. But so slow and so vast is Neptune's orbit-movement, that it would have moved but little, and as it moved, the ray-mechanism would be turned constantly a very little so that its great ray would still be directed ceaselessly toward the star in Sagittarius, and so that when that ray struck that star, Neptune and Triton would be just between or in line with the sun and that distant star.

"Thus half of our great task was finished, and there remained but to complete the other half, to make ready for the sending forth of the other great force-ray, the first one as we called it, toward the sun. In the years that followed, while the great force-ray traveled ceaselessly, on and on through the great void, toward that distant star that was its goal, we Neptunians were busy here upon Triton with the making ready of the newer force-ray. On Triton's sunward side, directly opposite to the other force-ray's source, we constructed again the great generators that would be used for this newer ray, massing them there beneath the great roof. With those generators finished, we began again to construct a great pit or well in the roof, and to place at its bottom the ray-mechanism that would send this newer force-ray in through the solar system toward the sun.

"Terrible years were those for us, though now at last this terrible time approaches its end. For in those years we had not only to keep on the immense task of constructing generators and mechanisms for the newer force-ray, and to keep operating the other great generators and mechanisms that were sending forth ceaselessly the great force-ray toward Sagittarius; we had also to fight against the ever-encroaching cold that was deepening ever its dread menace over us, and that seemed on the point of overcoming us even as we reached the climax of our giant fight against doom. For ever that cold on Triton grew greater as it grew still cooler at its heart, and ever we must make greater and greater efforts to keep operating the innumerable heat-mechanisms that alone held death back from us. Yet we spurred ourselves onward by the thought that now at last we were approaching victory over this dread menace of cold that had beset us for so long, for at last the dozens of years required were drawing to an end and the great force-ray was fast nearing the star in Sagittarius that was its goal.

"SO we labored on with all our strength, and soon the mechanisms of the new giant force-ray were finished, its great pit ready in Triton's sunward side, and the twenty control-boxes set in that pit's walls. Now at last was approaching the crucial moment of our great plan, that moment in which all must be calculated and performed with infinite care lest we meet disaster. The greatest of our scientists had many times, in those years, calculated the exact moment when the huge force-ray we had shot forth would meet at last the star in Sagittarius, would strike against that star. It was necessary that the other giant force-ray that we were to send forth against the sun would strike the sun's edge at the same moment exactly as the other ray struck that star, and with the same power exactly. So all was anxiety unutterable as we approached this great climax of our plan.

"By this time, scores of your Earth-days ago, Neptune in following its orbit had moved so that it was almost exactly between the sun and that distant star in Sagittarius toward which the ray was shooting. The fact that Triton revolved about Neptune did not impede that ray, of course, since as you know Triton moves about Neptune in an orbit slanted greatly, inclined greatly from the ecliptic, and so even when on the outer side of Neptune its ray would be able to go straight toward the sun, through the upper limits of Neptune's atmosphere, and so in the same way, even when it was on the sunward side of Neptune, its great ray, that we had sent forth years before, could shoot directly toward the star in Sagittarius. The only thing needful was that the ray we sent forth toward the sun be of the same power and strike it exactly when the other ray struck that distant star, so that they would push back against Triton with the same force at the same time.

"So in tense anxiety we remained and at last there came the moment for which we waited, more than four hours before the time when we calculated the other ray would strike the star in Sagittarius. And when that moment came the signal was given and the new mighty force-ray was shot forth, from Triton's sunward side, shot forth toward that edge of the sun turning away from us! That ray, of course, had no planets directly between it and the sun, we having chosen long before a time for the whole plan when this would not happen. But in the four hours and more that followed, we millions of Neptunians waited here on Triton with suspense unutterable. The moment was approaching when this giant force-ray would strike the sun. If we had calculated wrongly, if the other giant ray did not strike that star in Sagittarius at the same moment, Triton would be hurled out to doom in the great void by the sun-ray's pressure! Tensely we waited and then at last there came the moment for which we had waited. That moment came, and passed—that moment in which the new giant ray struck the sun—yet Triton did not move beneath its pressure.

"We knew that we had won! For the other ray had struck the star in Sagittarius at the same moment, balancing Triton against the pressure of the sun-ray, and now as we observed the sun, we saw by our instruments that it was turning faster already! Its huge mass was spinning faster as our great ray stabbed from Triton to press against that mass' edge with colossal force! Within the first Earth-day the pressure of that great ray against the sun's edge had increased the sun's speed of spin at almost the exact amount we had calculated, had decreased its rotatory period by four hours. And each day thereafter the steady pressure of that colossal force-ray has turned the sun ever faster at the same steady rate, has decreased its rotatory period by four Earth-hours more. So that even as we had calculated, we saw, within 150 Earth-days from the first sending forth of the sun-ray, that the sun would be spinning so fast beneath that ray's pressure, its rotary period decreased to the critical period of one hour, that it would no longer be able to hold together and would divide into a double star!

"And even now that great plan which we, the Neptunians, and we, the Council of Thirty, carried out, comes at last to its fruition! For already more than one-half of that time, more than eighty days, have passed, and there remains hardly more than three-score days before the great sun cataclysm comes. Hardly more than three-score days from now the end, for all your inner planets, for all the planets save Neptune, will come, the sun reaching that critical rotatory period of one hour and spinning then so fast, beneath the pressure of our great ray, that it cannot longer hold together, will divide into two suns that will whirl apart from each other and engulf in their fires all the planets save our own outermost one, sending them with all their peoples to fiery doom! For to that doom we Neptunians are sending them to save ourselves from a doom, in another way, equally as terrible."

CHAPTER ELEVEN
Desperate Chances

AS the great globe's voice ceased for a moment, that strange, staccato voice to which for many minutes Marlin and I had listened, I found my brain whirling with the things we had just heard. For a moment I glanced around as though to assure myself of the reality of what was about me, of what had just been told us. The great globe, the thirty silent Neptunians of the Council around it, the other disk-bodied Neptunians who guarded us—these, with the towering black walls and strange twilight about us, only deepened the strange trance of horror in which I had listened. And now the great globe was speaking again.

"Thus it is clear to you how unalterable is the doom that we are loosing upon the sun's other planets, upon your own planet, to save our own. Nothing now can save your world, and the other worlds of the sun, from annihilation, and it is to make that clear to you that we of the Council have told you this much of what we have done. Nothing can save your world from death, yet you two of that world shall escape that death with us Neptunians. For it is evident that your race and you must have considerable scientific knowledge to enable you to imitate our great force-ray and use it to venture out here to Neptune. So that, though lesser than our own great ancient race in science and knowledge, it may well be that you have certain knowledge, which would be new and useful to us. For that reason you have been saved, and have been taught our Neptunian tongue. From now on our scientists will question you, and whatever of new knowledge you are able to give to us, you shall give. You have heard, from us, how hopeless it is to think more of your own doomed world, and you know, of course, how entirely in our power you are. Therefore think well, when you are taken back to your cell, upon what you have learned here, since it is only for the sake of what little our knowledge might gain from you that you two have been preserved from the death."

The great globe was silent, and before we could reply to it, could gather even our whirling thoughts, the Neptunians guarding us had closed about us again, pointing to the door through which we had come. As in a daze Marlin and I were led through that door, the great globe turning and following us with its single vision eye as we went out. I think that neither Marlin nor I came to complete realization of our surroundings until we had been thrust once more into our little cell. For it was only then, staring toward me as though half-unseeingly, that Marlin repeated slowly the great globe-mechanism's last words.

"The death that in days will overtake our world! And the Neptunians are loosing that death on our world and all the sun's other worlds to save their own races!"

"And that is the explanation of all!" I exclaimed. "The great ray that turns the sun faster, the other ray shooting out toward the stars, the dead and deserted surface of Neptune, the crowded surface of Triton—God, Marlin, if we could only get back to Earth with what we know!"

"We *must* get back!" he cried. "Even if we escaped, we two could not turn off that great sun-ray, could not wreck all its twenty controls. But if we could only get back to Earth and lead back here the fleet of space-fliers that the World President planned to build!"

"It's hopeless, Marlin," I said, "We've thought of a thousand ways of escape in the days that we've been here, and not one has even the wildest chance of success."

Hopeless indeed it seemed to Marlin and me as we sat there silent in the dusky little cell. For the colossal epic of Neptune's past and mighty plan which we had heard there from the Council of Thirty, from their globe-mechanism that centralized their minds, had implanted in us a profound despair. We had found at last the explanation of all this vast enigmatic thing that was wrecking our universe, but had found in that very explanation new depths of hopelessness. Earth was doomed, the solar system as such was doomed! We saw it, now, beyond all doubt, we, who alone of Earth's races knew whence that doom was coming. And I think that neither Marlin nor I, sitting silent there in the dusk of our cell, gave any thought to the terrible fate that hung over us two who had been kept alive, as we now knew, for whatever possible knowledge we might be able to impart to the Neptunians. We forgot our own fate of a living death amid the Neptunians in our agonized contemplation of the great deepening shadow of doom that was darkening the sun and all its universe.

It seemed to me, as we sat there, that it was centuries, rather than weeks, since Marlin had given to Earth his first warning of that doom, his first news of the sun's increased spin. All that we had come through since that time seemed the events of countless years. The great meeting of the World Congress, and its adoption of the plan of Marlin and Whitely; the building of the space-flier and that start by night of Marlin and Randall and Whitely and myself in it; our hurtling flight out from Earth on our great mission, past Mars and through the dangers of the asteroidal belt, past mighty Jupiter and on, winning through the peril that almost annihilated us at Saturn, to our goal, Neptune; our amazement at finding that world roofed and enclosed, the venture of Marlin and myself down into its dead and deserted compartment-city; the attack of the Neptunians, the pursuit and destruction, somewhere out in the mists of Neptune, of our two friends, of Whitely and Randall in the space-flier; and our own capture, our own journey to Triton's swarming, strange world, and our days' imprisonment; and now, at last, this titanic tale of the past and purpose of Neptune's races, which had been told us by the great globe of the Council. It seemed incredible, indeed, that all of these things could have been so compressed into the time of a few-score days as they had been.

Yet they had been, I knew, and knew too that the sixty-odd days that remained to us before the end came, before the sun, spinning ever faster beneath the pressure of the giant ray from Triton, split at last into a double star, that these three-score days would seem centuries on centuries of agonizing torment for us two, who must wait, imprisoned here, for the doom that was closing down upon the solar system, to come to its dread climax. And at that thought, at the thought of that helpless inaction that must be ours, a blind unreasoning revolt arose in me as in Marlin, and like him I sprang to my feet, paced the little cell's length with clenched hands. All was unchanged about us, the towering black walls around us, the half-heard staccato voices of the Neptunian guards outside, the dim roar of sound that came to us through the twilight from Triton's swarming sunward side. The very changelessness of the things about us pressed upon my spirits with such suffocating force in that moment, that I was almost on the point of beating blindly against the cell's door, when recalled to myself by the suddenly tense tones of Marlin's voice, beside me.

"Hunt!" he exclaimed. "There is a chance to get out, I think! I've been thinking, and if we can make a great enough effort I think that we can win clear of this cell, at least!"

I shook my head. "It's no use, Marlin," I said. "We've gone over it all a thousand times—there's no way out but through the door, and that never opens but with a half-dozen Neptunian guards standing with ray-tubes outside it."

"But there is another way," he persisted. "Out the cell's top, Hunt, out the roofless top!"

"We tried it," I told him, "and it was useless. Even with the lesser gravitation here on Triton, even without these weights on our feet, we could only jump a score or more feet straight upward, and the walls are two hundred feet high and utterly smooth and vertical."

"But one way we didn't try," he insisted, and as I listened with dull lack of interest, he went on to outline to me his idea. And as I listened, my indifference suddenly vanished, for I saw that Marlin's keen, inventive brain had really found a plan that would give us a chance of escape. "It's our one hope," he finished, "and if we can use it to get out of this cell, we'll have a chance to steal one of these cylinders of the Neptunians and get back to Earth in it in time!"

"We'll try it at once, then," I said, excited now at this faint gleam of hope. "For the changing-hour for the Neptunians on the dark and sunward sides comes soon, and we don't know how soon those Neptunian scientists, who are to question us, will be coming here."

WE prepared for the attempt at once. Our first and main preparation was to unbind once more from our feet the little and great-weighted disks of metal, which increased our weight against Triton's lesser gravitation to its normal Earth-figure. With those disks removed, our lightest step sent us a few feet into the air, so greatly were the results of our muscular efforts increased. Then, since with my somewhat greater strength I was to be the first to try Marlin's plan, I stepped, or rather floated, toward the compartment-cell's side with a single step, crouching down there with my body braced against the wall behind me. From that position the square little opening of the cell, two hundred feet above, seemed infinitely distant, yet I did not despair, drawing a long breath and then with all the force of my muscles leaping obliquely upward. Upward and slantwise thus I went with the force of that leap for more than a score of feet, toward the opposite wall that much higher from the floor, seeming to float smoothly up—so much slower than on Earth was my progress through the air.

And as I shot smoothly toward the opposite wall I was twisting myself in mid-air, so that when I struck that wall, more than a score of feet above the floor, it was my feet that struck it. And as they struck it, bent with my impact against the wall, I abruptly straightened them again, shot suddenly away from that wall again on an upward slant again toward the other wall. Again, as I floated upward, I was twisting in mid-air to strike that wall feet-foremost, and again as I struck it I was kicking against it with my legs, so that hardly had I touched it than I was shooting back across the cell again toward the opposite wall, but again on an upward slant, gaining a score of feet on each strange leap I made thus across the cell! Thus, in zig-zag leaps from wall to wall, I was progressing up the narrow cell toward its roofless top far above! It was just the same as when on Earth a man in a wide chimney can work himself up from bottom to top of it by bracing himself now against one wall and now against another. And the fact that the cell was much wider, could only be touched one wall at a time, was counterbalanced by the fact of Triton's far lesser gravitational power, which alone was making it possible for me to continue my strange progress upward!

On Triton alone, indeed, or on a world of similar size and gravitational power, was such a feat possible, for only thus could one leap with such new impetus each time from wall to wall, and twist in midair to strike braced for another leap. And as I leapt up in that criss-cross fashion from wall to wall, my heart beating rapidly, putting all my strength into each great leap, I could see Marlin on the cell's floor below gazing up tensely through the dusk, knew what depended upon our escape, and so struggled upward with a superhuman strength. Up—up—back and across—across and back—in leap after slanting leap upward I progressed, until with a half-dozen more leaps the cell's open top lay close above me. By then, though, the energy which I had summoned for this superhuman feat seemed fast waning, and as I shot from wall to wall I realized that I was gaining less and less toward the top with each leap!

Another leap—another—and as I shot back across the cell's width from wall to wall I was aware of the wall's top but a few yards above me, yet felt at the same time the exhaustion that had gained upon me, now almost near to overcoming me. Another leap—with agonized muscles I propelled myself back to the opposite wall, with the top of that wall but a few feet above me. One more up-slanting leap would take me back up and across to the opposite wall's top, I knew, but in that tortured moment I felt that I could never make it, and knew that if I missed it I must inevitably fall downward. So, as I struck that wall feet-foremost, I put the last of my strength into a great effort and shot floatingly across the cell's width for the last time. And this time, with hands outstretched, I struck the top edge of that opposite wall, fumbled with it for an agonizing moment, and then had grasped it and had drawn myself up on the thick wall's top!

For a moment I lay across its top, oblivious to all else in the exhaustion that possessed me, inhaling and exhaling great panting breaths. Then as I drew myself up a little I peered about me. Far away on all sides of me stretched the walls of the compartment-city that covered all of Triton, those walls' tops intersecting like a great checker-board, and all level with the thick wall's top on which I lay. Twilight layover a broad band of that compartment-city about me, the twilight band between the dark and sunward sides, the brighter day of the sunward side stretching away to one side, humming with activity and with many cylinders moving to and fro above it, while to the other side stretched the silent, sleeping dark side, beneath its unchanging night. Now I gazed down through the dusk toward the cell's floor far beneath, and saw Marlin gazing up toward me anxiously, gestured silently to him. And in a moment more he was coming up toward me by the same great zig-zag leaps from wall to wall that I had used.

In anxious suspense I watched him as he came gradually up toward me, shooting from side to side of the cell in upward slanting leaps that brought him each many feet upward. Gradually, though, I saw that the force of his leaps was lessening, his upward progress slowing, as he, too, began to feel the waning of his strength. I knew that, older than myself as he was, those leaps were telling against Marlin even more than they had done against me, and in utmost suspense I watched as he came more and more slowly toward me. At last he was but a score or more feet beneath, his face tense and strained as he shot from wall to wall, gaining now but a few feet each leap. With clenched fingers I watched him, powerless to help, saw him by a last gathering of his strength making another up-slanting leap and another and another, until but one more was needed to reach up to the wall on which I crouched. And even as Marlin made that last leap, even as he shot across the cell's width and up toward the wall on which I crouched, I realized with a thrill of horror that he had leaped short!

In that moment, as Marlin shot across the cell's width toward me with hands outstretched, I saw his white, strained face and knew that even as I did he realized the shortness of the leap that he had made with his last strength, realized that his outstretched hands would miss the wall's top by feet. That moment in which he shot across the cell, as his own hands struck the smooth wall of length, yet as he shot toward me it was more by instinct than by conscious thought that I acted. Swiftly hooking my knees over the wall's top upon which I crouched, I hung with head and body downward into the cell, reached downward with hands open, and as Marlin shot across the cell, as his own hands struck the smooth wall of it many feet below the top, I reached and grasped them tightly. A moment thus we hung there, he held by my own down-swinging body, and then holding his own hand by one of mine I reached upward with the other, drew myself slowly and with an infinite effort upward. In another moment I had drawn myself and Marlin on to the wall's top, and there crouched with him again in a silence of exhaustion for the moment. Only his and my own lessened weight, on Triton, had made it possible for me thus to save him.

For but a moment we crouched there, then raised ourselves and looked quickly around us. Cylinders were moving to and fro from time to time over the compartments of the twilight band, from the sunward side, and we knew that if we remained upon the wall's top long we would inevitably be discovered. We must descend into one of the compartments as swiftly as possible. But into which one? In an endeavor to solve the question, we began to crawl quietly along the top of the wall, gazing down upon its other side as we did so. The compartment on that other side was a cell like our own, and it was empty; but its only egress was into the hall between the cell-rows, and that was guarded by the Neptunian armed guards. To descend into it or into any of the other compartment-cells was useless, so along the wall's top we crawled, through the dusk, until in a moment or so more we found ourselves looking down into one of the irregular-shaped anterooms to the great circular compartment of the Council of Thirty.

IN the ante-room compartment stood the usual files of Neptunian guards, and as we saw them, far beneath us, we heard a sharp staccato order from one of them, saw them standing aside from the entrance to the great circular Council compartment. Then, as we watched, we saw emerging from that circular compartment in a moment more, thirty Neptunians, the supreme Council of Thirty before which we had been so short a time before! They were conversing now in their staccato speech, no longer held silent by the synthesizing of their minds in the great globe-mechanism, and as we watched them from far above, we saw them, surrounded now by the files of guards, passing across the ante-room compartment and through a door in it, toward the sunward side of Triton. When they had gone, the ante-room compartment empty beneath us, Martin pointed downward.

"Down here, Hunt!" he whispered. "If we stay longer on the wall-tops we'll be seen by some cylinder passing above, and if we get down into this compartment, we can make our way to the dark side!"

"You're going to try to steal a cylinder on the dark side?" I asked, and he nodded.

"Yes, in the darkness there, where the Neptunians are sleeping, we'll have a chance to get at one. But we must hurry, for there's little time left before the great signal comes for those on dark and sunward sides to change places!"

So, spurred on by that necessity, we swung ourselves over the wall's edge and then dropped down through the dusk two hundred feet toward the ante-room compartment's floor. Yet that great drop was to us not more than a drop of a tenth that distance on Earth, so slowly did we float down toward the floor, breaking our fall a little by scraping along the smooth wall. We struck the floor, tumbled in a heap there, and then straightened, gazed about. The ante-room was quite empty and in it were but three of the broad low doors. One led back to the cell-compartments from which we had escaped, another led to the sunward side. Through that had just passed the Council of Thirty and their guards. The other led into the great circular Council compartment itself. The last, it was clear, was the only one that held out to us any prospect of reaching the dark side, so we passed through it quickly and into the great Council compartment, moving now in great floating leaps each step.

The great circular compartment was as empty of life as the one which we had just left, the twilight dusk in it dispelled somewhat by the soft-glowing disks in its walls. The great ring-table in it had in the seats around it no Neptunians of the Council now, but at that table's center stood still the great metal globe whose strange mechanism made of the thirty minds of the Council members a single mind, in perception and action. Knowing even as we did that it was but a lifeless mechanism now, without the Council's members connected to it, it was yet with some awe that we stared toward that great mechanism, to whose voice we had listened so short a time before. Much would I have given to have examined it, to have inspected whatever strange mechanism lay within the globe, but time now was our enemy. Soon the signal would come that would send the millions of Neptunians on dark and sunward sides streaming across Triton to change their sides. And unless we could steal one of the cylinders and escape before that signal came, we would inevitably be discovered.

So, sparing only a glance toward the great silent globe, Marlin and I moved silently across the great Council compartment, toward one of the low doors in it that led apparently toward the dark side of Triton, to our right. Cautiously we passed through that door, finding ourselves in another ante-room compartment, as empty now as the one through which we had already come. Swiftly we moved across it, in the great floating leaps that each step of ours made now, toward the door in it that led in the direction of the dark side. But even as we moved toward that door, as we stooped to pass through it, Marlin and I shrank suddenly back, appalled. For as we bent toward that door, the sound of staccato voices had come to us from just ahead, and we had seen in that moment that there were Neptunians in the next compartment, several armed with ray-tubes, who were coming straight toward that door, straight toward us!

A moment we glanced wildly about through the dusky compartment as they came toward us, then we had leaped aside from the door, had reached one of the compartment's corners, leaping more than a score of feet toward that corner and crouching there in the dusk, even as the dozen Neptunians came through the door! It was our one chance of escaping them, the chance that they might not perceive us in the compartment's corner through the twilight dusk that reigned in it. But I knew that so keen were their great bulging multiple eyes that it was against hope that I hoped. The

Neptunians who had come into the compartment, however, seemed not to notice us as they entered, passing across it toward the great Council compartment, conversing among themselves in their snapping speech-sounds as they did so. Tensely we crouched there, stiffening suddenly, as we saw one of the disk-bodied monsters suddenly turn and glance back across the compartment in our direction. But in the next moment he had turned back, not seeing us, and then they had passed through the opposite door, their strange voices passing from our hearing.

Marlin and I straightened, with long breaths of relief. "Close, Hunt!" he whispered. "But on to the dark side—we've little enough time left!"

"We're almost out of the twilight band now," I told him, "and in the dark side we'll be a little safer."

And now we were moving quietly through the door from which the approach of the Neptunians had startled us, through the compartment beyond it and on through another and another. These compartments of the twilight band seemed for the most part quite empty, filled neither with masses of working Neptunians like those of the sunward side, nor masses of sleeping Neptunians like those of the dark side. We had found, however, that the compartments of the twilight band were in fact used only for the housing of the Council of Thirty and of the other activities and departments of the rulers of the Neptunians, their only purpose aside from that being to provide easy access from the dark to the sunward side of Triton, and vice versa. So it was that now as we crept through the twilight dusk of those compartments, we found them almost wholly empty and tenantless, though once or twice we were forced again to seek hiding in the shadows as we heard the staccato voices of Neptunians in the distance. Once, too, we were startled by one of the cylinders throbbing by close above us, and since we had had no time to hide from it, thought ourselves discovered by it, though after tense minutes it became plain that its occupants had not seen us.

But soon the twilight of that narrow band was deepening, and almost at once, it seemed, we were moving from that twilight dusk into a deep darkness that obscured all things about us. We had reached the dark side of Triton, we knew, and now moved more carefully still, for upon that dark side, we knew equally well, slept half the massed millions of the Neptunian races. The first few compartments which we traversed in that darkness, however, were as empty as those in the twilight behind us. But then, as we moved silently on, we came into the first of the great sleeping-compartments. Even like those which had puzzled us so on Neptune it was, with its towering walls lined with intersecting shelves whose openings, twice as long as they were high, were ranged in rows, one above the other, like giant pigeon-holes.

This sleep-compartment, though, was not empty like those upon Neptune, for in its hundreds of shelf-openings, its great pigeon-holes, there slept hundreds upon hundreds of the disk-bodied Neptunians! Their seven short limbs folded up around their disk-bodies, they reposed in those openings with their bulging, glassy eyes as open as ever. It was evident they all were sleeping, since the dimness of the day upon Neptune had made lids for those eyes unnecessary in the evolution of their strange race. And eerie was that sight to Marlin and myself, as we stepped silently into and across the great sleep-compartment. For it seemed to us that the hundreds of Neptunians reposing thus in those wall openings were regarding us fixedly with their great multiple eyes, watching us as we moved across the compartment. None stirred, though, as we made our way across it to the opposite door, and moved into the next, which we found to be another sleep-compartment also, its wall-openings, too, holding hundreds of the sleeping monsters.

Through a dozen such sleep-compartments we went, moving with infinite quiet and care, lest any of those sleeping thousands about us be aroused by any sound. And almost it seemed to Marlin and me as we crept on that that hope was ended in any case, since so far we had found none of the landing-compartments for which we searched, none of the cylindrical fliers in which alone we could escape. We had passed through other compartments that held the great heat-radiating globes, now, great glowing globes whose intense heat was not radiated out horizontally at all, but sent up in vertical heat-currents, which by convection in some way warmed all Triton's atmosphere. Past these and through still more sleep-compartments we went, pausing now and then as from the distance in the dark side there reached us a few staccato voices; still we came not upon any of the landing compartments for which we searched.

Despair was growing in me as we crept on through the sleep compartments, through the thousands of slumbering Neptunians. For soon would come the signal that would awaken all those Neptunians about us, I knew, and unless we found a landing compartment, a cylinder that we might steal before then, all was lost. Even with such a cylinder, indeed, little enough hope was ours, since we dared not attempt to get to the twenty controls of the great sun-ray across the swarming sunward side. Our greatest hope would be to escape from Triton in it, if possible through the great roof that surrounded Triton, but even that hope seemed a futile one now, since, as we went on and on through the dense darkness of this sleeping side of Triton, we were moving still through a maze of sleep-compartments, groping blindly through the vast checker-board maze of intersecting, towering walls. And as we came into still another of the sleep-compartments, with its massed sleeping Neptunians in the wall-openings around it, I halted beside Marlin, twitched his sleeve.

"Marlin!" I whispered. "That signal will be coming soon—this dark side's sleeping millions will be waking around us, and we've seen no sign of cylinders yet!"

"We must go on, Hunt!" he whispered tensely. "It's our only chance now—to get to one of the cylinders before they awaken!"

"But if we were to head in a different direction—" I began, then was abruptly silent, stiffening suddenly, as Marlin did, beside me.

For there across the dark compartment from us it had seemed to us that one of the sleeping Neptunians in the wall-openings had moved! Fixedly, in that moment, we stared at it, its own glassy eyes staring back at us like those of all the other sleeping monsters. Was the creature asleep or waking? The question was in our brains at that moment as Marlin and I stood motionless, gazing toward the Neptunian. It was but the merest moment, though, that we gazed thus at the thing transfixed, for in the next instant it and the one in the opening beside it, roused by its own movement, had moved again, and then with their low staccato cries of surprise sounding together as one, the two Neptunian monsters had leaped down to the floor from their openings and were confronting us!

CHAPTER TWELVE
Through The Roof

EVEN as the two creatures leaped down to the floor, and before they could change their low cries of astonishment into louder cries of alarm, Marlin and I had leaped across the compartment toward them! For a full two-score feet in one great leap we shot toward them, a feat only possible with Triton's lesser gravitation, and only possible, too, because we knew in that moment that a single loud cry from the two creatures would bring to their aid the hundreds of Neptunians sleeping about us. Before either could utter such a cry, we two had shot through the air and were upon them!

So astounded were they with our appearance and our supernatural leap across the compartment, that before they could put themselves into a posture of defense, we had struck them, had knocked them to the floor and were grappling with them. In that first moment of contact I had reached for the mouth-opening of the disk-bodied monster at whom I had leaped, had gripped that opening in the top of its disk-body to prevent its outcry and then had striven to lift the thing sidewise, to hurl it against the floor. But great as was my strength against Triton's lesser gravitation, the strength of the Neptunian I held was greater still, and its weight, due to the weight-disks worn by it, was enormous. In an instant its seven great limbs were clutching for me, grasping me, and as I strained there against that great monstrous disk-body's grip, I knew with fatal certainty that never could I match my strength against its own. For even as I struggled desperately with it, Marlin struggling as wildly with the other beside me, the thing was lifting me with its own great limbs from the floor!

Upward it drew me with those powerful limbs, its bulging glassy eyes staring from its disk-body's edge straight into my own, as we grappled desperately in the dark compartment with the sleeping Neptunians all about us! I felt myself being overcome, my strength puny beside the strength of that monster, and as I clutched wildly still at the mouth-opening in the top of the disk-body, I thrust my clenched fist down into that small round mouth-opening, half by chance and half by design, closing it thus with my balled fist. Instantly the creature's body turned and twisted frantically, its grip upon me forgotten for the moment, its whole body's mass seeming to heave and twitch as my hand thus cut off the passage of air into that mouth-opening, into its body! I was throttling it, I knew, and hung fiercely to my grip upon it, my clenched hand still within its mouth-opening, while the thing swayed and tore at me with ever decreasing strength. A moment more and its struggles ceased, it collapsed limply to the floor, and I staggered up again to my feet.

In a single glance I saw that the other Neptunian had gripped Marlin and was crushing him against a corner of the compartment's shelving and instantly, with a single great leap, I was upon that other monster, had gained upon it the same throttling grip which I had found was so deadly to these creatures. In a flash the Neptunian had released his hold upon Marlin, was whirling me around the compartment, shaking me this way and that, and wildly attempting to tear itself loose from me, but with the last of my strength I clung to it, and in a few moments, it too, had weakened, then had slumped down in a lifeless, grotesque mass. And as I rose from it I saw that Marlin had staggered up likewise, was coming toward me. None other of the Neptunians had been aroused by the noise of our mad combat, because in the first excitement of that combat the two Neptunians we fought had not thought to cry out, and after I had gained that throttling hold upon them they could not. So around us the silent ranks of Neptunians slept on unaroused, their open, glassy eyes full upon us, even in their sleep, while Marlin and I were stumbling toward the compartment's door.

"On, Hunt!" he whispered hoarsely. "We still have a chance, if we can find a landing-compartment, can steal one of the cylinders before these sleeping Neptunians wake!"

Through the next compartment we went, and the next, and the next, all sleep-compartments, filled with rows of slumbering Neptunians like those behind us, but in our progress we had come upon no landing-compartment. And though we knew that such there were here and there on Triton's dark side, we could not tell, in the darkness and with the huge walls towering all around us, in what direction from us they might be. We could but blunder aimlessly on through the maze of adjoining sleep compartments in the blind hope that we might chance upon one of the landing-sections, and as we went on, staggering in great, irregular leaps through compartment after compartment, all filled either with masses of sleeping Neptunians or with great heat-radiating mechanisms, we knew that at any moment might come the great signal of light that would awaken the hordes around us.

Never could there have been flight more nightmare-like than that of Marlin and myself through the dark compartments of Triton's dark side, in blind search for the cylinders which alone held out to us any chance of escape. Through the sleep-compartments, with their masses of open-eyed and sleeping disk-bodied Neptunians, through the compartments where reared the great glowing globes whose radiated heat alone held back the cold doom that so long had threatened these strange beings, through compartment after compartment in a flight made more grotesque and unreal to us by the strange method of our progress; by the strange, great, smooth leaps that we made instead of steps, great floating leaps of a score of feet in which we rushed through the dark sleeping compartments, reckless now of the few Neptunians who might be waking and moving upon the dark side. Then suddenly as we leaped toward the door of still another sleep-compartment, poised an instant to leap through that low door, we halted, gazed with abruptly-flaring hope ahead. For the next compartment, we saw, was a rectangular one and greater in size than any we had passed through as yet, and in it there stood the great gleaming shapes of a score or more of the cylinder-fliers that we sought!

With hearts pounding Marlin and I crouched in the low door, gazing through the darkness toward those great cylinders, that gleamed a little in the feeble light that came down upon Triton's dark side from the stars through the great roof overhead. We saw that the low doors in the sides of those cylinders, near the bases, were open, and from them there came to us the throbbing of their mechanisms, inside! It was evident that these were part of the countless cylinders used to help in transporting the Neptunian hordes from dark side to sunward side of Triton, and *vice versa,* and it was equally evident from those throbbing mechanisms' operation, that the hour of awakening for those hordes was at hand

and that these were waiting for that awakening. For there stood also, between us and the nearest of the cylinders, three tube-armed Neptunians who were conversing in brief, snapping speech as they waited!

FOR the moment, at sight of those cylinders, Marlin and I came near to throwing ourselves toward them regardless of the three, but that we knew would be suicide, so despite our torturing agony of soul we waited there in the doorway, gazing desperately toward the cylinders. And in a moment, as we sought in vain for some way to get to the nearest of those cylinders, there came a final staccato order from one of the three Neptunians and at that order the other two turned and passed through a door in the landing-compartment's side opposite from us. It was our chance, the chance for which we had hardly dared to hope even, and no sooner had the two Neptunians disappeared through the opposite door, the other standing with his eyes following them for the moment, than Marlin and I had crept out a little bit into the landing-compartment and then with a great simultaneous leap had shot through the air toward that remaining Neptunian!

There was no chance for resistance on the creature's part. For even as we knocked it sidewise with the force of our leap Marlin had grasped the creature's limbs and with fierce, desperate strength I had with my clenched fist closed its mouth-opening in that method whose deadliness had been proved to me in our other battle. The thing threshed wildly, then it, too, had gone limp, and had collapsed. And in the next instant Marlin and I were rising from it, were leaping across the compartment toward the open low door of the nearest great cylinder, from whose great gleaming upright bulk before us came the throbbing of its powerful generators. And then, a dozen feet from it, we stopped dead, and from Marlin came a hoarse cry.

For at that moment there had swept over us, through us, past us, from the direction of Triton's sunward side across its surface, a band of intensely brilliant white light, white light that blazed brilliant for the moment all around us, turning the changeless night of Triton's dark side around us for the moment into a white and blinding day, and then sweeping swiftly on, around Triton's surface! It was the great signal of awakening, the signal for the millions of sleeping Neptunians about us to awake and change places with the swarming millions upon the sunward side! And even as that dazzling signal came, as Marlin and I stood stupefied there for the moment before the looming cylinder's open door, there came from all around us, from over all the dark side's great extent and from all its maze of sleep-compartments, a rising babel of staccato voices, the voices of its awakening Neptunian millions! Then, before ever we could recover from the stupefaction that in that instant held us rooted to the spot, there had poured into the great landing-compartment from the compartments on all sides of it swarms of hastening Neptunians, swarms of disk-bodied monsters, who in that moment saw us, uttered as one a sharp great cry of discovery, and in the next moment were rushing from all sides toward us!

"The cylinder!"

It was Marlin's wild cry that aroused me from the stupefaction of amazement that held me. Straight before us, a dozen feet away, was the open door of the nearest cylinder, and in the next split-second Marlin and I, as one, had leaped toward it, had shot through that door, into the cylinder's interior, even as the Neptunians raced toward us. The next instant I had reached frantically for the door, had with one swift motion slid it clanging shut, and then as the Neptunian masses outside hurled themselves toward it, Marlin and I were throwing ourselves up through the openings toward the cylinder's uppermost section. In one leap I was at the central control-standard, fumbled frantically with the green control-studs for an agonizing moment, and then, just as we heard the Neptunians below flinging themselves against the door, the great throbbing cylinder shot upward!

Up over Triton's dark side we rose, a dozen slender force-rays criss-crossing about us from beneath in that moment, and as we glanced momentarily down we could see the Neptunians in the landing-compartment beneath rushing toward the other cylinders there! And glancing far across the surface of Triton, we could see all its mighty compartment-city, dark and sunward sides alike, swarming now with Neptunian hordes as the end and beginning of their strange day and night periods was signaled. Over the great compartment-city, over all the countless millions of Neptunians that swarmed through it, there was spreading a crackling roar of excited tumult, as our escape was discovered. And from far away on either side and from beneath us, scores of great cylinders whirled toward us!

"Up—*up!*" Marlin was shouting now beside me, "They'll have us in another moment!"

I pressed swiftly again the studs before me, and as the cylinder shot up and sidewise with terrific speed on an upward slant I shouted back to Marlin over the roar of air about us. "The roof openings!" I cried. "We'll make for the nearest one!"

But as the cylinder flashed obliquely upward, Marlin and I crouching in the two opposite seats at the control-standard, I became aware of the swarms of racing cylinders behind closing in upon us. And over the dark and sunward surfaces of Triton that great mounting roar of sound was spreading, as the Neptunian hordes saw our wild attempt at escape. Up—up—and now we were racing close beneath the great roof, transparent from below, with the pursuing cylinders drawing ever nearer, their Neptunian occupants more skilled than I in their operation. And now, too, from those uprising, pursuing swarms were directed toward us slender pencil-like rays of pale light, visible only near their source, concentrated force-rays, that would cleave through our cylinder as through paper!

On and upward—and now as we shot on, with the swarming cylinders hurtling hotly after us in wild pursuit, with the throb of our generators and the roar of air about us thundering in our ears, with the wild tumult of the massed Neptunians on Triton's surface coming dully up to us from beneath, Marlin and I were gazing with tense eyes ahead and upward. The great opening, the great sliding section of the roof down through which we had come—that was our one chance to escape from Triton, I knew that unless we could win through that opening, out of Triton's enclosed world, we were doomed. On and on we went—our eyes still upon the vast roof overhead in search of that opening in it, when suddenly Marlin cried hoarsely in my ear, and pointed ahead. And there from ahead were rushing toward us other scores of cylinders, other swarms of racing cylinders answering the spreading alarm, while still others were shooting up from below toward us! From behind, from ahead, from beneath, the cylinders' swarms were converging upon us in that moment, and as instinctively I slowed our cylinder's mad rush I looked upward, toward the great roof—

"The opening-section!" I cried suddenly. "But it's closed against us!"

For there above, indeed, was that great circle in the vast transparent roof that we knew could be slid aside and opened by its Neptunian guards in the bright-lit little cage-room suspended beside it. My one hope had been that in our stolen cylinder we might deceive those guards of the great orifice into opening it for us to pass. But that hope was gone. Behind and below and before us were the pursuing swarms of cylinders and the Neptunians in the cage-room above knew that something was wrong, and had not opened the great circle for us. There were other similar circles, similar opening-sections, in Triton's roof, but it was too late now to seek them because from all about us the swarming, racing cylinders were rushing upon us. In another moment their rays would shatter us! I heard Marlin, beside me, utter a low exclamation of utter hopelessness as those cylinders rushed upon us, held our own cylinder for the moment motionless there in mid-air beneath the great roof's opening section, and then suddenly reached toward the control-studs, even as Marlin's hoarse cry was sounding beside me.

"The end, Hunt!" he was crying. "The cylinders are almost upon us—and the opening-section is closed!"

"The end maybe—but not this way!" I shouted fiercely, at the same moment sending the cylinder flashing straight upward with all its speed. "Hold to your chair, Marlin—*we're going to smash through that opening-section of the roof!*"

Even as I cried out thus, our cylinder was rising upward toward the roof with all the power of its throbbing generators, hurtling upward at speed unthinkable toward the great circle of the opening-section! I was aware in that moment of the crowding swarms of cylinders about and beneath us loosing toward us a storm of crossing force-rays that we drove clear of in that instant. I was aware of the Neptunians in the cage-room beside the great opening-section rushing wildly about as we shot upward like the cylindrical projectile of some giant cannon! The next instant I caught the gleam of the transparent roof, of the opening-section just above us, Marlin and I instinctively crouched lower in our seats, and a moment later there was a blinding, stunning shock that seemed to split the universe with its detonation. We were dragged up from our seats with awful force. And then as we straightened up and looked out, we saw that the cylinder had smashed through the great opening-section and was throbbing above Triton's mighty roof!

The cylinder's ceiling, above us, was crumpled and bent badly, but in that moment it seemed a miracle that we had lived through that terrible collision. It was only our awful speed that had saved us, driving us through the opening-section's thick metal even as a cyclone will drive fragile straws and twigs unbroken through a board. Now as we looked downward we saw that the swarming pursuing cylinders were massed beneath the crumpled opening-section and that that circle of the opening-section was slowly sliding aside, bent and crumpled as it was, to allow those cylinders to emerge through Triton's roof after us! And up they came, a full hundred of them, racing up after us at utmost speed, up from the great metal roof of Triton, dark and opaque to our eyes from above, and up through its atmosphere close on our track!

THROUGH the rushing roar of air about us, the throbbing of our generators, I was aware of Marlin shouting something beside me. I was gazing ahead for the moment, as that wild flight and pursuit passed on through Triton's atmosphere. Giant Neptune's cloudy green sphere bulked gigantic in the heavens before us, and far beyond it was the little fire-disk of the sun. Then I turned back to see the hundred pursuing cylinders, getting ever closer behind us. As I started at the sight, I became aware of Marlin shouting beside me, and at the same moment realized the import of his words, I realized that the throbbing of our generators was halting, hesitating, failing! Our great crash out through the roof had broken some part of their mechanism and now they were failing rapidly, and the speed of our cylinder was slowing!

And behind us the scores of onrushing cylinders were closer— closer! Already toward us again from them were leaping the slender pale force-rays, missing us at that distance but sweeping close about us. With an utter tenseness of body and spirit, Marlin and I watched them drawing closer, as our cylinder shot on through Triton's atmosphere. Suddenly another storm of rays had shot and swept toward us from behind, and one of those wild whirling rays, in a single instant, clove through the cylinder's uppermost sides like a sword of fire through cardboard, slicing away completely the already crumpled roof above us and the upper half-dozen feet of the walls! Instantly a flood of icy-cold air rushed in upon us and seemed in that moment to freeze us through. At the same moment the throbbing generators ceased completely to operate, the cylinder slowing swiftly on its rush forward, drifting helplessly there in the outer reaches of Triton's atmosphere, while from behind, like leaping creatures of prey, the scores of cylinders rushed upon us!

Neither Marlin nor I voiced a cry in that moment. We could only stare as if we were automatons, toward the onrushing cylinders, the oncoming doom. We had run our course at last. It seemed in that moment that all our bitter battle for freedom, our toilsome escape from our cell, our flight through Triton's sleeping side, our stealing of the cylinder and wild crash upward through the great roof's opening-section—that all this futile flight of ours was reenacting itself with lightning swiftness before my eyes. The swarming cylinders were almost on us, holding their rays now as they saw us helpless until they were closer, their great mass whirling straight toward us. And then, as I gripped the control-standard before me, expectant in that instant of the end, I saw that onrushing mass of cylinders suddenly shattered as though by gigantic blows from above. I saw the scores of cylinders driven this way and that in a single instant with colossal force, even as they rushed to annihilate us! And I looked dazedly up, was looking up—

"The space-flier!" Marlin's insane cry was sounding there beside me. *"It's the space-flier—and Whitely and Randall!"*

The space-flier! There high above us and above the pursuing cylinders it hung, a gleaming faceted ball, at sight of which I could only gaze stupefied. I saw in that moment that down from its lowest ray-opening there was radiating toward the cylinders that had been hurtling in a mass toward us, a pale, almost invisible great force-ray and that it was that ray's giant pressure that had shattered the mass of our pursuers, and in an instant had driven their massed cylinders to all sides! Then, as they broke thus in wild confusion before that swift great force-ray from above, the space-flier was flashing down toward our roofless, drifting cylinder, was hovering just beside us, touching that cylinder, with the round outer door in its facet within our reach! In an instant Marlin and I had clambered to the drifting cylinder's edge, had whirled open that outer door of the space-flier. When we threw ourselves into the little vestibule-chamber or air-lock, shut the outer door, and turned toward the inner one, that inner one was opened and Whitely—Whitely!—was pulling us inside!

"Whitely—Randall—" we were babbling in our excitement, "we thought you dead—saw fragments of the space-flier and thought it destroyed—!"

"No time now to tell you, Marlin—Hunt—" Whitely was hurriedly saying. "Those cylinders are forming again. They're coming up toward us! Head out from Triton, Randall—full speed!"

But even as he had spoken, Randall, in the control-chair, had flashed his hands over the six control-switches, and as Marlin and I clambered with Whitely into the other three chairs, we felt ourselves pressed down with terrific force against them as the space-flier shot out from Triton with colossal speed! But at the same moment the cylinders that had formed again into their close-grouped mass, had leaped forward with us and the next moment saw space-flier and cylinders alike whirling out from the atmosphere of Triton into the empty void of space! I glanced back, saw that the cylinders were close behind our hurtling space-flier, flashing after it somewhat beneath it, so as to clear its great force-ray shooting back toward Triton and flinging it outward. And as I glanced back, I saw Triton's dull-gleaming sphere, with the pale giant force-ray that stabbed from its side toward the sun, growing each instant smaller! But dead ahead of us, though somewhat beneath our level, there loomed the colossal green sphere of Neptune, growing in size as we rushed on at immense speed from its moon!

A Serial in 3 Parts
Part III

By Edmond Hamilton
Author of "Locked Worlds," "The Other Side of the Moon," etc.

In an instant Marlin and I had clambered to the drifting cylinder's edge and to the open outside door.

On we went, and as Randall's hands flashed over the control-switches, Marlin and Whitely and I staring tensely forth with him, we were aware that from the mass of on-racing cylinders behind slender force-rays were again questing toward us, though the range was too great for them to loose them accurately at this terrific speed. At any moment, though, one of those concentrated, pencil-like rays might cleave through our space-flier in a lucky hit, and unless we escaped from these relentless pursuers, the space-flier and ourselves were certain of destruction. This I saw, and saw too that Neptune's colossal cloudy sphere lay close before us, so awful was the speed of our flight and pursuit, and as it loomed gigantic before us, filling the heavens, it was apparent that we would pass close above its surface. Suddenly I turned to Randall, shouted in his ear above the thundering throbbing drone of our generators.

"Neptune!" I cried. "There's a chance to smash these pursuing cylinders there!"

"But how—?" he began. Shouting in his ear, I explained to him the desperate inspiration that had come to me. I saw his eyes and those of Marlin and Whitely widen as they heard, and then he nodded grimly, clutched the control-switches tighter.

And now about us was sounding again the roar of air as we shot through Neptune's atmosphere, shot above the surface of the huge planet with the cylinders rushing still at equal speed behind us, their deadly rays stabbing this way and that in slicing sweeps toward us. Through the cloudy mists of Neptune's upper atmosphere we flashed, straight onward, with the dark metal surface of the giant world's vast roof clear now to our eyes far beneath. And as we shot over it I saw Randall's grip tighten on the control-switches, saw him glance back toward the pursuing cylinders, behind and a little beneath us, and then abruptly he had flung open the switch of the great force-ray that was driving us on, our rear-ray! Instantly the speed of the space-flier slowed, and in a split-second the onrushing cylinders, racing on unslowing in that moment, were hurtling past beneath us. And as they did so, another switch had clicked under Randall's hands and straight down upon those cylinders from the space-flier's bottom was driving down another mighty force-ray!

In the next instant we had a glimpse of those massed cylinders that had been rushing thus beneath us driven down by the power of our great force-ray with inconceivable speed and force, driven down in a whirling, confused mass toward the vast metal roof of great Neptune below! And as our great ray, traveling across their mass, drove them thus downward with colossal power, we saw a moment later the cylinders of that mass crashing downward against that roof, shattering into crumpled, wrecked masses of metal upon the mighty structure, annihilated with all inside them on that roof as our great ray drove them down against it! Half at least of that mass of cylinders perished thus in the first crash downward and before the rest could gather again to whirl up to the attack, our great ray was playing upon them also, crashing them down upon the great roof of death, until in only a moment more but a half-dozen of the cylinders remained intact! And these, as their fellows crashed to death beneath us, were gathering and speeding away from this death that smote from above, were going back toward the dull-gleaming disk of Triton!

Marlin and Whitely and Randall and I were all crying out in that moment as the surviving cylinders flashed away in flight, and then Marlin and I had turned toward our two friends. "Whitely—Randall—!" Marlin was saying. "You escaped those Neptunians that first discovered us, then? We saw the fragments of wreckage your pursuers brought back, and Hunt and I never dreamed you might still live!"

"It was a trick that enabled us to escape," Whitely explained.

"When they discovered us there beneath Neptune's roof—chased us up through that roof and up into the great cloud-belts, I saw that we could not long escape those pursuing cylinders. So, while Randall drove the flier through the mists and while they searched in those mists for us, I battered and broke with blows of a large tool some of the spare plates and instruments we carried. Then, as they came closer to us, their force-rays slicing through the mists in search of us, I cast those fragments loose from the flier, and when they struck against the pursuing cylinders in the mists, when those cylinders saw the wrecked fragments, they had no doubt but that their force-rays had struck us somewhere in the cloud-layer and annihilated us. We lay in the shrouding mists until

THE UNIVERSE WRECKERS

we saw them returning toward Neptune's surface. We realized then that you two had been captured by whatever manner of creatures these Neptunians were, and saw the cylinders, with you in one of them, going down beneath Triton's roof. For days, therefore, Randall and I waited around Triton's surface, hoping against hope to get down inside in some way and find you, and had almost given up hope, when we saw the cylinder you had stolen racing up from Triton, and were able to save it and you from the pursuing cylinders."

"But you, Marlin—Hunt—" Whitely continued. "You have learned how and why these Neptunians are sending forth the great ray that is turning the sun faster? We saw that ray and another great ray on opposite sides of Triton— Is it not possible that we alone might be able to halt that ray?"

Marlin solemnly shook his head. "No chance, Whitely, for us," he said. "Perhaps no chance even for all the forces of Earth!" And quickly he told, while Whitely and Randall listened enthralled, of the captivity of us two in Triton's strange and swarming world; of the gigantic tale of Neptune's past and the purpose of its peoples, as it had been told us by the great globe of the Council of Thirty; of our desperate escape and flight across the dark side of Triton and our wild crashing upward through the roof and out from Triton. "We alone," Marlin concluded, "can never halt either of those great rays, for each has countless cylinders and Neptunians within to guard it, and each has twenty control-boxes of which one alone can keep it operating. No, our one chance is to get back to Earth, to gather there the great fleet of space-fliers which the World President and the World Congress planned to build in our absence, and to come out in that great fleet with the most powerful weapons available and endeavor to crush these strange Neptunians, to halt that great ray of doom that is turning the sun ever faster! For unless we can do that, unless we can bring Earth's fleet of space-fliers out here and halt the great sun-ray, that ray will in sixty days more have finished its work, will have split the sun and loosed doom upon all its planets except Neptune! And so it is back to Earth that we must race now at our utmost speed!"

Marlin's solemn voice ceased, and there was silence for a moment in the space-flier, we four gazing toward each other without speaking. By then the flier, with the tremendous impetus of its flight still driving it forward, had swept on and out over great Neptune now, out of the giant world's cloudy atmosphere and into empty space beyond it. And, with Neptune's giant globe filling the firmament behind us, Randall snapped on again our rear force-ray, sent that ray radiating back toward the vast disk of Neptune itself. And then again we were forced deep in our chairs as the flier's tremendous speed accelerated once more, the flier hurtling with greater and greater velocity through the gulf of space toward the far little disk of fire that was the sun, far ahead. For it was toward it, toward our Earth, that we were going from Neptune, from the solar system's edge, to carry back word to Earth of the nature of the doom that hung above it and to gather Earth's forces to forestall that doom!

CHAPTER THIRTEEN
The Gathering Of Earth's Forces

STARING ahead into space from the control-chair of our racing flier, I heard Whitely's voice from beside me. "Seventeen days," he was saying. "And in two more days we ought to reach Earth."

I nodded abstractedly, gazing ahead. "Two days at the most," I said. "We're inside Jupiter's orbit now, and once through the asteroidal belt, there'll be nothing to delay us."

For as Whitely and I gazed outward, Marlin and Randall sleeping now in two of the space-flier's bunks, we could see that we were approaching, indeed, that belt of whirling asteroids that marked the division between the four inner and the four great outer planets of the solar system. To the left, dropping behind us, gleamed the gigantic cloud-belted sphere of Jupiter with its stately train of attendant moons, as great a mystery to us as when we first had passed it. A side force-ray was holding the flier out still from the mighty planet's attraction, while ahead and to the right from us now gleamed crimson Mars. Yet it was not these that held the eyes of Whitely and myself, nor even the increasing fiery circle of the sun before us, but the bluish-white little spot of light that was expanding slowly in size and brilliance as we shot on toward it, the little spot of bluish light that was our planet, Earth.

For days we had gazed toward that little light-spot as our space-flier went on and on through the solar system's vast reaches toward it. For seventeen days, now, even as Whitely had said, we had been racing inward from Neptune at utmost speed on our desperate journey back to our own world. The space-flier's great rear force-ray, pushing back against giant Neptune, had hurled the flier in through the outer reaches of our universe with an acceleration of velocity that was so great as to prove almost our undoing. For more than once that terrific pressure of that acceleration on us, despite our shock-absorbing apparatus, had so affected our bodies as to overcome us with successive fits of nausea and unconsciousness. And once, just after we had swept in past great Saturn and its mighty rings, fearful of those great rings after our former misadventure with them, I had awakened from my sleep-period to find Randall and Marlin, in the control-chairs, quite unconscious from the flier's terrific acceleration, the flier itself speeding onward without any guiding hand on its controls.

Yet despite this we had grimly driven the flier to the utmost acceleration possible, its speed steadily mounting toward the maximum in those succeeding days that we flashed inward from Neptune. For behind us Neptune's calm, green little disk of light, though diminishing steadily in size as we receded from it, seemed like a baleful signal of doom shining there behind us. For out from Neptune, or rather out from its moon, Triton, the giant force-ray of the Neptunians, was still radiating toward the sun, thus shadowing all the solar system with the cataclysmic doom to come. For, as we flashed inward, Marlin had used his astronomical instruments to determine the fact that the sun's rotatory period had now decreased to a little over eight days, and was decreasing still by the same amount of four hours each day, its spin accelerated each day by the same amount as the colossal force-ray from Triton kept upon its side its unrelenting pressure. And within half a hundred days more, as we knew, that rotatory period of the sun would have decreased until its huge mass would be spinning once in every hour, would be spinning then so fast that it must inevitably be riven asunder into a new double star by its own centrifugal force, engulfing all its planets save Neptune alone!

So it was that we spared not ourselves but drove the space-flier in through the solar system toward Earth with a speed unthinkable, almost, using an acceleration that was all but death for us. For the one hope of preventing that colossal sun-cataclysm, as Marlin had said and as we all knew, was to reach Earth soon and then at once fly back out from Earth toward Neptune again with the great space-flier fleet, which, if the World-President and the World Congress had not failed us, would be waiting on Earth for us. With that fleet we must sally back across the solar system once more to its outer edge, to great Neptune, and must fall upon Triton and the giant force-ray that was shooting from Triton to the sun, with all our power. If we could vanquish the Neptunians long enough to destroy the giant sun-ray's mechanism, to halt that ray, we would have halted the acceleration of the sun's spin, would have saved the sun and its planets from the cataclysmic doom that now threatened them. But if we could not, if the Neptunians with their countless cylinders and great weapons were too strong for us, then we could but perish there in struggling with them, since in that case nothing could halt the doom that they were loosing from Triton upon the sun and the solar system.

And as Whitely and I gazed out through the flashing flier's windows, we knew that scant enough was the time left for us in which to do these things. Even if we were safe on Earth in the next two days, as we hoped, there would remain but little more than forty days before the coming of the dread cataclysm that threatened, and it would require half that time for the space-fliers of Earth to make their way back out across the solar system to Neptune. So that now there layover my mind that deepening shadow of impending colossal disaster that had hovered over all our minds during the strange days of our racing inward through the solar system, making me gaze somberly enough toward the bluish light-spot in the darkness of space far ahead that was our goal now. To the left, though, Jupiter's great globe had dropped far behind now, and as I saw that I cut out our side-ray, and turned toward Whitely.

"We're at the edge of the asteroidal belt now," I told him, "but I'm not going to slow our speed. We'll just flash on through it and take our chance."

He nodded gravely. "I'll wake Marlin and Randall now to help me keep watch," he said.

A moment later, having done so, Marlin and Randall freed themselves of the straps of the bunks and climbed across the flier to take their places beside Whitely in watching for the great menacing asteroids. And as we passed on through the belt of those whirling perils, Marlin and Whitely and Randall watched for hour on hour there beside me, though so vast was the maximum speed at which our flier was going now, more than eight million miles an hour, that before they could more than get a flashing glimpse of a nearby asteroid we would have passed it. We were relying almost wholly on blind chance to take us through the asteroidal belt at that lightning speed, yet so desperate was this grim race back to Earth from the solar system's edge, that we preferred to trust thus to chance, rather than to slow our speed or to delay by an hour our arrival on Earth. And chance, for the time, favored us, for some hours later we had won through the perils of the asteroidal belt without more than a few split-second glimpses of the great whirling spheres of peril. And then, as we shot across the orbit of Mars with the planet's dull red shield still farther to the right, I began to slow our terrific speed, for by this time the Earth was expanding rapidly before us.

And now, too, the sun was flaming before us, in all the halo-like glory of its great corona, with a brilliance blinding to our eyes after the dim shades of Neptune and its moon. Yet even with that brilliance dazzling us we could make out plainer and plainer the sphere of Earth, seeming to our eyes a thin silver-blue crescent as it spun there between our inrushing flier and the sun, its tiny moonspot growing brighter too. Marlin and Whitely and Randall watching tensely beside me, I cut out altogether the great force-ray at the flier's rear, which, even when our speed had reached its maximum, drove us straight onward and kept that speed unvarying against the gravitational influences from either side which were not large enough to require an opposing side-ray. Snapping that rear-ray out, I sent another force-ray from the flier toward the Earth-sphere ahead, and as that ray struck and pushed us back with immense power, the space-flier's colossal speed was gradually decreasing.

ONCE more we felt terrific upward and forward pressure in our chairs as the flier's speed steadily slowed, dropped swiftly from eight million miles an hour to six and then to five and then to three. And as we shot in thus toward Earth, the millions of miles dropping slower behind as our flier's great faceted ball clicked through space at slower and slower speed, I knew the same question was in the minds of my three friends as in my own. It was reflected in the tensely anxious eyes of Marlin and the imperturbable eyes of Whitely and the unwontedly grave eyes of Randall as the three stared ahead with me. Would the space-fliers that the World-President and the World Congress had promised to build be ready? If not, we knew we certainly could not venture out to Neptune and put an end to the great doom-ray that the Neptunians were stabbing toward the sun. So that it was in a growing suspense of spirit that we watched Earth's sphere, with its crescent of bluish-white light at one side, expanding before us.

At ever slower speed we were rushing in toward it, and at last, moving at but a few hundred thousand miles an hour by this time, were driving in out of the void and past Earth's shining moon, gleaming in space to our right, its great ranges and strange craters clear to our eyes from its airless surface. But now all our eyes were on Earth ahead, since now through the drifting cloud masses that floated in its atmosphere we could make out the great bluish globe's surface features, could see that western Europe and North Africa lay in the sunlight in that crescent of light at Earth's side, but that the North and South Americas lay in the shade of Earth's outer side, in the darkness of night. It was toward the dark half-seen outline of North America that I was heading the flier, for by this time, traveling still more slowly, our velocity now being less than a thousand miles an hour, we were entering Earth's atmosphere, the rarefied air of its outer reaches roaring about the flier as it shot through it.

"Straight to New York—to the World Congress," Marlin was saying. "There's not a minute to lose."

I nodded silently, at the same time snapping out the front-ray of the flier that was slowing our speed as we shot toward Earth's surface, and as its gravitation gripped the flier we were turning until instead of rushing onward we were falling to its surface from high above, as it turned in space before us, falling down toward the surface of the North American continent, whose outline was visible from our great height through the shifting cloud-screen. I felt my heart beating rapidly as we shot thus downward, forgot almost the mighty import of the mission on which we were returning in the mere fact of our return; for we were first of all men to venture thus into the outer void and to return from that void to Earth! And as we shot downward I saw the same thought mirrored in the faces of the others, staring down with me.

Down—down—with an oblique ray I was making the space-flier fall slantingly, more and more slowly, toward the northeastern coast of the continent beneath, whose broad, brown surface stretched out greater and greater beneath us. Moments more and as the roar of air about us intensified, mingling with the throbbing of our generators, we shot down from the sun's light into the darkness of this dark side of Earth, this night of Earth's one side. But now its great surface was changing from convex to concave beneath us, and now as we shot lower still Randall pointed downward and northward with a low cry toward a spark of bright red light, the beam of the great air-beacon of the Transatlantic air-liners, at New York. Slower—slower—and in moments more the vast mass of its towering cylindrical buildings, ablaze with outlining lights, was coming into view, with midmost among them the greatest of all, the huge mass of the World Government building.

As our space-flier dropped slowly toward that mighty structure beneath my controlling hands, as it dropped toward the swarms of bright-lit aircraft that were moving to and fro over the great city, so familiar was the scene beneath to us four cosmic voyagers that almost did our great journey, our mighty flight out through the sun's planets through the countless leagues of space to great Neptune, and our grotesque and dream-like adventures upon Neptune and its moon, seem to us indeed no more than dreams. But as we shot lower we were startled from this strange state of mind by one of the aircraft beneath, showing the customary red and green position-lights along its hull, driving up through the darkness toward our smoothly falling space-flier. We saw the three men in the control-room of the craft gazing amazedly toward the gleaming, faceted metal ball of our flier as they circled us, and then from their craft had burst out a score of brilliant vari-colored signal-lights. And as these blazed out there came a moment later an answering blaze of lights from each of the swarming craft below, that shot up now in hundreds toward our falling flier, crowding crazily about it!

Down through the darkness we dropped still, those swarms of aircraft almost jostling us as they seethed thickly in terrific excitement about us. As we shot downward over New York's surface we saw that across all the vast city, and far across the great air-docks to the south even, signal-lights were blazing out, a wild panorama of bursting lights stretching out in all directions! From beneath, too, there came up to us now a terrific roar of mingled voices, the vast crowds in the streets of the huge city sending their cheering cries up to us in a great thunder-roll of sound as we fell toward them. And as I held the space-flier to its smooth drop downward amid the swarming aircraft, I saw that Marlin and Randall, and even Whitely, were gazing across those vast, shouting throngs and across the swarms of madly-darting aircraft that encircled us, with somber, thoughtful faces.

Now we were falling a few hundred feet above the roof of the World Government building, on which a little knot of figures awaited us, and as I gazed from it across the other roofs of the great city I uttered a low exclamation. "On the roofs—you see?" I asked. "Those things of metal—those space-fliers—!"

But they too were gazing toward the roofs, toward the innumerable crystal-like metal forms that we could half-recognize on those roofs in the darkness. But a glimpse only we had of them before the space-flier was sinking downward to the great roof itself, and as Marlin saw the knot of figures on that roof he half-turned. "The World-President," he said, quietly, "waiting for us on the roof."

That roof's flat expanse was just beneath us, covered itself with other great crystal-like gleaming fliers, but with a clear space at its center where once had stood our space-flier's framework. There was no framework there now, but smoothly I brought the flier down upon that space, down to the roof, poised it a moment a foot above it, and then let it sink to the roof's surface and opened a half-dozen of the switches before me, the throbbing of the generators that had been enduring for so long ceasing and giving way to an unaccustomed silence that was strange to our ears. Then Marlin had turned, was opening the inner door, and in another moment the outer one had swung open also, a flood of cool, clean air rushing in upon us. Marlin leading, we stepped out, stood unsteadily for a moment on the great roof's surface beneath the brilliance of the lights that flared above it.

From beneath and above came still through the night the unceasing roar of the great crowds in the huge city's streets and the hum of its swarming, seething aircraft, and then we saw that the little group of men on the roof beside us were coming toward us, the World-President at their head. His strong, keen eyes were steady upon us as he came forward, his hands outstretched, and then he had gripped our own hands, was holding them for a moment in silence. In that moment we were all four swaying a little as we stood there, gazing about us at the far-flung lights of the great city around us, at the men before us, at the strangely-dulled stars overhead, as though never had we seen them before. When the World-President spoke, his human-sounding voice seemed strange even to our ears.

"Marlin—Randall—Whitely—Hunt—" he said. "You have come back then from your mission?"

"We've come back—from Neptune," Marlin said simply. "The World Congress is already gathered—is waiting for you," said the other, as simply, and then with him and the officials about him we were walking toward the stair-opening in the great roof, were walking through ranks of the great looming faceted things of metal that I saw now clearly were replicas each of our own polyhedron-like space-flier!

Down through that opening we went, down stairs after stairs until we were emerging through a high door on the raised platform at the end of the great room in which the World Congress awaited us. Brilliant white light flooded that room and in it, in silent row upon row, were seated the twelve hundred members of the great

Congress. As we four entered, with the World-President and his officials, there was turned instantly toward us every eye, and a tense hush of utter silence settled in which our own steps seemed loud to our ears. There were no shouts or cheering cries from the Congress' members, in that moment, for all knew that what they were to hear now from us was the word of hope or hopelessness for Earth, the report of our great mission upon which rested Earth's single chance for life. And as I stared across the great, silent Congress in that moment, there flashed upon the screen of my mind, strangely enough, a picture of that other silent, solemn council before which Marlin and I had stood but a few days before, that Council of Thirty of the strange Neptunians whose great synthesizing globe mechanism had spoken to us. Then, as we stood there, the World-President was stepping forward to address the Congress.

"There is no need for me to tell you who are the four men standing here before you," he said. "Marlin—Whitely—Randall—Hunt—these four who went out to Neptune on the Earth's behalf, and whom Earth has tensely awaited now for weeks. I do not know, any more than you, what they found there, what chance for Earth they found or failed to find. And it is that, which we, the representatives of the world's peoples, now wait to hear from Marlin, the leader of this great expedition." Utter silence held all present.

AND as the World-President stepped back, Marlin, unsteady still from our unaccustomedness to Earth's gravitation, and with face drawn, but eyes steady and bright, was stepping forward. Facing the great rank on rank of members of the World Congress he stood, while we others slipped into the seats behind him, facing them for a moment in tense silence as he summoned his energies to speak. In that moment, as my eyes roved across the great hall, I made out the faces of many there known to me, the face, just beneath our platform, was that of my chief at the Intelligence Bureau, Markham, the faces of many others, strange and yet familiar, all turned now toward Marlin. And then, in a voice low at first but gaining in power as he went on, Marlin was speaking to them, his words sounding out through the great room in a hushed, unnatural silence.

He began by reviewing in a few sentences the colossal peril that had threatened and was threatening us, the increased spin of the sun beneath Neptune's mighty ray that soon must result in its division and the solar system's doom. Then, with a reference to that other gathering of the World Congress at which our venture out to Neptune had been decided upon, he came to the start of that venture. While they listened in utter tenseness he told of our start, of our going out from Earth first of all men into the outer void, out past the mysteries of Mars with greater and greater speed. Our onward flight through the terrible dangers of the great asteroidal belt and our narrow escapes in it, our outward rush past mighty Jupiter—these he described in his steady voice, and we felt the tenseness that held all in the great room in dead silence. He told them of what doom had nearly been ours at Saturn, of our fall toward its great rings of death and our narrow escape from them.

Then, with a little pause, he was going on, was telling of our onward flashing flight beyond Saturn out through the vast outer reaches of the solar system, out past the orbit of Uranus toward Neptune itself. In utmost suspense they listened as he told of our arrival at last at Neptune, of our amazement at finding that giant world shielded with an enclosing roof of metal, and of our greater amazement at finding that world, the colossal city that covered it, utterly dead and deserted. Low exclamations of surprise broke from his listeners then as he narrated how he and I had been surprised in the dead city of Neptune by the coming of the Neptunians in their cylinders, their attack upon and pursuit upward of Whitely and Randall in the space-flier, their capture of ourselves and their taking us from Neptune out to the moon-world of Triton. And a low wave of uncontrollable excitement swept across the great room as Marlin told those in it of the roofed and warmed world of Triton and the countless millions of Neptunians on it, and above all of the giant force-ray that was stabbing from Triton's sunward side toward the sun and loosing doom upon us!

And that excitement intensified when he told of what else we had found at Triton, of the other giant force-ray stabbing out from its other side toward a distant star of Sagittarius, of our captivity there and our learning of the Neptunian tongue, our being brought before the great Council of Thirty of the Neptunian races I saw the hundreds before us listening with abated breath as he told them that gigantic epic of the solar system's past that had been told us by the great globe-mechanism of the Council, that story of the Neptunians' past history and of the great doom of increasing cold that had driven them from Neptune to Triton and that now had caused them to seek to split the sun itself to thwart that doom. How they had sent out toward that star in Sagittarius another great force-ray years before, to brace Triton against the back-pressure of the sun-ray and to keep it from being hurled out into the great void, how they had finally sent out the great force-ray toward the sun also, turning the sun ever faster toward the doom of all the other planets, planning to wreck the universe to save their own race. These things he told them through the hushed silence that again had replaced their stir and murmur of excitement.

But excitement held them again when he told how he and I, desperate at the doom we saw hanging thus over Earth, had made our wild attempt to escape from Triton, had dared to cross its surface and had stolen a cylinder, crashing up through the great roof and out from Triton in that cylinder with their pursuit close behind us, how we had been saved from that pursuit by Whitely and Randall in the space-flier, who, although we had thought them dead, had managed to elude their own attackers by a ruse and had hovered near Triton in hopes of saving us; how in the space-flier we had fled back from Triton over Neptune and had smashed our pursuers, while we and they were over Neptune; these things, his voice deep now, he told to the hundreds of his listeners. And then, swaying a little from sheer utter weariness of body and spirit, Marlin told them how we, knowing that never alone could we halt or even reach that giant ray driving from Triton toward the sun, had headed back for Earth at the utmost speed of which we were capable, had flashed back like some great messenger-meteor through the solar system to Earth to carry to the peoples of Earth word of what we had found, to gather the forces of Earth and head back to Neptune with them for a last gallant attempt to halt that mighty ray of doom!

THE UNIVERSE WRECKERS

When Marlin's voice had ceased, when he had stepped unsteadily back from the platform's edge, his words seemed reverberating still through the hushed silence that prevailed among the twelve hundred massed members of the World Congress. Then again the World-President, his own face as set and strange now as those of the massed members before him, was stepping forward to face them.

"You have heard the report of Dr. Marlin and his three companions," he said, quietly, "and you, and I, and the peoples of Earth listening now, know what situation faces us, what last necessity, even as was foreseen, has arisen before us. That giant force-ray of which Marlin told you, that colossal ray which these Neptunians are stabbing toward the sun's edge from their far moon-world of Triton, is turning the sun ever faster, as all of you know, is decreasing its rotatory period by four hours each passing day. Within hardly more than forty days it will have decreased the sun's rotatory period to that fatal period of one hour, will have increased its spin to that critical fatal speed, at which the sun must inevitably divide into a double sun, a double star, engulfing our planet, and almost all others, in fiery death in that cosmic cataclysm. This is known to you and you know, too, that it is only by halting that giant force-ray from Triton that we can save our sun, our world, from that tremendous cataclysm.

"This much we have known, indeed, and now with what knowledge these four men have brought back from their unparalleled venture out through the gulf of space to the solar system's edge, to Neptune itself, you know also what lies before us. We have, indeed, built during the absence of Marlin and his three friends that great fleet of space-fliers, which we had decided to build. Using the plans of their original space-flier and applying all our efforts toward achieving a quantity production of space-fliers on those plans, we have been able, as you know, to construct in their absence no less than five thousand space-fliers exactly like their own, space-fliers that rest now upon the roofs of New York's great buildings around us, complete now with trained crews and ready to start! The gathering of Earth's forces has thus already taken place!

"And upon this great fleet of space-fliers rests now the fate of the solar system! For that fleet must go out through the solar system now to Neptune and halt the giant ray radiating from Triton's sunward side toward the sun, if the solar system is to live. What perils, what opposition that fleet will meet, Marlin has made clear to you. These Neptunians, most ancient and mighty of the solar system's peoples, are of colossal powers, such powers that they are scrupling not at splitting the sun itself! They have thousands of their great space-cylinders that can whirl through space as swiftly and as well as our own space-fliers. They have as weapons their concentrated force-rays, which we must provide for the fliers of our own fleet before it leaves. They have an ancient science and might that can produce we know not what weapons against us, and they know that our four first venturers escaped back to Earth, and will be expecting now an attack from us, will resist that attack with all their powers, undoubtedly, since they are fighting for the existence of their races, their world, even as we are fighting for ours!

"Thus this great fleet of five thousand space-fliers of ours goes out to battle, to battle between the races of Neptune and Earth that must decide the fate of the solar system for all time. There can be but one fit to lead this fleet out to such battle, and that is Marlin himself, who was the first to discover this peril that hangs over us, who was one of the first to suggest a means of struggling against that peril, and who has led this first daring venture out through a thousand perils to Neptune, and back again to Earth with the knowledge without which we could not act. So that it is he, with these three companions of his, Whitely and Hunt and Randall, who dared all with him and who have done for Earth what he has done, as his three lieutenants, who must command this great expedition of ours which we are sending out to halt the oncoming doom, these gathered forces of all the Earth!

"For it is this great fleet of space-fliers, with Marlin at its head, which alone can halt that doom now! If that fleet can win safely out through the perils of the interplanetary void to Neptune, can win to Triton's sunward side against the opposition of the Neptunians and can destroy the controls and generators of their great sun-ray, can halt that ray, the sun's spin will cease to accelerate and our planet and the other planets will have been saved. But if our fleet cannot do this, if the Neptunians prevent it from reaching the great sun-ray's source, and from halting that ray, then the sun will spin on ever faster and within two-score more days will split at last and engulf in the diverging fires of its two new suns, all the planets save Neptune. For it is this great space-fleet of ours, heading out now toward the last great battle of Earth's and Neptune's races, which alone now can prevent the accelerating speed of the sun and the consequent wrecking of our universe!"

CHAPTER FOURTEEN
An Ambush In Space

"MARS ahead and to the left—once more!"

As I uttered the words Marlin and Randall and Whitely, beside me, were gazing to the left with me, "Strange," said Randall, "it all seems, almost, as when we first went out past Mars."

Strangely similar, indeed, did it seem to all of us, the panorama that now again stretched all about us, visible through the racing space-flier's windows, as we sat in the four control-chairs before them. For ahead and away to the left gleamed again the dull-red disk of Mars, farther now from us than on our first trip out but seeming almost the same. Ahead too, and close to the right, shone mighty Jupiter, and beyond it on the left the yellow spot of Saturn once more, with far beyond it and straight ahead again the green little spark of light that was Neptune. Behind, too, the bluish light-spot of Earth and the lessened fire-disk of the sun were as before, and as before the blazing stars that jeweled all the deep-black firmament about us. But behind our flier we could barely see innumerable tiny gleaming points moving forward at the same speed as ourselves through the void, keeping pace with us in regular formation, a great V-formation of which our flier was the point and that moved steadily on through space. For those tiny points, extending back and out of sight in the void behind us, were the space-fliers of that great fleet of five thousand space-fliers which our own, the flagship, was leading out through the solar system to Neptune!

For two days, now, we had been flashing with that great fleet behind us from Earth, out toward the solar system's edge on our mighty expedition, and five days had passed since we had stood before the World Congress with Marlin rendering to it our report. In those intervening three days on Earth we had been the center of such a whirl of hectic activity as the world had never known before—the whirl of preparations for the start of the colossal fleet. For in those three short days Marlin with the energies of a world at his bidding, had strained every nerve to complete the last preparations of the great armada of space-fliers which he, with us three as his lieutenants, was to lead out on its unprecedented flight to Neptune.

The most necessary preparation was the equipping of the five thousand space-fliers with the concentrated force-ray weapons used by the Neptunians in their space-cylinders, those concentrated rays which, instead of pushing against what they struck, tore through it with driving power. Fortunately, the production of these concentrated rays required only the addition of special smaller ray-openings beside the regular ray-openings in the sides of the space-fliers, but even so it strained the capacities of the world's workers to install in each of the space-fliers those smaller openings in the short time available.

Each of the five thousand space-fliers held a crew of eight, their operators having been trained during our absence as fast as the fliers themselves had been built. We four in our own space-flier, the flagship of the great fleet, had four additional crewmembers now, four mechanic-operators who worked in shifts and tended ceaselessly the operation of the flier's various mechanisms, the great generators, and the other mechanical equipment, thus leaving Marlin and Randall and Whitely and myself free to devote all our attention to the command of the great fleet itself, though one of us retained the controls of the flier itself. Another preparation that had been made during our absence had been to equip each flier with space-walkers for its crew, and to equip each with efficient radiophone apparatus. This, while the Heaviside layer around Earth would prevent it functioning from Earth to space or from space to Earth, would allow free communication from space-flier

THE UNIVERSE WRECKERS

to space-flier while in space itself, and thus would allow Marlin and us to control with spoken orders all the great fleet we led.

Thus the last preparations had been completed and three days after our arrival at Earth the great fleet of space-fliers had taken its departure, the five thousand faceted polyhedron-like fliers rising as one from the flat roofs of New York's countless gigantic buildings. Once more we had started at night, and it seemed that all of the peoples of Earth had assembled in and around New York that night to speed us farewell. The vast crowds that had watched our single space-flier start out on its first trip weeks before, were as nothing to those vaster crowds that had watched the great fleet leave, since all on Earth knew now what word we had brought back from Neptune and knew that in two score more days, unless this fleet was successful in its tremendous task, unless it could win through the Neptunian opposition and halt the giant sunray, that all on Earth would perish in flaming death.

Thus surely there could have been no tenser moment in Earth's history than that, when, with the World-President and the massed members of the World Congress watching again around us, our flagship had risen from the roof of the great World Government building into the night, flashing up and outward once more toward Sagittarius, toward unseen Neptune. And behind us almost instantly there had flashed up in regular timing and formation our five thousand following fliers, racing out and after us with colossal speed like ourselves and flying in that hollow triangle or V-formation behind us. That formation had been adopted so that the rays of the fliers of the fleet, driven back toward Earth to push them on, would not strike against other fliers behind them, as would have been the case had our fleet moved out in a compact mass. And now for forty-eight hours our five thousand space-fliers had been hurtling outward, with our own flagship still at the apex of their formation.

And as we four sat now again in the four control-chairs, two of our mechanic-operators watching over the generators behind us and the other two asleep in their bunks, we had a somewhat different array of controls before us. Before myself were the controls of the flier itself, unchanged, with the six switches that directed its propulsion force-rays from the six openings. Marlin, though, to my right, had before him now as well as his array of astronomical instruments, the black mouthpiece and speaker of the radiophone, as well as a compact array of switch-studs by which he could speak to and hear from the various squadron leaders in the great fleet behind us. For convenience in giving orders, the five thousand fliers of the fleet had been divided into fifty squadrons of a hundred space-fliers each, and it was to the designated leader of each squadron that Marlin gave his orders, which were then transmitted by that leader to the hundred fliers of his squadron.

Before Randall, too, to my left, were new controls, the controls of the concentrated force-rays which were to be our fleet's weapons even as such rays were the Neptunians' also, and with which our flagship had of course been equipped. Those controls were two thick metal levers of no great size, with hand grips at their end, one of which controlled by its position the side of the flier from which the concentrated cleaving ray was shot forth, the other controlling the slant or exact direction at which that ray was emitted. With Randall handling these, our weapons, Whitely had before him all the space-flier's remaining controls—those of the generators, air replenishers, the various recording dials that were vital to its operation, and other essential things. So that as our throbbing flier drove on now at the great fleet's head, with Marlin and Randall and Whitely and myself gazing to the left toward the nearing crimson shield of Mars, we had each before us some vital part of our great fleet's or our flier's control.

Gazing toward Mars' red disk, Marlin broke the silence. "We'll need no side-rays this time to hold us out from it," he said, and I nodded.

"No, it's far enough from us now, and the speed of our fliers will take them safely past—is taking them past now. But it's the asteroids ahead that I've been thinking of."

Marlin somberly shook his head. "There's no help for it, Hunt," he said. "We'll have to lead the fleet straight through the asteroidal belt and trust to chance that as few of our fliers as possible will be struck."

The following hours, therefore, were perhaps the most tense and terrible that ever we had experienced. For as we shot on past Mars and through the great belt of whirling asteroids, it was not possible for the five thousand space-fliers of our fleet to maneuver to avoid those asteroids. We must hold straight on in our regular formation, we knew, lest all our fliers crash one into the other, so in that formation we went steadily on through that great zone of death. And hardly had we entered it, Marlin and Randall and Whitely gazing forth as intensely as myself, than an expanding dark globe loomed suddenly before us, sweeping past us with terrifying closeness, and then as it shot past there came suddenly in the blackness of space behind us a soundless flash of fiery light, that flared for a moment and faded. The asteroid, we knew, had struck a flier close behind us!

From ahead and from either side still, as we sped on, other asteroids were rushing, following their complicated orbits as our great fleet's open triangle of space-fliers moved through them, and now again and again still behind us came other fiery flashes in quick succession, flashes of flame which each marked the instant destruction of a space-flier and all its occupants! Yet there came no word, no protest, from any of the space-fliers behind us, all were going steadily forward at unaltered speed and in unaltered formation through the great belt of whirling death. And though, within a few hours more than a score of our space-fliers had been annihilated in white-hot and soundless flashes of fire as they were struck by the hurtling asteroids, the rest had escaped unscathed, and Marlin was giving to them the cheering knowledge that we had won through the asteroidal belt and were out of its whirling death.

Thus again Jupiter loomed ahead and to our right though closer now and greater in apparent size, and again we four were staring toward it in almost as great a wonder as formerly, as its mighty cloud-wrapped disk and attendant four big moons loomed closer. By this time, Marlin had transmitted to all the fliers behind us a brief order, and already from each of them and from our own a side force-ray was shooting toward the gigantic planet to hold us out from its terrific attraction. The V-formation in which our five thousand space-fliers flew was so slightly tilted sidewise as to allow the use of side-rays by all our fliers, and a side-ray of immense power it required indeed to hold each of us out from the mighty monarch of the solar system's planets as we sped past its huge and enigmatic sphere.

BUT still on and on through the void our mighty armada of space-fliers was racing, on toward the green spark of Neptune that slowly waxed brighter far ahead of us. That little green spot of light held our eyes, even to the exclusion of Saturn's yellow disk, expanding again to the left before us as we shot toward it also, for all our minds were centered upon Neptune and what mighty task it was that awaited us at that great world and its moon, what mighty struggle would be ours. So that it was not until Saturn's disk had expanded almost to moon-size before us, surrounded by the great rings and by its whirling moons, that we gave that planet any attention. By this time, for more than seven days our huge fleet had been speeding out through the boundless void, out through the solar system, and so it was as a certain landmark to us that Saturn appeared as we neared it, the last planet between us and our goal of Neptune. With our great fleet close behind, as we drew abreast of the huge planet's mighty sphere and colossal rings, it was intently enough that we four, gathered again in the control-chairs of our flier, and gazed toward it.

"The most dangerous planet in the solar system—Saturn," said Marlin, as we looked toward the huge world from which our side-rays now were holding us. "It was death almost for us before when we ventured too close in passing it."

"Well, we're safe enough from it this time," Whitely commented, "for since then it's moved farther to the left—is farther away from us with no danger to us now of chance meteors from its rings."

"Yes, we're safe enough from it now," Marlin admitted, "yet at the same time—"

Before Marlin could finish the words they were interrupted by a thing that chills my blood to remember even now. One moment he was speaking beside us, our space-flier flashing steadily on at its tremendous speed at the head of its great triangle fleet, past huge Saturn to the left. The next moment there was a terrific whirling around us of our space-flier's walls, it spun for an instant with tremendous speed in space, and at the same moment then was being driven with colossal speed in a direction at right angles to that in which we had been moving, was being shot through the void toward the mighty sphere and rings and moons of huge Saturn! And even as in that awful moment it drove with sickening speed, with an acceleration terrible, toward Saturn, all its forward progress suddenly halted, reeling blindly and at unthinkable velocity toward the huge planet, I looked through the windows, and saw whirling about us, the thousands of space-fliers of our mighty fleet bunched in a great, irregular mass with us, and hurtling through the void at the same tremendous speed toward great Saturn as ourselves!

"Saturn!" cried Randall hoarsely as we whirled in that mad moment. "The controls, Hunt!—we're being shot in toward it!"

The controls don't answer!" I shouted, my hands frantically flashing over them. "Something's driving us into Saturn—our rays can't hold us out—"

"The Neptunians! There behind us—those great cylinders—they're pushing all our fleet into Saturn to death!"

As Whitely voiced that last mad cry we glanced back through the windows of the flier even as they whirled about us, even as our flier and all the thousands of space-fliers of our great fleet whirled madly in toward huge Saturn looming ahead, and we saw that even as he had cried out, there, behind us, hanging motionless in space and only visible to us for a moment, hung a great mass of cylinder-fliers! Half our own great fleet in number they seemed, those massed Neptunian cylinders, and mid-most among them were a score of greater cylinders of immense size, far larger than any of the others, that were grouped closely together and from openings in which there was coming toward us a pale force-ray of immense size, visible only as it issued from those greater cylinders! And that ray it was, as was plain even in that instant, that was pushing our fleet with colossal power in toward its death in great Saturn's maze of rings and moons! The Neptunians had come out with those great ray-generators, those greater cylinders, and with a portion of their thousands of cylinder-fliers, and had waited for us in space to the right of Saturn, knowing well that our own escape meant a great attack upon them, an effort to halt their great doom-ray! They had awaited us there and when we had come between them and Saturn, never suspecting their presence, they had loosed upon us this forceful ray that was now driving us swiftly in to death!

THE UNIVERSE WRECKERS

An ambush in space! They were being pushed into Saturn.

inders—they're pushing all our fleet into Saturn to death!"

As Whitely voiced that last mad cry we glanced back through the windows of the flier even as they whirled about us, even as our flier and all the thousands of space-fliers of our great fleet whirled madly in toward huge Saturn looming ahead, and we saw that even as he had cried out, there, behind us, hanging motionless in space and only visible to us for a moment, hung a great mass of cylinder-fliers! Half our own great fleet in number they seemed, those massed Neptunian cylinders, and midmost among them were a score of greater cylinders of immense size, far larger than any of the others, that were grouped closely together and from openings in which there was coming toward us a pale force-ray of immense size, visible only as it issued from those greater cylinders! And that ray it was, as was plain even in that instant,

"An ambush!" I cried. "An ambush in space—the Neptunians are pushing us in to Saturn—our fleet can't live for minutes then!"

"Try to bring our flier out of it—up out of their ray's push, Hunt!" Marlin shouted to me, and for a moment I worked frenziedly at the controls before me, but the rays I shot forward to push against Saturn, to hold us back or push us to either side were powerless against the vast pushing ray from behind! Larger and larger great ringed Saturn loomed ahead as our disorganized fleet shot on at awful speed toward it, pushed by the vast ray, and but minutes remained before we would have crashed to death in all our fliers against the mighty planet and its whirling rings and moons! The end of our fleet and the end of Earth's hope, crashed to annihilation by the Neptunian ambush that had been laid for us here in space!

The thought maddened me, and with a sudden desperate inspiration I ceased to direct our flier's rays ahead against Saturn in vain attempt to halt our reeling flash forward, but instead suddenly shot a ray back against the mass of Neptunian cylinders no longer visible in space far behind. As that powerful propelling ray struck their cylinders' mass, our reeling flier leaped forward with even greater speed toward Saturn, and as it shot forward thus faster than even the huge ray from behind alone could push it, it was slightly freed from that vast ray's pressure, and I could edge it upward a little from that great ray's path! Up—up—while Marlin and Whitely and Randall watched with white faces beside me, while our space-fliers and all the fleet's around and behind us came on at terrible velocity toward mighty Saturn that now filled the firmament before us. Up—up—and as I saw that we were winning gradually up from the great ray's path, I shouted to Marlin, heard him with his radiophone apparatus quickly order all the fleet's fliers to follow my example in an effort to win up from the great ray's pressure. Only the fliers uppermost in that ray's path, though, like our own, could hope to get clear in this way, but as we swept on, gradually our own flier and perhaps four or five hundred others out of our great mass of five thousand won thus upward until at last we burst up out of the vast ray's path and were out of its pushing pressure!

"Back to the Neptunian cylinders!" Marlin shouted into the mouthpiece before him. "Unless we can destroy the greater cylinders whose ray is pushing the rest of our fleet into Saturn, we're lost!"

And back now our flier and the five hundred others that were clear of the ray like it, were rushing, back away from Saturn, while the remaining thousands of space-fliers of our fleet, unable to get clear in that way of the vast ray's pressure, were being driven on by it with terrific speed and power toward annihilation against Saturn! We must destroy the greater cylinders that were sending forth that ray, we knew, before the mass of our fleet crashed into Saturn, and so our five hundred space-fliers, our own flagship at their head, went fast almost as light through the black gloom of space, back toward the two thousand or more Neptunian cylinder-fliers that were massed around those greater cylinders that were our object! Upward and backward we flashed, until in another moment it seemed that great mass of cylinder-fliers loomed before and beneath us in space, the score or more of greater cylinders that were pushing with their huge ray our fleet to doom. Before ever the Neptunians in those cylinders could see us we had rushed back high above them, and then, as Marlin gave a single order through the mouthpiece before him, our five hundred faceted space-fliers were diving through space upon that Neptunian mass of motionless cylinders!

Down like light we flashed upon them through the black gloom of space, and a wild exhilaration thrilled me through in that moment, as we flew downward. The immense blackness of empty space around us, the far fiery disk of the sun and the bright sparks of Jupiter and Neptune burning inward and outward from us, the vast ringed sphere of Saturn behind us—these seemed to spin slowly around our flier as with its fellows it dove down through the sheer darkness of the void toward the unsuspecting Neptunian cylinders below. Marlin was gripping the control-board's edge, staring downward with the radiophone mouthpiece close before him, Whitely at the other side gazing down with his calm eyes ablaze for once, while Randall grasped tightly, with his face set and stone-like, the two levers of our concentrated force-ray weapon, and while with my own hands I held the controls of the flier's propulsion-rays, and sent it swooping down out of the upper void now upon the Neptunians, even as the hundreds of our fliers around us swooped. Then, as those cylinders loomed greater close beneath us Randall had swung sharply the levers in his hands and as he did so there had emerged from our space-flier, and from all those about us, ray upon ray of concentrated, terrible force, slender and pencil-like rays of pale force, that crashed down with awful cleaving power through the massed cylinders beneath!

I SAW in that whirling instant score upon score of the cylinders below cloven through by those terrific slicing rays, saw a full half of the score of greater cylinders that had been our chief target break up into great fragments as our rays swept through them! For that moment it seemed that below us unharmed and wrecked cylinders were merged together in a wildly-confused mass, fragments of wreckage and disk-bodied Neptunians, slain instantly by the cold of space, and unharmed cylinders whirling together there in a great mass beneath us! In that instant we had stayed our downward rush, almost upon that great mass, had with a repelling ray shot our fliers over and beyond it, and then as we whirled upward once more, as Marlin again uttered a hoarse, swift command, we were leaping back toward the great mass of the Neptunians, leaping back with all in our flier shouting now as we drove toward the remaining greater cylinders to destroy them also!

But now, as we shot toward them, the Neptunians had rallied from the first surprise of our crashing attack down upon them, and before we could again swoop down upon them, their unharmed cylinder-fliers, still more than two thousand in number, had separated themselves from the confused wreckage of those we had destroyed and were driving boldly up toward us, to meet us! In another instant they would have overwhelmed us, would have wiped us from the void with their great mass crashing over our own, their concentrated rays directed toward us, but before they could come closer Marlin had given an order and from our own racing fliers there had shot out toward the on-racing Neptunian cylinder-fliers propulsion-rays that in an instant had pushed us back from their onrushing fleet, back through a great gulf of space in an instant! Before they could comprehend the maneuver, another order had sounded, and we were again leaping forward, this time on a lower level, leaping toward the half-score greater cylinders that still remained motionless where first they had been, their combined great ray still pushing our fleet on to Saturn! The cylinder-fliers above, their occupants seeing our object, darted down like falling meteors to prevent us, but were an instant too late. Before they could do so, our concentrated rays had cloven through the half-score greater cylinders and had annihilated them, their combined great ray ceasing instantly!

"The greater cylinders are all destroyed!" Whitely was saying. "We've saved our fleet from death against Saturn, at least!"

"Back toward Saturn—toward the fleet!" Marlin shouted. "We're outnumbered five to one by these Neptunian cylinders!"

For even as he cried out, the two thousand or more Neptunian cylinder-fliers, too late to save their greater cylinders, but made fiercer by the sight of their destruction, were diving down from above, with all their concentrated weapon-rays toward us! Against those outnumbering cylinders our own few hundred fliers had no chance, and even as the Neptunians whirled down on us, as Marlin shouted his order, our space-fliers were going on toward Saturn, the Neptunians leveling out instantly and raging through the void after us in close pursuit. On we shot, their questing weapon-rays taking toll now of our rearmost fliers, and though Saturn was again filling the firmament before us with his mighty cloudy-yellow disk, his colossal whirling rings and circling maze of moons, there was no sign of our fleet's main body ahead. Had we destroyed the greater cylinders too late? Had their combined great ray pushed our fleet in to death against Saturn before we could save it? It seemed so in that tense moment and then, close ahead, there loomed in black relief against Saturn's mighty heaven-filling disk, a great swarm of black dots that were whirling toward us.

"The fleet!"

As I cried the words, Marlin was giving swift orders through the mouthpiece before him, and then, even as our own few hundred fliers suddenly slowed their speed and halted, the great swarm of dots ahead had rushed up beside and around us, had taken form around us as the thousands of space-fliers of our great fleet, falling instantly into their regular formation and confronting thus the

Neptunian cylinders that had been so hotly pursuing us! Those Neptunians were too late to halt their cylinder-fliers as we faced them thus so suddenly in force, our five thousand fliers opposed to theirs, hardly half our number, but they swerved as they saw us, swerved upward and attempted to race above us, raking us with their weapon-rays of concentrated force! Before they could do so, however, Marlin had uttered another order and our fleet had shot up to meet them, so that in the next moment, Earth and Neptunian craft had rushed together in their two respective fleets, there beside mighty Saturn!

As the two great fleets neared each other there crossed and flashed from one to the other innumerable slender rays of concentrated force, and space-flier and cylinder-flier were being clove through and annihilated by those slicing rays as they neared one another! Almost it seemed that we must crash straight into the oncoming Neptunian cylinders, the whole firmament for the moment ahead of us being full of their onrushing mass. I saw openings in those oncoming cylinders from which gleamed light, looked inside and there as one sees things in a dream were the many disk-bodied Neptunians calmly manipulating the controls as their great mass of cylinders shot toward our greater mass of space-fliers. Cylinders and space-fliers were being annihilated in that moment by scores by the slender rays that drove across the closing gap between the fleets, and then just as we seemed on the point of crashing dead into their oncoming cylinders they had shot their propulsion-rays sidewise, had swerved aside and were rushing with our own great fleet, which had instantly swerved with them, through the void!

Side by side for the moment the Neptunian and Earth fleets flew, countless weapon-rays stabbing across the gap between them as at dizzying speed they shot through the void, and I kept our space-flier at our fleet's head, as Marlin gave his orders to the fliers behind us, Whitely swiftly opening and closing the controls of our generators to keep constant the flier's power and speed, Randall was sending our own slender and deadly rays shooting toward the opposite Neptunian cylinders like bolts of straight and half-seen lightning! For but instants it could have been that the two great fleets, our own of space-fliers and the smaller Neptunian one, whirled through the void, but eternities it seemed to me, so tense and timeless was that whirl of awful action.

Soon I became aware of a mighty yellow disk that filled the firmament from top to bottom before us, toward which our racing, struggling fleets were flashing, and then I saw Whitely bending across me and shouting to Marlin through the wild whirl of this terrific battle:

"We're heading with the Neptunian fleet in to Saturn!" he was shouting. "What this battle will mean in those rings and moons—!"

"We'll keep straight with them!" Marlin cried. "They are trying to escape from us in Saturn's rings and moons, and get back to Neptune to rejoin the main Neptunian body!"

So that now as fleet and fleet rushed forward I held our own flier at our own fleet's head, racing forward with the vast whirling system of Saturn's rings and moons stretching dangerously before us. Full before us was looming greater each instant the spinning dark globe of Titan, Saturn's largest moon, and now as our two fleets rushed side by side toward it at terrific speed, stabbing still at each other from space-flier to cylinder with the concentrated weapon-rays, it seemed that inevitably in the next moment we must crash against the big moon! Seeing this, though, Marlin shouted a swift order into the mouthpiece before him, and instantly in answer to it our great fleet's mass bore sidewise against the racing mass of the Neptunian cylinders! For an instant it seemed that the two fleets were merging into each other, space-flier crashing into cylinder and slender rays coming thick, and then the smaller Neptunian fleet had given way beneath the pressure of ours, had veered sidewise so that in the following moment the two fleets were rushing past Titan's whirling sphere!

And now we were inside Titan's orbit, and as we whirled farther in just across the path of another and smaller whirling moon, I saw that Saturn's colossal rings lay edge-on close before our racing masses of craft, gigantic spinning rings of mighty meteor-masses, countless great meteor-swarms whirling there about the vast yellow planet whose sphere now was stupendous in the heavens before us. In another few moments Neptunian cylinders and space-fliers of Earth would have rushed alike into those thundering swarms of meteors, in which no craft could live for a moment. Already chance meteors were whirling through space about us as we shot on, cylinder or space-flier here and there in the two racing, grappling fleets vanishing in white-hot flashes of heat and fire as a meteor struck them. But other and more cylinders and space-fliers were vanishing in wreckage beneath the cleaving rays from either fleet, and both were racing on so intent upon our terrific struggle as to notice hardly at all the vast whirling rings before us! I heard Whitely utter a hoarse cry to Marlin as we flashed forward, heard Marlin swiftly utter an order in the mouthpiece before him, and then our fleet, and the Neptunian cylinders at almost the same instant, had shot diagonally upward and instead of crashing into the great rings' edge were slanting swiftly up over them!

And now, as Neptunians and Earth fliers drove together up over Saturn's colossal rings, the intensity of the struggle seemed to deepen to a fierceness as yet unknown. For the moment it was sheer blind battle without need of reason or command, sheer awful combat there in space above Saturn's whirling rings, with beside us the vast cloud-screened yellow sphere of Saturn itself looming gigantic, and with outside the great rings its whirling maze of moons! Cylinders and space-fliers grappled in that moment with mindless fury, and with a swiftness and skill of which I had not dreamed myself capable, I whirled our space-flier this way and that amid the swarming, boiling ruck of the giant battle, amid the grappling hordes of space-fliers and cylinders that filled the air before us, their cleaving concentrated rays slicing this way and that in swift circles of death about us! I heard Whitely laughing a little from excitement beside me as the battle reached this
terrific pitch, saw Randall sending our own weapon-rays this way and that with lightning-swiftness, Marlin gazing out tensely into that hell of battle that filled space about us. Struggling there above Saturn's colossal rings, ever and again Neptunian cylinder or space-flier of Earth shot too low and was caught by the whirling meteor swarms of those giant rings, annihilated instantly by them! Hundreds of cylinders and space-fliers had gone to death already, but so far the battle had been almost even despite our greater force, and seeing this Marlin cried quickly into the order-mouthpiece before him.

INSTANTLY our whirling space-fliers shot back suddenly from the wild ruck of the battle, formed instantly into a long double column of fliers with our own flier at the head, and then before the surprised Neptunians could reform their own spread-out and disorganized mass, our compact column had leaped forward and had crashed through their formless mass with a great shock, fliers and cylinders perishing in scores in that reeling crash! And then our double column had divided, pushing out to either side and thus splitting and separating the Neptunian mass of cylinders, and thus separated and inferior to us in numbers we were in the next moment leaping upon them there above Saturn's rings and sending their cylinders into wrecked fragments by the hundreds with our whirling rays! Fiercely their own rays came back upon us, as they faced us, and then they seemed to waver, to hesitate. And before we could sense their intention their remaining cylinders, depleted by scores each moment now and numbering no more than fifteen hundred, had dropped downward almost to the giant whirling rings, had formed into a swift massed formation there, and then with all the power of their propulsion-rays were speeding away, away from Saturn, out through the void toward the calm green distant spot of light that was Neptune!

"They're fleeing!" I cried, as our own space-flier whirled around in that moment. "We've beaten these, at least—they're fleeing back to Neptune!"

"Regular formation—all squadrons!" Marlin was shouting into the mouthpiece before him. "Full speed out from Saturn—after the Neptunians!"

And as our space-fliers, still over four thousand in number despite the losses of that wild combat, massed swiftly together in their V-formation and then were hurtling out from Saturn through the gulf after the fleeing cylinders, I was crying to him over the sudden waxing throb of our generators: "There's far more Neptunian cylinders than these that waited for us at Saturn here—the rest must be waiting at Neptune itself!"

He nodded, grim-faced. "The main Neptune fleet is probably waiting there for us—and must outnumber us by almost two to one. But if we can overtake these fifteen hundred cylinders before us we'll keep them, at least, from rejoining their main fleet!"

Now Saturn and its rings and moons was dwindling swiftly behind us as our great fleet shot forward again from it, out toward Neptune's steady, pale green little light-spot, and after the hundreds of cylinders fleeing before us toward it. With an acceleration that never before had we dared to risk did we leap forward through the void now, and so awful was the pressure of that acceleration upon us that even with our shock-absorbing apparatus we were crushed almost into unconsciousness by it. Steadily, though, with the last of my consciousness and strength, I held the space-flier's speed and course onward, while close behind us there shot after us with the same terrific acceleration, the fliers of our own fleet. We knew, though, that the Neptunians were fleeing toward their great world at a speed and acceleration as great as ours, for we were not gaining upon them. Their massed hundreds of cylinders, indeed, were not visible to us in the great void ahead except by means of our telescope, but with it we could keep them in view and could check their progress and ours out through the great gulf toward the solar system's edge.

Out—out—for hour upon hour we throbbed through the void after those fleeing Neptunian cylinders, out once again toward great Neptune and toward the last mighty battle that was to be ours there. For well we knew that the two thousand and more Neptunian cylinders that had waited for us there at Saturn, that had laid that great ambush in space for us there and then had battled us so fiercely over Saturn, were but a portion of the Neptunian main fleet of cylinders, sent out to delay, and if possible, to destroy us. That great main body of their cylinders, we knew, must number almost double as many craft as our own, and undoubtedly was aware of our coming and was waiting for us at Neptune or near it. And it was the great main body of the Neptunian cylinders that we must overcome, I knew, before ever we could hope to get to Triton and halt there the giant force-ray that was turning the sun on toward the doom of the solar system. And well we knew, too, that in the interval the Neptunians had had time to build many more cylinders, to make their great fleet even greater, and that whatever mighty weapons they had devised in that time we now must face.

So that as our great fleet of space-fliers, holding to its regular formation, flashed on and on and on through the great gulf of space, on out through the outer vast reaches of the solar system toward its outermost planet, our every effort was bent upon overtaking the fleeing Neptunians before us and annihilating them before they could rejoin the main body. At the same colossal speed as ourselves they were fleeing from before us, on toward Neptune's tiny green disk far ahead, and though we held steady in our pursuit after them, we could not lessen the gap between us. Hour passed into hour and day into changeless day thus as we throbbed on in that tremendous pursuit, hours and days that we could not measure, all things seeming timeless now as our great fleet flashed on in this terrific pursuit. At maximum speed, at millions of miles an hour, the Neptunians and ourselves were hurtling on, yet they kept out of reach ahead of us, as Neptune grew larger ahead. And now that mighty pursuit of ours had become so strange and unreal and dreamlike that it was as men in a dream that we watched and slept and watched in our space-fliers as Earth's brave fleet shot on through the last reaches of the solar system toward its edge.

Timeless indeed seemed the day on day, the hour on hour, of that daring pursuit of our fleeing enemies out from Saturn toward great Neptune, but now we knew that that pursuit had begun to draw to an end, since Neptune's disk was steadily enlarging before us and we had begun slowly to draw closer to the fleeing cylinders! Closer and closer our fleet, our own foremost space-flier, was coming to those fleeing fifteen hundred cylinders, and the interval of hours and days of pursuit out from the wild combat at Saturn seemed as though it had not existed, so tense once more we became as we drew nearer to the Neptunians before us. At last, with Neptune's pale green disk and the bright little spot of Triton above and behind it within hours of us, we had come so close to the fleeing cylinders that their mass, hurtling on in a cone-like formation, was clearly visible to our unaided eyes in the void ahead. And by this time, in every space-flier of our onrushing fleet, its occupants were waiting impatiently for the moment when we would be near enough to loose our concentrated weapon-rays on the fleeing craft ahead.

"We'll overtake them before they reach Neptune!" Marlin declared, gazing intently ahead toward the gleaming points that were the fleeing cylinders far ahead. "Within hours now we'll be up to them!"

"Well enough for us that we can do so, too!" Whitely commented. "For if they rejoined their main body, the odds against us might be overpowering!"

And now as pursuers and pursued rushed nearer and nearer toward mighty Neptune's great pale-green sphere, they were also nearing each other, our onleaping four thousand space-fliers drawing closer and closer toward those fleeing fifteen hundred cylinders, though they were a great distance from us. Beside me Randall's hands were resting on the weapon-ray controls, and as we came closer still to the fleeing Neptunians, I saw Marlin leaning toward the mouthpiece, preparing to give his order to the great fleet behind us. Closer—closer—we could clearly make out now the massed fleeing cylinders far in the void ahead—already almost within accurate ray-range, a swarm of black dots against Neptune's cloudy green disk ahead. And as we came thus close Marlin leaned to voice his order, to spread the space-fliers of our fleet into a broad firing-formation and send their rays stabbing ahead. But that order was never uttered, for at that moment Whitely uttered a sharp cry, and we saw that the racing mass of cylinders ahead was suddenly slowing!

With unprecedented quickness its speed was decreasing before us and in moments more we would have crashed into those slowing cylinders had not Marlin's voice snapped a quick order that slowed instantly all the fliers of our fleet likewise. Fearful of some trick, slowing thus, we gazed intently ahead in that moment and then all of us had cried out together as we saw, beyond that swarm of black dots that were the slowing fifteen hundred Neptunian cylinders before us, other black dots that showed against great Neptune's disk also, which loomed great now in the heavens ahead! Other black dots, an immense swarm of them, that we knew were other cylinders, an immense fleet of them, rushing out from Neptune toward the fifteen hundred before us and toward ourselves! And then as in moments more the fifteen hundred cylinders before us slowed and stopped in space even as we had slowed, we saw sweeping from behind them, from great Neptune, those other cylinders, forming with them, there in space, a colossal semi-circular mass of fully eight thousand Neptunian cylinders in all, that faced our own four thousand or more space fliers there in the void! It was the giant assembled Neptunian fleet, gathered here outside their world to face our own fleet, in that great struggle in which Earth and Neptune were to come now at last to death-grips for the life or death of the solar system!

CHAPTER FIFTEEN
"You Of Neptune Or We Of Earth!"

"COLUMN formation—all squadrons full speed ahead!"

It was Marlin's voice that shouted that swift order in the next instant, and then, even as the gigantic semi-circle of the Neptunian fleet was leaping through the void toward us, our four thousand and odd space-fliers, outnumbered almost by two to one by the cylinders massed ahead, had shifted like lightning from their great V-formation to one of a long double column once more, and no sooner had its squadrons taken that new formation than the column slanted slightly to allow the free use of their propulsion-rays. They were flashing forward now like an enormous spear cast toward the curving front of the giant Neptunian fleet! For it was Marlin's intention to meet that outnumbering mass of cylinders by splitting it with a column as we had done over Saturn to our enemies, and then engaging separately the parts of the disorganized mass. So that now, even as the great half-circle of the Neptunian cylinders whirled through the void to overwhelm us, we had formed that long, double column and were dashing straight at them!

Holding the controls of our space-flier steady in that moment, I was aware for an instant of a sense of the utter strangeness of all the wild scene about me—of our space-flier's interior with Marlin and Randall and Whitely crouched in their chairs beside me, of the great column of polyhedron-like, gleaming, faceted space-fliers that came forward through the black gulf of star-sown space behind us, of the oncoming giant line of the Neptunian cylinders flashing toward us in turn, and of the immense green disk of mighty Neptune looming in the black vault behind them. All seemed for the moment the panorama of some strange nightmare stretched about me, but that momentary sensation that had gripped me so often in our wild rush through the solar system vanished in the next instant as stern reality loomed before us. There were the mighty curving line of gleaming Neptunian cylinders through which in the next split-second our great column must crash! I braced myself mentally for that vast crash that must almost inevitably mean death for the foremost of our space-fliers. I was aware as we drove upon the onrushing Neptunian line, that now unthinkable storms of deadly concentrated rays were raging from fleet to fleet; and then suddenly, at the very instant that we thought to crash into their great approaching line, that line opened swiftly before us to allow our great column to rush unharmed through it!

So astounded were we by that unlooked-for maneuver on the part of the Neptunians, that before we could check our speed, we were through, had shot in our entire column through that opening in their semi-circle, which instantly closed again behind us. And as it did so, there rushed toward each other the open ends of their semi-circle, thus closing that circle even as we rushed into it. Our fleet was held enclosed within the circle of their own! And then, from all those thousands of Neptunian cylinders that surrounded us, there were stabbing at us in countless number slender shafts of concentrated force, countless pencil-like weapon-rays that instantly clove through hundreds of our gathered space-fliers and that strewed space thick about us with their wreckage, even as we sought in vain to answer that terrible rain of deadly rays!

"Trapped!" Whitely was shouting. "They've trapped us inside their circle—are destroying us!"

For, though our own rays were fiercely springing forth and striking cylinder after cylinder of the vast fleet that had gathered about us, that fleet so outnumbered us and had such advantage of position, that it was decimating us in short order. Our space-fliers had broken from their column-formation now, and in a loose, disorganized mass were drifting at the center of that great ring of death which the Neptunians had formed about us. Swiftly our fliers were going into wreckage and death beneath the terrific storm of rays from all around us, and then Marlin's voice was flaring as he shouted an order into his mouthpiece.

"All space-fliers mass together," he cried, "and turn all your propulsion-rays outward!"

"You're going to—" Whitely began, but Martin cut him short.

"We're going to break up the Neptunians' circle in the only way it can be broken up!" he cried.

As his order sounded the thousands of our space-fliers were obeying it, were massing compactly together at the center of the Neptunians' mighty circle. Thus massed, they presented for the moment a perfect target for our enemies' rays, and for a moment those rays stabbed thick toward us from all sides. In the next moment our massed space-fliers were shooting their great propulsion-rays outward, outward in all directions around us, outward toward the Neptunians' encircling ring! As those rays shot out, they pressed with terrific power against that ring of cylinders about us, and since our own fliers were massed together and thus braced against each other, it was not they that moved but the cylinders, their great ring instantly broken up, disintegrated, as those cylinders were hurled out into the void from us by the pushing power of our great propulsion-rays! For the moment they were broken up completely, their formation entirely shattered, and before they could reform, there had come another order from Marlin and in a compact formation ourselves, our space-fliers were leaping upon their shattered masses!

To right and left, like light, drove the deadly weapon-rays of our massed space-fliers as we seized the opportunity and leaped upon the Neptunians. Ample was the revenge we had upon them in that moment, since the concentrated rays tore through and wrecked hundreds of their own cylinders as we sprang upon them! Fleeing from before us for the moment, flashing away toward giant Neptune's tremendous green disk ahead, they strove to reform, while we leaped after them and harried them with every weapon-ray which our space-fliers could emit. Swiftly, though, even as they rushed onward before us, the Neptunian cylinders were drawing together into a great mass again, into a great column-like formation, and as our own column-mass drove beside and after them with weapon-rays stabbing, their resistance abruptly stiffened, and they were racing in close formation once more beside our own mighty fleet, grappling once more with it in space as both rushed toward great Neptune. But we had struck a mighty blow at their disorganized masses in the moment of our opportunity. Fully two thousand of their cylinders had been swept to death by our rays before they had been able to mass again, and now but six thousand or less cylinders remained, racing ahead with our own four thousand or less fliers!

The great green sphere of Neptune was looming colossal ahead and slightly beneath our two oncoming fleets, with behind and above it the bright little disk of Triton. It was toward Triton even in that wild moment that all of us were gazing, toward the source of the giant sun-ray that we must, somehow, halt. But now the battle around us had become so furious that we could spare no thought to aught else, since the two mighty fleets, stabbing ceaselessly at each other with their slender rays as they slowed their flashing progress forward, were rushing into the outer reaches of the atmosphere of huge Neptune! Its air was roaring about our whirling space-fliers as we shot through it, but as we shot on we saw that the Neptunian cylinders were going into annihilation far swifter than were our fliers! For they had formed and were racing beside us in their half-circle formation, while our own fliers at Marlin's command had leaped forward in a long column that could concentrate all its fire of rays upon the side of the Neptunian formation nearest us! And though slender rays tore lightning-like through fliers here and there across our own column, we saw that their cylinders beneath our fire were being wrecked in scores, in hundreds! In that vast running fight we were fast evening the odds against us!

Marlin's eyes were gleaming with excitement as we saw the Neptunians thus falling beside us under our concentrated fire of rays, and Randall and Whitely and I were almost beside ourselves with exultation. Faster were falling the Neptunian cylinders beneath our rain of rays, the rays of their farther cylinders being held from us by their own cylinders in their fatal formation. Already, as we thundered through the mists of mighty Neptune and low over its gleaming surface, we saw that the Neptunian cylinders had been reduced by that deadly fire of ours to hardly more than three thousand, to hardly more than our own fleet of fliers, which had itself lost its hundreds in that vast running battle. As our rays tore into and through their shaken mass hundreds upon hundreds of their cylinders had been cloven through, had been reduced to whirling wreckage, and we had evened the odds in our raging battle at last!

Even as we cried out in triumph, the Neptunians must have seen that to continue in that running fight longer was suicidal for them. They could not change formation during that flight without exposing themselves to worse peril, so in desperation they did a completely unexpected thing. Their enormous mass of cylinders, battered out of its half-circle formation by our terrific fire of rays, suddenly swerved in toward our own fleet as the two great armadas rushed forward above Neptune, and then that Neptunian fleet of cylinders had crashed obliquely with immense power into our own space-flier fleet! The next instant it had so merged with it that the two fleets ceased instantly to exist as such and for the moment became one colossal, swaying, reeling mass of cylinders and space-fliers in utter merged confusion, striking and soaring and smashing each other!

As that great cylinder-armada crashed thus into our own it had seemed to me that the air all around us was filled in that instant with colliding space-fliers and cylinders, and with a hell of slender pale and deadly concentrated rays that raged thick in whirling death about us! I saw before us two onrushing cylinders, whirled the flier up to avoid that imminent collision, and then as they passed beneath us, saw Randall send our rays driving down and cleaving through them, saw them whirl in wreckage into which a battling cylinder and faceted space-flier had crashed themselves in the next instant! I heard Whitely's shout of alarm in the next split-second, instinctively flung the flier sidewise through the boiling ruck of the battle, just in time to escape a pair of stabbing rays from a cylinder beneath, and then saw those rays stab on up and strike another cylinder and destroy it! And even as I whirled the flier sidewise, Randall was driving our rays to right and left against other cylinders rushing upon us!

THE air about us seemed filled in that moment with a single wildly-swirling mass of cylinders and space-fliers, grappling with each other there in countless individual combats inextricably intermixed, their weapon-rays going out m destruction through the craft that whirled upon them, their propulsion-rays driving the ships about them crazily to right and left! With inconceivable fury cylinders and fliers soared and fought and fell above great Neptune's roof, the air filled with falling wreckage, our great battle reaching now an undreamed-of phase of intensity, as gleaming cylinders and faceted ball-like space-fliers were annihilated alike by hundreds! That giant merged combat of the two fleets had in minutes taken toll of half the force of each, and I wondered dimly even as I whirled the flier up and back through the wild, annihilating battle how either men of Earth or disk-bodied Neptunians could cling to a battle of such suicidal nature! Then suddenly from Marlin had come a hoarse exclamation, and I saw in that instant all the Neptunian cylinders intermixed with our space-fliers rising upward, as though in answer to a single command!

"Up!" cried Marlin, "The Neptunians are over us! They're going to—!"

But before he could finish the sentence, before our space-fliers could whirl upward in answer to his command, from the Neptunian cylinders massed above us had shot down upon us innumerable powerful propulsion-rays, rays that struck scores, hundreds, of our space-fliers and drove them down with terrific force to crash against the metal roof of Neptune beneath us! They were repeating the maneuver by which we four had escaped from our pursuers over Neptune weeks before, were driving our fliers down to crashing death in hordes! Instantly as Marlin shouted into the order-mouthpiece, our fliers leaped forward, to escape from that death that smote us from above, but as we drove forward in our column formations again, they went on above us, were with their powerful propulsion-rays driving us down to death in scores even as with those rays they prevented us from rising to meet them! We were being quickly destroyed now, and as we saw it, as our column flashed on with the Neptunian cylinders massing in another column above and driving our fliers down by scores, we saw that not much longer could that unequal battle continue! Then abruptly

Marlin pointed ahead and downward to Neptune's mighty roof beneath us, was crying an order to us and the fliers behind and about us.

"That opening!" he cried. "Down through it—down beneath the roof! It's our one chance to escape them!"

I caught my breath at that cry of his, for I saw that he was pointing down toward one of the great circular openings in Neptune's roof, openings that were set in it here and there, all being open now as when we had first explored Neptune's mysteries. To flash down beneath the roof through that opening was our one chance of escape from the relentless smiting death above. I saw it, too, so the next instant our own flier and all the long column behind us were diving downward at a dizzying angle toward that great circular opening; and in the next moment before the Neptunian cylinders above could fathom our purpose, we had passed through that opening and were racing forward beneath the great roof in an instant, though, the Neptunian cylinders had followed in their long column and were racing after us, through the dim Neptunian day above the dead and lifeless surface of the great compartment-city that covered all of Neptune!

On we flashed, with the Neptunian column some distance behind, numbering now some half-thousand more in cylinders than our own bare thousand space-fliers. On until above us we saw another similar opening in the great roof, and then at Marlin's quick order our narrow, long column of fliers were slanting up toward it, through it. And then, outside of the great roof once more, Marlin gave a swift order that revealed to me the purpose of his strategy. For at that order our fleet checked its upward rush and bent its long column lightning-like around to form a great circle, a circle hovering there around and above the great circular opening in the roof through which we had just emerged. And in the next moment, as the Neptunian column flashed up through that opening likewise in hot pursuit of us, never suspecting us of waiting there for it, from all the fliers of our great circle there had radiated toward them storm on storm of deadly concentrated rays, rays that smote them with blinding shock as their column rushed upward and that crashed through hundreds of their upflashing cylinders even as they burst up through the opening, before ever they could catch sight of us around them! In those seconds of dazing surprise there was no chance for them to recoil, and their column of cylinders, as if too astounded for the moment to answer with a single ray, was flashing up from the opening through a hurricane of rays that in that moment was annihilating their cylinders by hundreds! But a scant three or four hundred cylinders of those that ran upward through that gauntlet of death escaped it, and these swirled for a moment in stunned confusion above us, and then were without formation racing away from us over Neptune's surface, racing away toward the gleaming disk of Triton!

"Beaten!" I cried, as our own space-fliers whirled up now after the fleeing cylinders. "They're beaten—they're fleeing back to Triton!"

"The giant ray!" Whitely was shouting, as we thundered forward. "We've still more than a thousand fliers left, and if we can get now to that great sun-ray—!"

"Hold steady after them!" Marlin cried. "We've fought our way this far, and we've got now to get to that ray and halt it!"

Now out over Neptune's surface, out through its mists and outer atmosphere again, the cylinders ahead were roaring at utmost speed, almost leaping in a confused and disorganized mass, the remnants of that mighty fleet that had come out to meet us outside Neptune, toward their moon-world of Triton, whose disk gleamed bright ahead. A thrill of pride even in our wild excitement shot through me as we thundered on in pursuit of those fleeing cylinders. For whatever else that day might hold for us, whether or not we were able to halt that giant ray on Triton's sunward side that was reaching out to the sun and turning it ever faster, we men of Earth had at least proved our fighting ability to the solar system for all time, had come out to the solar system's edge and had shattered there the mighty armada of the Neptunians' ancient and mighty race! And now as we flashed on in swift pursuit of the fleeing survivors of that armada toward Triton, confidence and hope were strengthening in us each moment, for with the Neptunians' great fleet shattered what could hold us back from the shattering and halting of the giant sun-ray and its mechanism?

On—on—and now we were rushing after the fleeing cylinders out of Neptune's atmosphere and into the airless void again, with

Triton growing each moment more bright and big as giant Neptune fell behind us. Across the gulf from Neptune to its moon we sped, after those cylinders, with utmost acceleration and speed, and swiftly we drew closer to the Neptunians flying before us, and swiftly too drew closer to the gleaming sphere of Triton. And as it grew larger before us, as we pursued the cylinders in toward it, we all cried out as we followed with our eyes at the sunward side of it the giant pale beam, hardly visible, of the colossal force-ray acting on the sun, that mighty ray that was turning the sun ever faster to the doom of the solar system! We could make out that gigantic beam, leaping out into space toward the distant fire-disk of the sun, and could make out also in that moment a great number of great humped dark shapes gathered on Triton's roof around the great pit of the sun-ray. As our eyes shifted to Triton's other edge we could discern the other giant force-ray, which reached out toward the distant star in Sagittarius and by bracing Triton with its pressure kept the moon-world from being hurled out into space by the sun-ray's pressure. Around this other ray's pit, too, were a few of the strange great humped or domed dark shapes, but in that moment we gave them small attention, for the cylinders that had been fleeing from before us straight toward the great sun-ray's giant beam, had abruptly slowed, stopped, as they rushed into Triton's atmosphere, and had turned desperately to face us!

IT was a wild, fierce attempt on their part to hold us even to the last from their great ray, and as their three or four hundred cylinders massed so suddenly before us and faced us, our own column was leaping upon them with all the impetus of our thousand and more space-fliers! The next moment cylinder and space-flier were reeling in a wild last struggle there high in Triton's atmosphere, high above the pit of the giant sun-ray, with the mighty pale beam of that ray passing up and out toward the sun and still beside us! Like demons the Neptunians were fighting now, but we were wrought up to the fiercest pitch battle ourselves, and as Marlin gave his orders, we were swooping upon them with insensate fury, cylinder and space-flier crashing together there above Triton or falling beneath the slicing sweeps of the weapon-rays that again raged thick around us! Faster, ever faster, fell the outnumbered cylinders before our wild attack, until at last but a score were left—a dozen—a half-dozen—and then those, too, were gone, the last of the Neptunians' mighty fleet of cylinders annihilated! And now as from our hovering space-fliers, still over a thousand in number, there came muffled, wild cheers, our eyes were shifting downward, down to the great pit from which the sun-ray sprang, down to the twenty control-boxes in the sides of that pit!

"Down to the pit—down to the controls!" Marlin was shouting over the wild uproar in our and the other fliers. "Everyone of those control-boxes must be destroyed before we can halt the ray!"

"We'll halt the great ray now!" I cried to him, as our space-fliers swooped downward now toward the giant pit of the ray. "We've wiped out their last forces, and we can—"

"But look—those great domes around the pit below!" It was Whitely's hoarse shout that broke in upon me. "They're great domed forts—*great domed forts guarding the giant sun-ray's pit and controls!*"

For as we shot down toward the great pit of the mighty force ray we had seen clearly now the scores of giant domed, humped shapes on Triton's roof around that pit, which we had vaguely discerned from high above. And they were, as Whitely cried to us, great forts! Giant domed forts of inconceivably thick and strong metal, each hundreds of feet in height, with openings here and there in them from which countless deadly weapon-rays could be emitted. And these great domed forts, over a hundred in number, were moving, were wheeling this way and that smoothly and swiftly on Triton's roof, were circling slowly on that roof about the pit of the giant sun-ray, guarding that pit and the control-boxes in its walls! Even as we heard Whitely's cry in that moment, as we flashed down toward them, we realized that the Neptunians had constructed those mighty moving forts of metal to guard their great force-ray's controls from our attack, placing more than a hundred of them around the pit of the great sunray, and a half-score of them, as we had perceived, around the pit of the other great force-ray on Triton's other side! And then, in the moment that Whitely cried out and that we saw those great forts moving like smooth-gliding mountains of metal beneath us, there had rained upward from them toward us a staggering, withering storm of concentrated force-rays!

Reeling, staggering, falling, our fleet spun in crazy disorder in the next moment as that terrific fire from beneath decimated us! And though in the next instant Marlin's voice rang steel-clear with an order, though in answer to that order our own concentrated rays radiated down madly toward those gliding mountain-like domed forts beneath us, it seemed that our rays had no effect upon them! For so stupendous in thickness and strength were those giant domed forts of metal, that instead of cleaving through them our rays could do no more than crumple and dent somewhat their smooth outer surfaces! They were invulnerable, almost, to our attack, and though one of them was crumpled into twisted metal by scores of our rays happening to converge upon it, the others were almost unharmed and were raking us with a terrible, annihilating rain of rays as we shot down over them!

Down and down—and then as I shot our space-flier down foremost of our mass of fliers through that wild tornado of deadly rays, I saw the great pit's opening looming full beneath us, the giant pale beam coming up from that opening, the twenty vital control-boxes set at equal intervals around its walls! Toward one of those control-boxes our own flier was whirling beneath my hands, and then Randall drove out like light our piercing weapon-rays toward that control-box, clove through and wrecked it instantly! But it was but one of twenty, and in the next instant our space-fliers, unable longer to withstand that terrific fire of rays from the gathering domed forts around the pit, were staggering upward, none other of our fliers having progressed as far down as ours, and none other of the twenty control-boxes being destroyed! And as our space-fliers reeled thus upward, unable to reach the control-boxes in the pit against the awful fire of the gathered domed forts about it, we saw that more than a hundred of our fliers had fallen beneath the terrific fire of rays from the forts in our mad rush downward!

"Those twenty control-boxes!" Marlin was crying, "We've got to destroy everyone before the sun-ray will halt!"

"But we can't with these giant moving forts against us!" Whitely cried. "They're wiping us out—they will have destroyed us in minutes!"

"We'll hold it to the end, then!" Marlin shouted. "We've fought our way out through the solar system to this great ray, and unless we halt it now it means death for the solar system in a score more days! Down again to the attack!"

And down—down—down—like striking, rushing meteors our hundreds of space-fliers shot, to one side of the giant beam, down with the great domed forts beneath swiftly flashing over Triton's roof to mass beneath us at the pit's side. Through the little window-openings in those forts we saw the disk-bodied Neptunians inside, and knew that beneath the great roof of Triton also were swarming the millions upon countless millions of all the Neptunian races, all the disk-bodied monsters in their great compartment-city, who, with this great ray, were turning our sun faster and faster to divide in a score more days and doom the solar system! And with a desperation born of that thought we shot down once more, down with the hell of rays from the great domed forts again raging up around us and taking toll of our fliers as we shot over them, curving back upward once more, and stabbing again toward the control-boxes in the pit's wall our weapon-rays as we reached that curve's lowest point! But this time, though the great forts took toll again of scores of our fliers as we shot down over them and up again, over the pit and up again, our rays were so imperfectly aimed, that no control-box was destroyed this time!

Upward we swirled and then again, with a persistence more insensate than human, were racing downward again in a terrific swoop over the pit of the great ray! Again the deadly rays of the surrounding hundred domed forts crashed through our down-swooping fliers, sending masses of them again into whirling wreckage, while as we swooped down over the pit and upward again in that lightning-like rush through death we saw that our rays had missed once more and that none of the control-boxes had this time been destroyed by them! And as we reeled upward again over the great pit, from over the giant domed forts, we saw that but a few more than five hundred space-fliers remained to us of the thousand and more with which we had first flashed downward! In three downward swoops only, in three lightning-like moments of attack, the giant invulnerable forts beneath had annihilated more than half our force, and we had succeeded in destroying but a single one of the twenty control-boxes!

"The end!" cried Whitely. "The end of our chance to halt the great sun-ray!"

"The end of our great fight through the solar system—the end of Earth's and the solar system's last chance!"

For it was the end! Even as we cried out thus we knew it, beyond shadow of doubt, as the shattered mass of our remaining space-fliers reeled high above Triton's roof, high above the great pit of the ray and the colossal moving domed forts that guarded it! Marlin—Whitely—Randall—they were swaying in that moment, the knowledge of doom plain upon their faces as upon mine! Another great swoop downward and those giant, almost invulnerable moving forts would blast us entirely from the air with their storms of rays! All of the nineteen remaining controls below must be destroyed to halt the mighty sun-ray, and before we could destroy even one of them, we would be annihilated! The giant ray beside us would turn the sun on ever faster, turn it on until in a score more days the sun would divide at last into a double star and engulf its planets in its diverging fires—all save Neptune! And as we came thus to the end at last of our superhuman struggle to halt the solar system's doom there was coming up to us from beneath the great roof of Triton a vast, rolling muffled shouting of triumphant Neptunians, of all the Neptunian hordes upon Triton who saw as we did that for us the end had come!

"But if it's the end, we'll meet it trying!" Randall cried. "One more swoop downward—we can die that way at least—"

BUT from Marlin, who stood with crimson face and blazing eyes, there came a mad shout. "The end—no!" he cried. *"There's still a chance for us—to halt the other ray—the ray on Triton's outward side!"*

The other ray! The other giant force-ray that went from Triton's outward side, its dark side, into the gulf of interstellar space toward that far star in Sagittarius, the other mighty ray that braced Triton against the great sun-ray's pressure and that kept that sun-ray's pressure from hurling Triton out into the great interstellar void! The other ray—and if it were halted—then Triton— I felt my mind reeling as the stupendous meaning of Marlin's mad shout came home to it! The other ray guarded by only a half-score of the giant moving domed forts, instead of the hundred beneath us—and then Marlin's voice was tearing across the throbbing, rushing din to my ears and instinctively I had obeyed his order, had shot our space-flier forward at immense speed even as there rushed forward beside us our five hundred and more remaining fliers! I whirled it away from the great pit of the giant sun-ray and over Triton's roof at lightning speed toward its dark side, toward the other giant ray that reached out into interstellar space from that dark side!

And as we rushed thus away with reeling speed, we heard the mighty thundering cheers of the Neptunian millions beneath the great roof changing to wild cries of alarm, saw the hundred great domed forts around the sun-ray moving over Triton's roof after us with immense speed, themselves, gliding at utmost velocity on around that roof's smooth surface after us in sudden wild alarm! But, more slow by a little than our massed space-fliers that split the air above Triton they dropped behind us even as we shot forward, even as that colossal roar of rising alarm rolled across Triton's surface beneath the great roof. On—on—like rushing meteors massed close together our space-fliers flashed now, toward Triton's dark side around its surface, and then were whirling around that dark side, were whirling straight toward the colossal other beam, the giant other force-ray that stabbed out opposite from the sun-ray, that stabbed out toward Sagittarius' bright star and by its pressure towards that star kept Triton braced against the sun-ray's outward pressure! Marlin was shouting, screaming an order as we flashed downward, and we caught sight for a moment of the half-score domed forts, left as guards of this other ray's great pit and controls, and then like comets of metal our fliers were thundering down upon them!

Slender beams sprang quick to meet us from those ten great domed forts, but though those beams drove crashingly upward upon us in narrow rays of death, it was not toward the domed forts that we were rushing, but toward the twenty control-boxes set in the wall of the giant pit from which this other mighty ray issued! Through the wildly-whirling beams that sliced the air about us we flashed downward, and then as the pit's walls loomed close ahead, as beside us, almost thundered into by us, loomed the pale, gigantic beam, we saw the out-jutting control-boxes full before us, set around the pit's great wall, and the beams of our massed space-fliers were driving thick toward them! Crash!—crash!—crash!—and we were shouting crazily as we saw half the twenty control-boxes smashing inward, annihilated by our first wild rush! And then as we spun around there in the pit, around the giant beam to annihilate the other control-boxes, the rays of the ten domed forts sweeping insanely about us, Whitely cried out hoarsely and pointed away across Triton's metal roof surface toward the hundred mighty shapes of the great domed forts rushing to the defense of this other ray, rushing to annihilate us!

"The control-boxes!" Marlin cried. *"The last control-boxes!"*

And even as he cried that, even as with their utmost immense speed the hundred colossal domed forts of metal rushed over Triton's metal roof to join with the outnumbered half-score beside us, to annihilate us with one combined mighty blast of their countless rays, our massed space-fliers had whirled around the great pit, around the mighty ray, and were driving toward the remaining control-boxes in its wall with all their weapon-rays stabbing ahead! *Crash!—crash!*—and those remaining control-boxes were crumpling, crashing, beneath our rays, with but a single control-box in the wall remaining intact in the next instant, a single one that sufficed still to keep the giant ray beside us going upward, outward, though! And even as we gathered, whirled to rush upon it also, the colossal rushing domed forts had appeared at the pit's edge around and above us, seeming to pause for a split-second before their combined countless rays came down to annihilate us! But in that instant, when the giant domed forts paused above us, Randall had whirled back the ray-switches in his hands, and from our space-flier and from a score more around us in the same instant there had flashed toward that last control-box a converging score or more of driving rays that instantly had crashed through and had annihilated that last control! And as that last control-box of all the giant ray's twenty was thus destroyed, there came what seemed a blinding flash of light at the great ray-mechanism far in the mighty pit beneath us, and then the giant pale force-ray that radiated upward and outward from that mechanism had abruptly snapped out beside us!

There was a pause, a silence of a single instant, a pause in which all the universe about us seemed holding its breath, in which our rushing space-fliers were whirling up out of the great pit, in which the giant domed forts at the great pit's edge beneath us seemed held in an enchantment of stupefaction. And then as our massed space-fliers whirled thus upward over Triton's surface, as Marlin and Randall and Whitely stared downward, swaying, we saw the great metal-roofed world of Triton reeling beneath us as though from some colossal shock, saw it rushing outward from beneath us with colossal, unthinkable speed! Saw it rushing out with velocity inconceivable away from the sun, away from Neptune, away from the solar system, rushing out into the vast void of interstellar space, *hurled into the void with all the countless millions of the Neptunians upon it, hurled into the void out from the solar system never to return!*

Hurled into the void, we four knew even as we watched it whirl away from beneath us, by the pressure of its own colossal sun-ray, that continued to emanate from it! For that giant ray which the Neptunians had directed toward the sun had pushed back upon Triton with pressure inconceivable, even as we had known, and it had been only the other ray radiating out toward Sagittarius' distant star that had braced Triton thus against the sun-ray's unthinkable outward pressure! And with our halting of that immense other ray, with our halting of that bracing ray, the moment that saw its connection of bracing force or pressure broken between Triton and that distant star saw Triton hurled out instantly by the pressure of its own giant sun-ray against the sun, that awful outward pressure breaking the moon-world loose instantly from the hold of great Neptune, its parent planet, from all the solar system, hurling it out from the solar system's edge into the boundless outer void forever!

Marlin—Whitely—Randall—myself—as we reeled there at the window watching, as our space-fliers whirled up and outward from Triton even as it shot outward from beneath us, we saw its gleaming sphere swiftly diminishing as it hurtled out in the great void, saw that it was spinning as it shot outward from the impetus of that gigantic push, that the great sun-ray issuing from it was whirling with its spinning now! And then as its gleaming sphere shot out into the void away from us, away from great Neptune behind us, away from the solar system's edge, shooting out into the cold and sunless outer void and bearing upon it all the Neptunian hordes to death, Marlin flung out his hand toward its diminishing gleaming little sphere in the black void before us, was crying out to it as though to the Neptunian millions upon it as it shot out, never to return.

"You of Neptune or we of Earth!" he cried. "One had to go to death—to doom! You fought for Neptune and your races as we fought for Earth and the solar system—but Earth and the solar system win!"

CHAPTER SIXTEEN
Space-Rovers

BEFORE us Earth and its little moon gleamed brilliant in the blackness of space when our five hundred space-fliers shot in toward them once again, days later. Again we four held our familiar positions in the four control-chairs of our space-flier, and again Marlin and Randall and Whitely were gazing forth with me as at the head of those massed space-fliers we moved in with slowing speed. It had been for a score of days that we had reeled back through the solar system from Neptune, from its edge, had reeled back from the border line of that vast void of space, in which Triton long days before had become invisible, hurtling out into that void forever. Past perilous Saturn, and past mighty Jupiter, and through the dangers of the asteroidal belt and past red Mars once more we had sped, within us only a strange sick desire for Earth once more; that Earth which we knew, would be shaken even now with unimaginable rejoicings as its peoples saw the acceleration of the sun's spin that had menaced all our universe halted at last with the hurling forth of Triton days before. And now, as we sped in at last toward Earth, it was in mutual silence that we gazed ahead.

Once again the outlines of Earth's great continents were coming clear to our eyes as we shot nearer, and once again, now, we were heading toward that side of it that lay in shade, in night, toward the North American continent, to hover out from it, over it, and then to drop down toward it, down through the darkness of Earth's night toward New York. Again beneath us Earth's surface was widening to a vast dark plain as we sank down toward it, and then again through the darkness we had seen, beneath us, the gleaming lights of New York, and were sinking lower toward them. Down—down—until New York stretched beneath us but one colossal bed of brilliance, one vast mass of blazing lights above which there flashed to and fro the innumerable brilliantly-lit aircraft like countless shuttles of light, the giant World Government Building and all the colossal buildings that stretched far away around it burning with unequalled brilliance, and their roofs and the ways between them thronged once more with crowds, such crowds as never yet had the mighty city seen.

A strange dumbness held us, as we sank slowly downward with our massed space-fliers. Then, as a great whirling lightbeam from beneath caught our fliers' descending mass, held us in its glare, other beams were swinging toward us, holding us bathed in a white flood of light as we sank downward. And as we were discovered thus to the vast thronged city beneath, the swarming aircraft above it abruptly shot downward from about us, while the great roaring voice of the city's crowds abruptly ceased as the city saw us. Down through a great silence, the most tense and utter silence surely ever to reign in the mighty city beneath, we dropped, our fliers separating and falling smoothly over the crowds, over the seas of white, upturned faces, falling through that hushed silence toward the roofs of the great buildings beneath, our own toward the roof of the great World-Government building.

As we shot downward we saw that upon that roof waited now for us a massed and silent crowd, as in the streets below, that had given back to the roof's edges to make way for our own space-flier and those with us to descend. Smoothly I lessened the power of our lower ray, and smoothly we sank downward through the brilliant lights above that roof, until at last our own and the fliers about us had come gently to rest upon it, the throb of our generators ceasing. Then, with the same dense silence reigning outside, Marlin slowly was opening our space-flier's doors, and with Whitely and Randall and me behind him was stepping forth upon the great roof's surface, into the white brilliance of its lights. Hesitatingly, wearied, with the men of our other fliers gathered now about us, we looked around. Beside us there stood, and around us, the massed members of the World Congress, with the World-President with them. Over these silent figures we looked, a little dazedly, and out over the superhumanly brilliant, superhumanly silent city that stretched about us, and then up toward the great constellations as though in reassurance. For they stretched above us as before, as always, Capricorn and Sagittarius and Scorpio and the rest, with Jupiter and Saturn and Mars shining there, and with great Neptune, invisible here to our eyes, and farther still than Neptune its moon-world of Triton hurtling on toward those distant stars. Dazedly, slowly, we looked, up and around us, while still around us that hushed, thick silence held, and then saw that the World-President was coming toward us.

Across the roof he came toward us from those silent crowds about us, his hands outstretched, his voice unsteady.

"Marlin—Randall—Hunt—Whitely!" he said. "You have come back once more—back to the Earth that you and your forces have saved."

"We have come back," said Marlin, his voice low, strange. "Have come back with what remains of those forces."

And then, while the World-President and the World Congress stood silent before us, beneath the brilliant lights, Marlin was speaking slowly to them, was speaking in short, halting words of our flight outward, our escape from the great ambush at Saturn, our wild pursuit onward to Neptune and the colossal battle that had ended there with our halting of the other ray, with our hurling of Triton and all the Neptunians on it out into the void forever. In a hushed, strained silence the crowd before us was listening, and as the speech-apparatus beside us took Marlin's slow words out to all the crowds in all the vast city about us, and beyond, they, too, were listening in that same tense stillness. Then, when he had finished, that stillness continued unbroken for moments.

"Marlin—Whitely—Hunt—Randall—!" he was saying, again. "There is no way in which we can tell, there is no need for us to tell, what gratitude Earth's peoples have now for you and for your men, who saved Earth and all the solar system from a dreadful death." Marlin slowly shook his head. "That gratitude is not for us alone who came back," he said, "but for those others of us who did not come back—who went to death out there for Earth."

"We of Earth know that," the World President said, "and our gratitude is for them as for you—our silence now for them as for you. But you who came back—you four who dared first of all men out through the void, and who came back to lead Earth's forces out to the terrific struggle that saved us—is it gratitude only that Earth can give you?"

Marlin half-turned, his eyes meeting our own. "There is nothing Earth can give us, more," he said, "for we have that which never men have had before, have the space-fliers and have now all the solar system's worlds before us! For to us four could be no greater gift, no greater thing, than that—to be space-rovers once more together!"

And as Marlin's eyes met ours, standing there on the great building's brilliant-lit roof with all about us the assembled masses of the World Congress, silent, with those other vast silent throngs in all the mighty city around us, we were looking together upward. Marlin with his brilliant eyes; Whitely with his calm, strong upturned face; Randall with a new light flaming into his tired eyes; I with a strange new eagerness clutching at my heart; we all were looking upward. Upward past the brilliant lights around us toward the constellations and toward the planets that shone among them, crimson Mars and yellow Saturn and white Jupiter! Upward with a sudden strange tenseness, forgetful for the moment of the hushed world around us that we had helped to save from doom, upward across the immensities of space where we four had roved toward the great planets that moved there across the star-sown summer sky!

THE END

If you've enjoyed this book, you will not want to miss these terrific titles…

ARMCHAIR SCI-FI & HORROR DOUBLE NOVELS, $12.95 each

- **D-131** **COSMIC KILL** by Robert Silverberg
  BEYOND THE END OF SPACE by John W. Campbell

- **D-132** **THE DARK OTHER** by Stanley Weinbaum
  WITCH OF THE DEMON SEAS by Poul Anderson

- **D-133** **PLANET OF THE SMALL MEN** by Murray Leinster
  MASTERS OF SPACE by E. E. "Doc" Smith & E. Everett Evans

- **D-134** **BEFORE THE ASTEROIDS** by Harl Vincent
  SIXTH GLACIER, THE by Marius

- **D-135** **AFTER WORLD'S END** by Jack Williamson
  THE FLOATING ROBOT by David Wright O'Brien

- **D-136** **NINE WORLDS WEST** by Paul W. Fairman
  FRONTIERS BEYOND THE SUN by Rog Phillips

- **D-137** **THE COSMIC KINGS** by Edmond Hamilton
  LONE STAR PLANET by H. Beam Piper & John J. McGuire

- **D-138** **BEYOND THE DARKNESS** by S. J. Byrne
  THE FIRELESS AGE by David H. Keller, M. D.

- **D-139** **FLAME JEWEL OF THE ANCIENTS** by Edwin L. Graber
  THE PIRATE PLANET by Charles W. Diffin

- **D-140** **ADDRESS: CENTAURI** by F. L. Wallace
  IF THESE BE GODS by Algis Budrys

ARMCHAIR SCIENCE FICTION CLASSICS, $12.95 each

- **C-58** **THE WITCHING NIGHT**
  by Leslie Waller

- **C-59** **SEARCH THE SKY**
  by Frederick Pohl and C. M. Kornbluth

- **C-60** **INTRIGUE ON THE UPPER LEVEL**
  by Thomas Temple Hoyne

ARMCHAIR SCI-FI & HORROR GEMS SERIES, $12.95 each

- **G-15** **SCIENCE FICTION GEMS, Vol. Eight**
  Keith Laumer and others

- **G-16** **HORROR GEMS, Vol. Eight**
  Algernon Blackwood and others

If you've enjoyed this book, you will not want to miss these terrific titles…

ARMCHAIR SCI-FI & HORROR DOUBLE NOVELS, $12.95 each

- **D-141** **ALL HEROES ARE HATED** by Milton Lesser
  AND THE STARS REMAIN by Bryan Berry

- **D-142** **LAST CALL FOR DOOMSDAY** by Edmond Hamilton
  HUNTRESS OF AKKAN by Robert Moore Williams

- **D-143** **THE MOON PIRATES** by Neil R. Jones
  CALLISTO AT WAR by Harl Vincent

- **D-144** **THUNDER IN THE DAWN** by Henry Kuttner
  THE UNCANNY EXPERIMENTS OF DR. VARSAG by David V. Reed

- **D-145** **A PATTERN FOR MONSTERS** by Randall Garrett
  STAR SURGEON by Alan E Nourse

- **D-146** **THE ATOM CURTAIN** by Nick Boddie Williams
  WARLOCK OF SHARRADOR by Gardner F. Fox

- **D-148** **SECRET OF THE LOST PLANET** by David Wright O'Brien
  TELEVISION HILL by George McLociard

- **D-147** **INTO THE GREEN PRISM** by A Hyatt Verrill
  WANDERERS OF THE WOLF-MOON by Nelson S. Bond

- **D-149** **MINIONS OF THE TIGER** by Chester S. Geier
  FOUNDING FATHER by J. F. Bone

- **D-150** **THE INVISIBLE MAN** by H. G. Wells
  THE ISLAND OF DR. MOREAU by H. G. Wells

ARMCHAIR SCIENCE FICTION CLASSICS, $12.95 each

- **C-61** **THE SHAVER MYSTERY, Book Six**
  by Richard S. Shaver

- **C-62** **CADUCEUS WILD**
  by Ward Moore & Robert Bradford

- **B-5** **ATLANTIDA** (Lost World-Lost Race Classics #1)
  by Pierre Benoit

ARMCHAIR MYSTERY-CRIME DOUBLE NOVELS, $12.95 each

- **B-1** **THE DEADLY PICK-UP** by Milton Ozaki
  KILLER TAKE ALL by James O. Causey

- **B-2** **THE VIOLENT ONES** by E. Howard Hunt
  HIGH HEEL HOMICIDE by Frederick C. Davis

- **B-3** **FURY ON SUNDAY** by Richard Matheson
  THE AGONY COLUMN by Earl Derr Biggers

If you've enjoyed this book, you will not want to miss these terrific titles…

ARMCHAIR SCI-FI & HORROR DOUBLE NOVELS, $12.95 each

- **D-151** **MAGNANTHROPUS** by Manly Bannister
  BEYOND THE FEARFUL FOREST by Geoff St. Reynard

- **D-152** **IN CAVERNS BELOW** by Stanton A. Coblentz
  DYNASTY OF THE LOST by George O. Smith

- **D-153** **NO MORE STARS** by Lester del Rey & Frederick Pohl
  THE MAN WHO LIVED FOREVER R. De Witt Miller & Anna Hunger

- **D-154** **THE CORIANIS DISASTER** by Murray Leinster
  DEATHWORLD by Harry Harrison

- **D-155** **HE FELL AMONG THIEVES** by Milton Lesser
  PRINCESS OF ARELLI, THE by Aladra Septama

- **D-156** **THE SECRET KINGDOM** by Otis Adelbert Kline & Allen S. Kilne
  SCRATCH ONE ASTEROID by Willard Hawkins

- **D-157** **ENSLAVED BRAINS** by Eando Binder
  CONCEPTION: ZERO by E. K. Jarvis

- **D-158** **VICTIMS OF THE VORTEX** by Rog Phillips
  THE COSMIC COMPUTER by H. Beam Piper

- **D-159** **THE GOLDEN GODS** by S. J. Byrne
  RETURN OF MICHAEL FLANIGAN by S. J. Byrne

- **D-160** **BATTLE OUT OF TIME** by Dwight V. Swain
  THE PEOPLE THAT TIME FORGOT by Edgar Rice Burroughs

ARMCHAIR SCIENCE FICTION CLASSICS, $12.95 each

- **C-63** **THE OMEGA POINT TRILOGY**
  by George Zebrowski

- **C-64** **THE UNIVERSE WRECKERS**
  by Edmond Hamilton

- **C-65** **KING OF THE DINOSAURS**
  by Raymond A. Palmer

ARMCHAIR SCI-FI & HORROR GEMS SERIES, $12.95 each

- **G-17** **SCIENCE FICTION GEMS, Vol. Nine**
  Ben Bova and others

- **G-18** **HORROR GEMS, Vol. Nine**
  Emil Petaja and others